THE DEVIL TO PAY

The Story of Alice & Petronilla

HUGH FITZGERALD RYAN

THE LILLIPUT PRESS
DUBLIN

First published 2010 by

THE LILLIPUT PRESS

62–63 Sitric Road, Arbour Hill

Dublin 7, Ireland

www.lilliputpress.ie

ACKNOWLEDGMENT

Excerpts from *The Latin Poems of Richard de Ledrede, O.F.M.*,
from *The Red Book of Ossory*, edited by Edmund Colledge
(Toronto 1974), are reproduced by kind permission of the
Pontifical Institute of Mediaeval Studies (PIMS).

ISBN 978 1 84351 1793

1 3 5 7 9 10 8 6 4 2

Set in 10.5 pt on 15 pt Dante by Marsha Swan
Printed in Scotland by Thomson Litho of Glasgow

THE DEVIL TO PAY

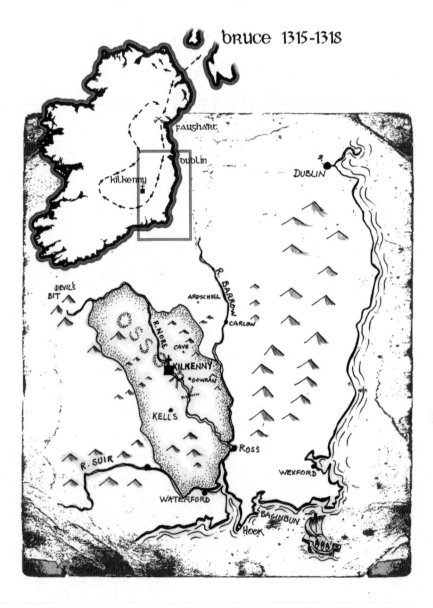

bruce 1315-1318

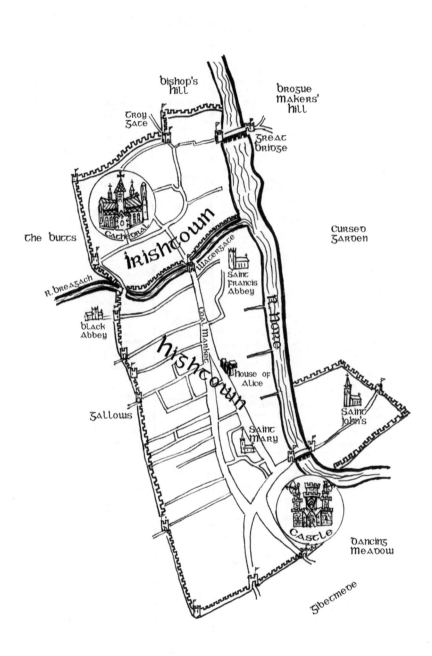

Ireland / Kilkenny	Timeline	World Events
	1150AD	
LAUDABILITER BULL	**HENRY II (1154)**	
(1169) NORMAN INVASION		DEATH OF THOS. BECKETT (1170)
(1172) HENRY II IN IRELAND		
KILKENNY CASTLE	1175	
(1176) DEATH OF STRONGBOW		
	RICHARD I (1189)	MAGNETIC COMPASS
		THIRD CRUSADE/ SALADIN
WILLIAM THE MARSHAL LAYS OUT 'HIGHTOWN'	**JOHN (1199)**	GOTHIC ARCHITECTURE
	1200	ARABIC NUMERALS (FIBONACCI)
(1210) CHARTER FOR KILKENNY		ROGER BACON (1214 – 1294)
CATHEDRAL OF ST.CANICE BEGUN	**HENRY III (1216)**	MAGNA CARTA (1215)
FIRST ANGLO NORMAN BISHOP OF OSSORY		
	1225	ST. FRANCIS OF ASSISSI D. (1226)
FRANCISCANS, DOMINICANS AT KILKENNY		GENGHIZ KHAN D. (1227)
		AQUINAS (1225 – 1274)
	1250	
		MARCO POLO (1254-1324)
		DANTE (1265 -1321)
	EDWARD I (1272)	GIOTTO (1267 – 1337)
	1275	PAPER
(1280) BIRTH OF ALICE KYTELER		EYEGLASSES
		GUNPOWDER
		FALL OF TRIPOLI
ALICE M. WILLIAM OUTLAWE	**1300**	FALL OF ACRE / END OF CRUSADES
BIRTH OF WILLIAM OUTLAWE THE YOUNGER	**EDWARD II (1307)**	PETRARCH (1304-1374)
ALICE M. ADAM LE BLOUND		WILLIAM WALLACE D. (1305)
		POPE AT AVIGNON (1309)
ALICE M. RICHARD DE VALLE		BOCCACCIO (1313-1375)
(1315) INVASION OF EDWARD BRUCE		BATTLE OF BANNOCKBURN (1316)
RICHARD DE LEDREDE APPOINTED BISHOP OF OSSORY		DESTRUCTION OF TEMPLARS
ALICE M. JOHN LE POER		
(1324) WITCH TRIALS	1325	MURDER OF EDWARD II (1327)
(1329) DEATH OF SIR ARNAUD LE POER	**EDWARD III (1327)**	ROBERT BRUCE D. (1329)
(1332) COLLAPSE OF BELFRY		SALISBURY SPIRE COMPLETE (1334)
(1334) PAVING OF KILKENNY/ MARKET CROSS		FIRST MING EMPEROR
		HUNDRED YEARS WAR BEGINS (1340)
(1338) THE GREAT FLOOD		GEOFFREY CHAUCER B. (1343 – 1400)
(1349) FRIAR JOHN CLYN D.	1350	BATTLE OF CRECY (1346)
		BLACK DEATH (1347)
LEDREDE RESTORED GLAZING OF THE GREAT WINDOW		BATTLE OF POITIERS (1356)
(1362) DEATH OF LEDREDE		
(1366) STATUTES OF KILKENNY		
	1375	
	RICHARD II (1377)	CANTERBURY TALES
	1400	DEATH OF CHAUCER (1400)

PROLOGUE

Multi reges ante fuerunt
Mundi passus qui transierunt
Ubi iam sunt?
(Where now the many kings of former
times who ran this earthly course?)
—Richard de Ledrede

IN THE YEAR of Our Lord 1169, a full century after Hastings, a company of desperate Norman knights established a foothold on a rocky headland in south Wexford. They came with guarantees of reward from Dermot, the banished king of Leinster, should they succeed in restoring him to his lands. They had Dermot's word, but as security for his promises they brought weapons, armour and horses.

They had, as further justification, the notion that the Pope had, at some time in the past, urged the king of England to bring the Irish people back to the true practice of the faith. The king, the flamboyant Henry II, had other concerns but after the feudal custom of the time, he farmed the task out to his vassal, Richard de Clare, the formidable Earl of Pembroke, known to all as Strongbow.

These first knights spent a bleak winter on that windswept promontory. They constructed a fortification. They repelled attacks by the natives. They butchered emissaries of peace, hurling them from vertiginous crags to the jagged rocks and the surging waves. They let it be known that English law, backed by Norman might, had arrived in Ireland. They waited for Strongbow and within a bare four years Strongbow was Lord of Leinster and son-in-law to the devious Dermot of the Foreigners. He could have been king but he was constrained by his word to Henry Plantagenet.

Henry came to look over his new lands. He entertained the Irish chiefs over a long Yuletide and bound them to him as sworn vassals. The chiefs enjoyed the feasting and gleemen, the jesters and the bonhomie. They drank the wines of this great king's French dominions. They pondered how they might use him against their neighbours in their incessant tribal wars. Departing, they shrugged at the oath, but they were ensnared in a web, tripped by their own words. The web was loose and flimsy, but it was enough to start with.

∾

The Irish called the little river *Bréagach*, the river of deceit. In summer it was bland and peaceful, but in winter it became a torrent, breaking its banks and bringing floods to the low ground at its junction with the mighty Nore. It separated the church of Saint Canice and its surrounding settlement, Kilkenny, from the higher ground and the Norman castle to the south. The Normans had lost no time in placing a fortress on a bluff dominating the crossing at a bend of the Nore. Stone castles became the backbone of their new colony. The Norman lighthouse at The Hook, where the Nore and its two sister rivers meet the sea, guided more and more settlers to Waterford and William the Marshal's new port at Ross.

There was no deceit. By judicious marriage to Strongbow's daughter, the Marshal gained sway over much of Leinster. By shrewd administration of the new laws, he nurtured the colony. He became the pre-eminent knight of his time. He might well have made himself a king, but he also was bound by his word, to the Plantagenets.

He acquired land by legal means, from the Bishop of Ossory, enabling him to lay out a town extending from the castle to the deceitful little river. He opened a quarry, providing free stone to the new settlers. He intended that they should stay. They paid him a rent of twelve pence, due at Easter and Michaelmas. He enabled the appointment of Hugh de Rous, the first Anglo-Norman Bishop of Ossory. Hugh also was a builder. He demolished the old Irish church and began to build a new cathedral. That work was to go on for over a hundred years. The old Kilkenny became Irishtown, while the new settlement appropriated the name to itself. The friars, both Grey and Black, came there to safeguard the souls of the citizens. In 1207 William the Marshal, pleased with his work, granted a charter to Kilkenny, a mere thirty-eight years after those Norman adventurers clambered to the safety of that windy headland in south Wexford.

In 1275 the Irish chiefs offered a grant of seven thousand marks to King Edward I, asking him to extend equality under English law to all of Ireland. This was long overdue. He needed the money, but he was wary of deceit. He had inherited a deep distrust of the Irish, his reluctant subjects.

Two years later Walter le Kyteler, a prosperous banker from Flanders, moved his family and wealth to a thriving Kilkenny, in search of further profit. His wife marked the momentous occasion by presenting him with a strong and healthy daughter. They called her Alice.

As a precursor to the cruelties of that terrible century, the trial for witchcraft in 1324 of Alice le Kyteler and her maid, Petronilla de Midia, introduced a new horror to Ireland. Their story still haunts the stone-flagged streets and narrow lanes of that ancient town beside the gliding Nore.

ONE

Thure Deum altissimum
auro regem et dominum
sed mirra mortis gremium.
(Incense to God on high; gold to king and lord,
but myrrh to Death's cold embrace.)
—Richard de Ledrede

HER FATHER always walked with a staff, a long stick cut from the fork of a blackthorn. The stump of the thicker branch formed a knob, polished now by years of handling. The staff reached almost to his shoulder and when he stopped to deliver himself of some observation, he leaned his right forearm on the knob, bending slightly forward, with his left thumb hooked into his belt.

Alice was always amused by his stance. He looked like a labouring man resting a moment on his spade, drawing breath, before bowing again to the stubborn soil. But those long, blue-veined hands had never handled spade or mattock. Mottled with age, they sped over the lines of the counting-table and bundles of tally sticks. They stacked and sorted coin of every denomination, mostly the Easterling silver he loved so well. They held invisible reins on many lives in Hightown and Irishtown and far beyond the encircling walls.

He liked to walk for a time during each day, maybe as far as the Great Bridge or the castle, feeling the pulse of the town, taking the greetings of the people in the street with a gracious nod. He knew their thoughts and fears and they knew that he read them well, these people of the Middle Nation. The inhabitants of the walled town feared their lord and his laws, even though he spent years away from them in England and France. They feared the lord's seneschal with his armed men. Also they feared the wild men outside the walls, the barbarous Irish of the hills, a people detestable to all civilized men and to God Himself. Beyond lay the great world and outer darkness, where the Enemy of Mankind prowled ceaselessly, seeking to drag them down to eternal fire and damnation. Their only hope was in God, His Son and His Holy Mother, but the way to God was steep and beset with many pitfalls. God's servants took their dues and tithes and eked out salvation at a price, just as Walter le Kyteler lent out his silver coin and took his interest twice a year on the feasts of blessed Hilary and holy Michael.

'Why are you not damned for usury, like the Jews?' Alice asked.

'Ah,' he replied, scratching his straggling beard, 'because I am not a usurer. Like the Temple Knights, I charge no interest. The sin is in the interest. I charge a percentage for the service. The Jews are damned anyway for many crimes, but true Christians are entitled to a wage for their services.'

'This is sophistry and you know it,' she retorted. 'Are you not afraid for your soul?'

Walter cleared his throat and spat into the dust. He pointed his staff at the great bulk of the cathedral looming over Irishtown.

'That holy place was built for the glory of God, but every mason, every artificer, the ingeniator himself, was paid a wage. Every stone was paid for by service, or by silver and a portion of that silver trickled down from the hill and through my door.'

He chuckled. 'They need me, you see, and others like me. When the time comes I shall purchase Masses and my bones will lie safely inside those walls. I shall leave money after me to protect you and my seed forever.'

He swept the tip of his staff in the dust. 'I sweep it towards my door, just for luck. All the wealth of Kilkenny town lies in the dust, the stone, the dung, the soil and the work of the people. I ask only for my share.'

Alice looked up at the cathedral. The clouds fled across the summer sky, making the massive building appear to move. The high east gable rose above the narrow street like the prow of a great ship. The round bell tower, left over from a former age, appeared to lean as if it might totter onto the small, half-timbered houses below. She let him talk. He could be ponderous and sententious, but she humoured him by drawing him out. In return, he indulged his strong-willed and often wilful nineteen-year-old daughter, his only child. He gave her reading and the mathematics. Especially the mathematics. She would inherit his property and his creditors. He admired her insatiable curiosity about life and the world and sometimes he feared for her. The only security for his 'bele Aliz' would lie in money and a firm husband. That, however, was a matter for another day. He leaned on his staff, looking up, with his head to one side.

'Every stone,' he mused. 'Even the long-legged king needs his Flemings and his Jews. Without us he could not keep his throne.' She shushed him, putting her finger to her lips.

'Be quiet,' she said urgently. 'You never know who might be listening.'

He laughed again, softly.

'Where I grew up in Flanders the merchants built a great hall. They trade their wool and their fine linen there. The bankers set up their benches there.'

He paused, remembering the smell of lanolin, the odour of fresh linen and the chink of coin. He had fallen in love with the hubbub of the commerce reverberating in the vaulted chambers of the Cloth Hall.

'When the spire is finished it will be taller than the cathedral.'

He paused, letting the point sink in.

'Is that not tempting the vengeance of God?' she wondered. 'Will He not strike down such a challenge?'

'No, they are good neighbours. Mutual interest, you see. Anyway the cats take all the blame and the bad luck with them.'

'The cats?' She knew the story already, but he would tell it.

'Yes, the cats. Every year the merchants hurl cats from the four corners of the tower. The cats carry with them all the sin and any evil that lies in trade.'

Involuntarily he looked up, measuring the distance from the top of the tower to the street below. In his mind's eye he saw cats flying through the air, twisting and flailing as they hurtled downwards to smash their nine lives in one bloody impact on the granite cobblestones. There were always one or two to be finished off by the clogs of the laughing onlookers.

Except for Lucifer. 'Lucifer', because he also was cast out and fell from Heaven. Walter had found him under a stall. A pang of pity prompted him to take the broken creature and carry it home, hidden under his coat. He concealed the cat in an outhouse and nursed it back to a semblance of health, although Lucifer's nightly excursions were forever curtailed by a crippled leg. Walter said nothing to his parents, knowing that they would not permit bad luck to be brought over their threshold. As time went by, Lucifer assumed a proprietorial air in the stable yard and fathered many offspring who earned their lodging by keeping the mice in check. The name lived on in Lucifer's son and grandson. When Walter le Kyteler secured safe conduct from the English king to bring his money to Ireland, along with his family and retainers, he had no more devoted a follower than Lucifer, the third generation to bear the name.

Walter straightened up and grasped his staff.

'We must return to our toil, daughter,' he declared, setting off purposefully up the sloping street towards the Watergate. Alice followed briskly, stepping fastidiously over ruts, outcropping stones and dung. The smell of the tanners' vats gave way to the odours of the fish market and the shambles. She reflected that even if she were blindfolded, she could find her way around the town and its environs by mapping its many smells, from the sweet air of the tenter fields to the abbey mill and bakehouse or the communal privy and dunghill by the river. Every smell, in its own way, was the smell of money.

They crossed over the little bridge at the Watergate. She looked into the rushing stream, as it carried its tribute of water to the parent Nore, just below the abbey weir. The guard at the gate saluted as they passed from the Bishop's town into that of the lord of the castle. The guard knew his betters, but all the same, he looked after Alice with a rueful glance. He liked the way her costly gown swirled as she walked. He liked how her girdle emphasized her small and graceful waist and how her dark hair peeped from beneath her hood. Not for me, he thought, rubbing the back of his forefinger over the stubble of his upper lip. Not for me, but as they say, a cat can look at a king. He sniffed. He scratched his armpit, where the leather jerkin chafed him in the summer heat. The river sang below the bridge.

∾

Although there was an outstanding harvest that year and there was peace on the marches, the Irish found cause to fight among themselves. The feuding families of the north, south and west continued their incessant wars, but at least this left the towns of the east in peace, to consolidate their holdings and expand their trade with England. Ruling with a firm hand, the Norman lords played one petty princeling against another, assisting here, making punitive raids elsewhere, using English law when it suited and exacting fines under the Irish system, the laws of the Brehons, when it seemed more advantageous. This was not a stratagem open to the Irish. Their attempts to bribe the hard-pressed king and his justiciar in Dublin had not had the desired result. At rowdy parliaments the barons of the Middle Nation protected their exclusivity. The rot would set in if the 'Hibernici servilis conditionis' were ever to gain the privileges won by hard conquest and maintained by constant vigilance.

❧

Alice had heard all the arguments many times. She turned half an ear to her uncle Guillaume's rasping voice and her father's persuasive tones. She enjoyed these exchanges, logic pitted against bombast, but on that day she delighted in the new flour and fresh bread in July, a rare occurrence. She rolled the dough, turning the lump in upon itself, pushing her knuckles into it, sprinkling flour to stop it sticking to the board. Her arms were white to the elbow. She set a small piece aside for the next batch, always a pinch of the ancestral yeast to carry on the line. There were those who regarded this as magic.

She wished that she could see into the seeds of every thing. There must be an explanation for it all. She had always asked 'Why?' Charming enough in a small child, but irritating in an adult and, at times, even dangerous.

'Because that's the way it is,' her father would say. 'There are laws binding everything. There are things we should not enquire about.'

She knew that the seasons came and went; that the dome of the sky with all its many lights revolved over the disc of the world; that the swallows that twittered all summer under the eaves, spattering the patch of paving with their droppings, would leave when the winter began to advance from the north, shortening the days and bringing cold, stinging rain and sleet. But why?

'I'll tell you why,' bellowed Guillaume in the inner room. She heard his fist on the table. He was a man who would maintain standards. No longer a mere Fleming and certainly not an Englishman, he had become in his own mind one of the conquering Normans, with all their suspicion of those they had dispossessed. He mangled the French language on a daily basis, but after a few drinks, the truculent Fleming emerged again. Guillaume would have been more at home on foot in a Flemish phalanx, but he saw himself as one of the noble knights, even though they were, as often as not, unhorsed by the long and lethal halberds of the infantry.

'Because there are too many Irish skulking inside our borders and too many of our own people willing to tolerate them.'

She knew where he was going with this argument. She knew the two corpses that hung from the gallows on Gibbetmede. She saw them frequently, scarecrows turning in the wind and blackened by time. She knew their mocking grins and eyeless sockets. Even in death, in typically Irish style, they laughed at the humour of their predicament. Their long straggling hair, hanging down over the brow, 'a perfect haircut for a thief', as Guillaume declared all too frequently, had been thinned out by carrion birds to thatch their high, swaying nests. The plight of the two thieves was hopeless, but still a cause for mirth.

Guillaume and his servants had caught them in the act of taking stock from Outer Farm. It was the most natural thing to them. In a few hours they would have been in the hills, lost in the straggling woods and mountain bogs. They laughed at Guillaume and put up their hands in surrender. They gibbered at him in the Irish tongue, but he would have none of that nonsense.

In the castle court they explained, through a clerk learned in their barbarous speech, that they were merely carrying on the trade of their ancestors. They offered to pay a fine. They smiled innocently at the seneschal, but now they would smile into eternity.

Guillaume was proud of his achievement. If only other people did their duty, the king's people would be safe in their houses. He called for more ale. Alice wished that he would go. She knew that her father found his brother exhausting.

He referred to his brother as a corner boy. Guillaume de Ypres was a natural brawler. Ypres stood on a crossroads of trading routes. Guillaume had fought with French, Burgundians, English and the followers of the Count of Flanders. He had seen the ebb and flow of war, but eventually he had come with Walter to Ireland to make his fortune. Everything would be well as soon as the Irish were extirpated from English lands and left to exterminate one other. The sooner the better.

She sighed and wiped her floury hands. She brought the pitcher of ale into the inner room. She refilled the tankards. Her father caught her eye and smiled. He raised one conspiratorial eyebrow. Guillaume held out his tankard for her to pour. He perspired and breathed heavily, adjusting his weight to a more comfortable position, settling in for the evening. The third man, William Outlawe, regarded her closely. She filled his tankard. He thanked her graciously, watching her face as she poured.

William Outlawe, despite his name, was a quiet-spoken man in his middle years. Like Walter, he was a banker of considerable wealth, a good friend and frequent fellow investor. He owned a fine stone house not far from the Coal Market, with a long burgage plot stretching down to the river.

Alice knew his orchard and garden well. She had loved to go there as a child and look over the low wall at the dark waters of the Nore. She watched the frogs coupling, almost inert, in the green slimy waters of the New Quay, a narrow slot of slack water, cut between two gardens. She fished their spawn into a pail and waited for weeks to see the tiny black spots sprouting tails and then, wonder of wonders, arms and legs, even toes and fingers. But why?

Once, on a golden autumn day when she was very small, she had stepped out onto the level surface, a pavement of tiny weeds. She remembered the terror of the green pavement yielding beneath her feet and the rank smell of stagnant water. Her fingers clutched the soft mud of the bottom. Even in the depths of the green darkness she heard a shout. She could still feel William Outlawe's strong hand on her collar, pulling her up into the air. She bawled with the shock. Her summer gown was smeared with black mud. Swags of weed hung from her hair and shoulders. She spluttered the vile-smelling water from her lips and bawled again. Her father was speechless, trying to hide his laughter, but William comforted her, wiping the mud and tears from her face. He gave her to his young wife to be cleaned up and wrapped in warm towels. He plucked a peach and gave it to her to take the taste away. She blinked away her tears and looked at the sun, at the blue sky and the high, white clouds. It was good to be alive and not lying with the frogs in the cold and fetid darkness.

Her father carried her home, holding her safe and warm in a heavy woollen shawl. He felt guilty for laughing and anxious to make light of the incident.

'At least, my love, we know that you are no witch,' he said, patting her gently.

'Why?' she asked, inevitably.

'Because if you were a witch, you would not have gone under.'

She pondered this for a while.

'Why?'

'It's all silly nonsense. There are no witches in the real world. Only in tales to frighten children.'

Despite her experience, she still loved the house of William Outlawe. She went there to see the cot men bringing fish into the narrow dock. They paddled small, crude boats dug from a single log. The boats were laden with nets and fish. They brought salmon and trout, char and eels, lampreys, whatever the river condescended to give up in each season. They grumbled about the castle weir and its fish traps and those of the monasteries downriver. Throughout the winter and into Lent they brought casks of salted herring from Ross, balanced precariously in their little bobbing cots. The tide carried them to Innistioge, but after that came the cursed portages around the weirs and mill races.

'Allecia for la bele Aliz,' said a fisherman, lifting a cask of herring onto the dock. His companions sniggered. She wondered about that, figuring that they shared some coarse joke at her expense. She resolved to find out and punish them.

If I were a real witch, she thought, I could bring storms and floods and sweep them all out to sea. I could destroy their nets and starve their families. But these things are not possible. Better to give these Irish churls a wider berth, avoid their smirks and false gallantry. Better in fact, to do as her father wished, to marry the wealthy and recently widowed William and then charge those fishermen through the nose to unload at her dock.

She looked at the three men seated by the window. Guillaume had lapsed into a contemplative silence. He held his tankard in his enormous paw. Occasionally he grumbled or belched. 'Yes, indeed,' he said several times, to nobody in particular.

William sat quietly, drawing wet circles with his tankard, on a small side table. She noted his elegant, yet restrained garb, a short coat trimmed with vair, and wide fashionable sleeves. His shoes were soft and pointed, of the best cordovan leather. His greying temples were lit by a shaft of sunlight through the leaded glass. His neck was somewhat slack and wrinkled. He was getting old, but his elegance compensated. He seemed absorbed in his thoughts.

Walter looked at her again and raised his eyebrow. She smiled a little smile. 'Yes, indeed,' she said. He raised his tankard to her in a silent toast.

TWO

Dies ista gaudij.
Dies leticie.
(This day of joy and happiness.)
— Richard de Ledrede

A STAKE WAS set up in the market-place, a great beam set into a pit of stone and mortar. Nothing would shift it, not even a bear. William spared no cost in making his wedding a memorable event. Butts of ale were hoisted on trestles. His servants poured for all who wanted it. Even the seneschal, Sir Arnaud le Poer, and his lady Agnes, graced the assembly, seated on a high tapestry-covered wagon. The tapestry depicted a hunting scene, a tribute to Sir Arnaud, renowned for his hunting of both men and the beasts of the forest.

Arnaud le Poer, seneschal of the palatine counties of Kilkenny and Carlow, lord of Gras Castle, Croghan, Moytober, Kenles and others too numerous to mention, was a figure to be reckoned with. In English they punned on his name. He was the personification of Power. He epitomized the men who kept the peace and guarded the marches against enemy incursions. He smiled upon William and his new bride.

The bear's cage was manhandled into the circle. The crowd cheered and surged forward to gaze at the monster. The bear roared. The people fell back in fear. Small boys with dirty faces tripped over the feet of those behind them. The chain linking the gyves on the animal's hind paws rattled against the bars. The keeper drew the loose end of the chain out under the door. Henry the Smith, proud of his skill, picked a glowing rivet from his brazier and strode into the circle, holding it aloft in his tongs. The crowd cheered his dexterity. With a few blows of his hammer he shackled the chain to an iron ring at the base of the stake. He stood back and bowed with a flourish. The people admired his muscular arms and his panache. The keeper unbarred the door. The bear lumbered forth.

The crowd fell silent, masters and apprentices, friars and good-wives, urchins and nobles, cripples and men at arms, all waiting in fear and glee to see some sport. The bear lunged to the length of the chain. The people flinched again, cringing from the enraged creature. Nothing like it had ever been seen before. The shackle held. Their courage returned.

The bear stood upright. He looked around at the faces. He raised his forepaws, as if in benediction. The people laughed. Then the dogs were loosed, mastiffs and baying hounds, bulldogs and yapping terriers. There arose a crescendo of barking and snarling, to the cheers of the crowd, when the bear eviscerated a hound or sent a yelping terrier flying through the air with a swipe of his bloody claw. Blood, foam and snot spattered the dusty street. Sometimes a dog fastened mighty jaws around the bear's leg, flailing and snarling as the monster shook him off or tore him to pieces. Sometimes the bear fell on all fours, surging this way and that, wreaking havoc among his assailants, blood pumping from the many gashes in his limbs and face. It was the most magnificent spectacle of courage and strength that anyone had ever witnessed, a fitting accompaniment to the union of two of the most important families in the town.

The circle was strewn with broken and dying dogs. The survivors were called or beaten off and dragged away, to the mockery of the onlookers. Money changed hands and arguments flared. The keeper and some helpers used poles and lances to urge the bear back into the safety of his cage. Henry struck off the shackle and the door was barred again. The crowd cheered.

Sir Arnaud stood and shook hands with William. Walter looked around in satisfaction. Guillaume, red-faced from the heat and too much wine, applauded a fellow brawler. In high good humour, he slapped William's son, Ivo, on the back. The boy scowled and hung his head. Alice, in her lustrous wedding clothes, looked at the stake with its iron ring. She saw the blood and the viscera of the broken dogs. She saw the crowd scattering to the ale butts and other diversions. She felt the hairs rising on the back of her neck. A cold shiver of dread prickled all over her body. The houses swayed before her eyes. She hesitated. Sir Arnaud offered his arm and conducted her to her wedding feast.

∽

The harvests were good. Parliament underscored the peace. Attacks on the Irish at peace with the king were expressly forbidden, but still, no true subjects of the king might style their hair in the notorious culan, that drooping frond of hair that concealed a man's eyes and thereby his intentions. Highways were cleared and bridges repaired. A curb was put on the keeping of idle men, kerns and hobbelars surplus to requirements.

Moreover, it was a good year for money. The king forbade the introduction of bad monies, pollards and crockards into Ireland. He threatened a revival of the custom of castration and amputation of the right hand, for those uttering debased coinage. Only sterlings of the king's coinage might circulate throughout his realm. He forbade increases in wages. He brought stability at last.

Alain Cordouanier was glad of the peace. Although careful to stick to the main roads and to travel in company, it enabled him to wander in search of a better life. As a free man and a master craftsman he could follow any impulse and rise in the world, if God willed it. He could yoke his little horse to his cart and go.

The splendour of the scene brought him to a halt. He turned to his wife, Helene, and to his daughter, where they sat together on their little cart.

'Look,' he said. 'Is it not magnificent? Are you not glad that I brought you here?'

The town glowed in an autumn sunset. The river mirrored the sky, broken only by the curving line of the castle weir and a straggle of willow and osier along its banks. The dark reflection of the mighty castle stood in the glassy water above the weir. All below was a tumble of white. The houses sent up a haze of blue smoke, out of which rose the spires of churches, James and John, Mary and the Magdalene. From the height they could just make out, above the trees, the bulk of the cathedral, a blur of violet against the sunset.

'Oh, it is beautiful,' she replied, slipping down and tucking her hand into his elbow. 'Petra, what do you think?' Petra jumped eagerly down from her perch. She leaned on the low stone wall. She looked down into the river. She smiled.

'It is like the city of God that I have heard of in church. A city of gold.'

They loved the innocent joy of her twelve years. They loved her vivacity and gentleness, her beauty and instinctive delight in God's creation. She was the treasure that they laid up against old age, the reason why Alain toiled and Helene cared for them so well.

They had not cared for Dublin. It was, said Alain, a city of foot-pads and filth, of nightwalkers and guerriers who would cut your throat for a penny. Even the watchmen refused to stir abroad at night, for fear of dogs and men of evil intent. Better than Dublin and better than the low, grovelling towns and villages of Meath, where he had begun his life, was this glowing town on the great river Nore.

'I can see from your poor beast, that you have travelled a long way,' said a voice behind them. They turned from their contemplation of the sunset, to see a young man, a Greyfriar, regarding them with interest. He spoke the heavily accented English of south Leinster. He patted Adam's little horse, a superannuated hobby, not much more than a pony. The horse tore at the lush grass by the roadside, with a soft, rending sound. It shook its ears at the swirling midges. Alain noticed the friar's worn and dusty sandals.

'We have indeed, reverend sir,' he replied 'but now I think our journey has come to an end.'

'Very good,' said the friar, 'but have you made provision for lodgings for the night?' Alain shrugged. 'Surely we will find somewhere in the town.'

'But of course, and it will be my pleasure to conduct you to our abbey, where all Christian people may find a welcome.'

Alain looked at Helene. She seemed relieved. This was a good start.

'We are grateful, reverend sir,' he said, bowing his head. 'In truth the journey has fatigued us greatly.'

'I am Friar John,' replied the friar, pushing back his cowl. 'I have finished my pastoral work for the day and would be happy to walk along with you and hear the news of the country. I like to record everything that I hear, so that the race of Adam will remember.'

'I go by the name of Alain Cordouanier.'

'Well now,' smiled the friar. 'A useful man to have around. There will be plenty of work for you in Kilkenny, I have no doubt. Let us walk down by the Great Bridge and you will see our abbey across the river.'

Friar John liked to talk. It was a reaction, he said, to the long hours of silence enjoined upon his community. He liked to write also. He showed them his ink-stained fingers. '*Rian ár gcoda*, as the Irish say. The mark of our kind. Impossible to remove.' He was nonetheless proud of the stain. 'I am not permitted to write my own opinions.' He spread his hands in a Gallic gesture of helplessness. 'Of which I confess, I have many. Facts, Father Prior insists. Only facts. Too many opinions can stray into error and heresy. And you know where that can lead to.' He assumed a serious mien.

Alain twisted the reins securely in his right hand. The horse clopped gently along. The harness creaked.

'We have few opinions, Friar John. We have our work and our prayers. We are content to listen to those who know better.'

'Very wise, very wise,' nodded the friar, with a gravity that sat uneasily on his young and cheerful features. 'Our great teacher, Roger, the doctor mirabilis, has shown us the dangers of error. Error is an instrument of the Evil One.' He crossed himself at the name.

'I know nothing of that,' said Alain lightly, lifting the mood. 'We are not lettered people. We will accept what you tell us. You are obviously a learned man.'

The friar shrugged. 'It is my task in life. I teach the truth and I record the facts as faithfully as I can, but the funny thing …' He frowned. 'The funny thing is, Roger himself spent much of his life in prison for heresy and error.'

'Perhaps,' suggested Alain, 'he knew too much. Where I come from we learn enough words and enough skill to put bread on the table. Perhaps your great teacher went astray in himself with too much knowledge.'

The friar put his head to one side, turning the idea over in his mind.

'I never thought of it like that. Maybe he did. He was lucky to avoid the stake.' He shrugged again and pointed across the river to the abbey. It stretched like a village along the western bank, a spired church and arched cloisters, a tower, low sunlight glinting on fish ponds and orchards, a white weir and the abbey mills. Alain,

Helene and Petra gazed in admiration. The friar smiled proudly.

'We own nothing and yet we are rich. Rich enough to serve God and his people in the right way. Roger disputed this wealth in poverty, but little good it did him. However, we must hurry now or the gate will be closed.'

They crossed the Great Bridge and entered into Irishtown.

'Welcome to Dublin,' said the guard genially. Alain looked at him in surprise.

'Take no notice of him,' said the friar. 'Herebert likes his foolish joke.'

The guard laughed. 'You will be late for vespers, my brother, and then there will be penance.' He waved them on.

'There is no harm in him,' confided the friar. 'He is the Bishop's man, but he likes to remind people that the Bishop holds his power from Dublin. All Church lands are under Dublin law.'

'Strange,' said Alain. 'I will never understand these matters.'

'Sooth pley, quaad pley, as my friend Walter says,' murmured the friar.

'What is that?' Alain frowned.

'A true joke is a bad joke. Walter is a Fleming. Some day there will be strife between the Bishop and Dublin. Maybe not this bishop, but some day.'

Petra watched birds swooping about the cathedral tower. Their evening squawking filled the air.

They lodged that night in the guest house, warm and well fed. It was their first night under a roof for many weeks. They were inclined to whisper, in awe of the silence all about.

A bell rang for Compline. Petra lay in the darkness, listening to the distant voices chanting in unison. They sang in Latin, 'nunc dimittis', the Canticle of Simeon, an old man who had lived to see salvation. She knew no Latin. The voices rose and fell as the wind gusted. She found it comforting, the sound of safety and security, of voices echoing in darkness, entrusting themselves to God.

In the stillness before dawn Alice heard the chink, chink of the bell calling friars to prayer. She knew that they prayed, 'Let us then cast off the work of darkness and put on the armour of light.' What was that work of darkness? For the friars it was merely sleep. There was an old song, 'Hey how the chevaldoures woke all night', like the hum of flying beetles in the soft autumn darkness. Little golden horses with iridescent wings, flying wherever they wished, swooping over the moonlit river, making love under the over-hanging willows. Perhaps that was the work of darkness.

She listened. She heard a soft 'thud' on the roof, Lucifer returning from some night-time expedition. He seemed to levitate from rooftop to rooftop. There was silence and then another 'thud' and a scramble of claws on slate. She wondered what he would bring for her, a field mouse, a vole, a tattered bird lying cold on the doorstep.

It amused her that Lucifer had decamped from her father's house and followed her to her new home. William's dogs gave him a wide berth, fearing his needle-sharp teeth and flashing claws, but his devotion to Alice was total. Sometimes he came in by her bedroom window, a dark shape flowing through a half-opened casement, to curl up at her feet with a deep, vibrating purr.

William hated the cat. He would rise from the bed in his long night shirt and take Lucifer by the scruff of the neck.

'Get out, get out,' he would say, swearing under his breath as he opened the door. Sometimes he stubbed a toe against a chair in the darkness or stopped to relieve himself with a groan into a jordan. He was not quite the figure of fashion in his long shirt. His arms were thin and white, protruding from the sleeves like peeled elder sticks. In the half-light of dawn there was a white stubble on his usually clean-shaven chin.

'Infernal beast,' he grumbled, pulling back the drapery around the bed. He climbed in and, wrapping the blankets around himself, he turned his back. Soon he was asleep again and snoring, while Alice, feeling the early morning chill, attempted to retrieve some blanket for herself. She looked up at the rafters and drifted into a dream.

She rode with Sir Arnaud and his retinue over the hills of Muckalee. They galloped through forests and over high moorland. The horns sounded, echoing in the frosty wind. The stag led them on, until darkness enfolded them and they came to a lonely castle. The gate was open. They entered the bawn, the horses milling about in the darkness. A feast was prepared in the hall. Braziers glowed with warm, red coals. They drank wine. They spoke only in French, a glittering assembly of noble knights. Sir Arnaud laid her down on a bear-skin robe before a fire. He leaned over her, his dark eyes glinting like rain-washed coal.

She awoke, thwarted by the sound of birds and the tickle of what might have been a flea or even a spider. She had heard once that spiders drink from the eyes of sleepers.

She blinked and scratched the spot. She could not retrieve her dream. She was awake. Thoughts of the day intruded, Sir Arnaud, his voice, his touch, his smile, far away in one of his many manors, perhaps even in England with his liege lord and the king. Her skin crawled at the thought of lice. She would gather some wild lark-spur and make a tincture. Lark's heel, lark's toe. It went by many names; lark's claw, royal knight's spur. Her mother had known all these names and had taught her something of the lore of herbs and flowers. Royal knight's spur. She heard the clinking of his armour and the jingle of harness.

William turned and farted, an old man's fart, careless of any who might hear it. He mumbled in his sleep. She sat up and looked at him in the dawn light. He was a mild and generous man, making few demands on her and granting whatever she asked for. At her request he had sent his son, Ivo, to the household of Guillaume, to learn about hard work and something of the profession of arms. 'To put some backbone into him,' she had suggested, but mainly to remove his surly presence from her household. In the house of Guillaume le Kyteler he would learn to drink and bellow and with a little luck, might fall and break his neck in some clumsy country tournament.

She knew that she had new life stirring inside her. It was something of a wonder, given that William was not greatly interested in the pleasures of the bed. She had imagined that a man twice her age, with a young and lusty wife, noticed by all the men of Hightown and beyond, might have luxuriated in his good fortune, storing up carnal delight before old age shrivelled him up like an empty husk. But no. William was measured and courteous when he came to her, brief in his lovemaking and she knew that all was done when he groaned, 'O Jhesu! Jhesu!' and fell back exhausted. Where was the soaring ecstasy, the blazing union of … ?

There was that flea again. She lifted the sheet carefully. There he was, humping his way across the broad, white expanse of her nightdress. He stopped as if deep in thought. She moved to capture him, to feel the satisfying click of an enemy extinguished between fingernail and thumbnail, but he knew her mind. He toyed with her for a moment, feigning ignorance of the approaching finger and then he sprang. He vanished. She wondered how. It was a kind of magic. How might he come to earth again without dashing himself to pieces?

It was a foolish speculation. She knew that she would get him some time. She slipped from the bed and sat pondering the day. She thought that she might go to the abbey to be shriven of the lustful thoughts brought on by her dream. She would ask for Friar John, newly ordained and innocent of the world. She would tell him of her sinful lust and how her body reacted every time Sir Arnaud came into her thoughts. She would ask for his advice and watch him squirm in an agony of embarrassment. She would kneel before him and implore his blessing. She would look up at him with wide, tearful eyes. He would make the Sign of the Cross over her and flee from the room. She could crush him between finger and thumb if she wished. She smiled at her power, but still she liked Friar John. She liked his cheerful kindness and his love of knowledge. She had seen the manuscripts he copied and had heard him discuss his annals with her father. She would not destroy Friar John for sport. Not yet anyway.

∽

'I see,' said Walter, drumming his fingertips on the table. 'You require a loan to secure a place to set up in trade.'

'My friend is a master cordwainer,' interjected Friar John.

'A cobbler,' said Walter.

'No, good sir,' Alain put in. 'A master cordwainer, not a cobbler.'

'I see.' Walter conceded the difference. 'Why therefore are you wandering the country? Should you not have a workshop and apprentices?'

'He has come to our town to find a peaceful place for his family,' said the friar.

'Hmm, and how do I know that you will not wander off again and leave me at the loss of my money? Have you anything that you might place with me as an earnest of good faith?' Walter looked from Alain to the friar and back again.

Alain held out his hands, palms upwards.

'Do you see these callouses? I have my skill and my good name. I have the safety of my wife and child in these hands. I have the bones of Saint Hugh. Your money will be safe with me.'

Walter looked to Alice where she stood by the window. She could see Alain's pony and cart with a woman and a child standing by it. It was a pretty child with long fair hair.

'What do you think, Alice?' asked Walter with the ghost of a smile. 'Should we risk our silver on this cordwainer? Does he strike you as a steady man?'

Alice turned from the window. She dropped a demure curtsey

to Friar John. The friar blushed. He felt the heat rising even to his ears.

'I think you should, Father. Our soles are always in need of protection in this rough world. Is that not so, Friar John?'

The friar mumbled in some confusion.

'Well it is done, then,' said Walter expansively. 'I have a premises, albeit outside the walls, which should suit your purposes. It lies just beyond the Great Bridge, but convenient to the town and the tanners. Your family should be comfortable there.' He extended his hand. 'The good friar will direct you and if it proves satisfactory, come to me in the morning and we can draw up the indenture.'

He liked Alain's firm handshake. He brought them to the door. He spoke to Helene and patted the child on the head. He returned to the room, pleased with the transaction.

'What did he mean about the bones?' Alice had been puzzling about it as she watched the family departing.

'Saint Hugh. He was a shoemaker and a Christian martyr. The Emperor had him crucified like our Blessed Saviour. He forbade his companions to take the body from the cross and over time, his bones fell to the ground.'

'So our friend carries relics of the saint. Very strange.' Alice frowned.

'No, not quite. Hugh's companions gathered up the bones and made them into shoemaker's tools. Every shoemaker carries the bones of Saint Hugh.'

'I see,' said Alice thoughtfully. 'The power of the saint lies in the tools.'

'More so in the hands that wield them,' replied her father absently. He picked up a tally stick of soft poplar wood and began to write on it with a quill. The ink blurred in the soft grain. He wrote on one half and then repeated everything on the other half. He drew a jagged line across the centre and looked at his work with an air of satisfaction.

THREE

Cruore nam rubente – in carne fulgida
Tolluntur nostra mente – patrata scelera.
*(By crimson blood our consciences are
cleansed of sin.)*
—Richard de Ledrede

BROTHER FERGAL LOVED his work. For almost seventy years he
had lived in the abbey, the last of the Irish friars to survive the great
changes. He was no threat to the English king in his possession of
his Irish lands. Neither was he a threat to the great men of the order
in their wisdom and piety. He just loved to tend the gardens and
the orchards, to sing in his cracked voice of the glory of God and
to mix the inks for the clever calligraphers of the scriptorium. His
understanding of the written word was not great, but he knew that
books contained power to triumph over time, to preserve the truth
against all vicissitudes.

But the clever men could not work without ink. That was his
particular skill. He made sturdy workaday black, by grinding charcoal so small that he could not feel the grains between finger and
thumb. He bound it with rainwater and Arabian gum. It served well

enough, but it tended to flow down the sloping parchment and form little feet at the base of each letter. He always smiled at the idea of the words dancing in little black shoes, tapping out their hidden meanings to a piper's tune. For grander work he gathered oak galls in the woods outside the walls. Oak apples, people called them, but they contained no nourishment. Each gall was pierced by a pin hole, where a tiny wasp had escaped from his dark cradle. Did the creature know, wondered Fergal, what a contribution it had unwittingly made to learning? In the great days of Outremer, before the Holy Land was taken back by the heathens, the best oak apples came from Aleppo. All very fine, but in those days he had no excuse to wander in the autumn woods, kicking through leaf mould, listening to the wild creatures and the rushing of the wind. He had known those woods as a boy. He had poached the lord's rabbits, in fear of his life. He recalled the sweet smell of a blown thrush's egg and the early morning thrill of new mushrooms.

He ground the galls as fine as the charcoal. He infused them in wine and let them sit for a few days. Then he added the sal mortis, brought all the way from Moorish Spain. Finally, drop by drop, he added the obedient Arabian gum. He stirred the mixture carefully with a fig stick, always a fig stick, from the orchard of the lady Alice, and strained it into the ink-horns of the learned men.

Of all the colours, though, braise was the most exciting, the heart's blood of the brezil tree. Deep in the forests of India lived the wondrous tree, its heart-wood as red as burning coals. Brother Fergal reflected with pride on the great reach of his order. In every part of Christendom the Greyfriars could be found. Friar John maintained that if new races were ever to be found, even on the moon, the Greyfriars would be there, spreading the Gospel of the Lord. They would go in poverty and humility and in the name of Blessed Francis. Their houses would become part of the great chain of monasteries that bound the civilized world together and enabled a poor lay-brother in Kilkenny to handle the precious goods of Araby, Portugal and Spain.

He felt a warm glow of pride to play a small part in such a great organization. He stirred the precious scarlet fluid and strained out the flecks of wood. This was the colour for rubrics and gaudy days and for little flourishes around a capital letter. He tapped the fig stick to release the last drops into a glass jar. He held the container up to the light of the window. It glowed like the blood of Christ Himself.

He heard a low cough. The Father Prior stood in the doorway. A strange monk stood beside him, his hands tucked into his sleeves. Something in the stranger's bleak expression sent a chill of fear through Brother Fergal's veins. He put down the jar of ruby ink and stood deferentially. The prior beckoned to him.

∽

Alice watched her infant son tumbling on the floor. He was a merry, laughing boy, with a stubborn streak. He was handsome, as his father had once been. It was a great pity that her own father, Walter, had not lived to see the continuation of his line. Nevertheless, he had left her comfortably provided for, independent of the wealth of William Outlawe. Soon, she reflected, the bulk of that wealth would be hers also. She had seen to it that her husband had drawn up a new will, to the virtual exclusion of the son of his first wife, the surly and resentful Ivo.

William Outlawe was fading fast. The flesh had shrunk off him. He plucked at the bedclothes. His breath came in rasping gasps. It was as much as he could do to swallow a mouthful of broth or one of his wife's vile-tasting herbal brews. He could not deny that she was attentive. He took consolation from the fact that she had a son to keep her company and, in the fullness of time, to take over the administration of her affairs. Another William Outlawe.

He took comfort too from the sacrament brought to him daily by the kindly Friar John and the knowledge that Masses would be said for him in the cathedral, that holy words would reverberate among the rafters and protect his soul on its flight to Heaven. He feared the outer darkness that he must traverse and kept a candle lighting near him, as he told his beads.

Alice prodded the little boy with the tip of her father's staff. She teased him, making a sweeping motion in front of him.

'All the wealth of Kilkenny town come to the door of William, my son,' she rhymed. The boy laughed, trying to seize the stick. She let him take it. He straddled it like a horse and toddled about in great good humour.

This William was a lucky child, born exactly thirteen hundred years after Christ, thirteen being the number of Christ and His Apostles. With her guidance he would be the wealthiest man in all of Ireland. Great noblemen, even the king himself, might come to him for the favour of a loan.

The boy clattered the end of the staff against the furniture. Alice smiled indulgently. In his bed in the room above, William Outlawe started at the noise. Lucifer the cat slid in by the open window. He looked at the sick man in the bed and arched his back. William flapped an ineffectual hand at the animal.

'Get out, you demon,' said William. The cat stared at him with hostility flaring in its eyes. It backed away and disappeared out the window. William crossed himself and pulled the covers up to his chin. His hands were cold.

∼

Friar John paused in reading his office. He looked down the length of the arched colonnade. The wind whipped at the pages of his breviary. He closed the book and tucked it into a pocket in his sleeve. Down in the orchard he could see Brother Fergal at work, raking leaves. As quickly as he raked up a little pile, the wind whipped them away again, sending them whirling about the old man and scattering in all directions.

Friar John smiled. It was a saying of the old lay-brother in his long-unused mother tongue '*Ní hé lá na gaoithe lá na scolb.*' The day of the wind is not the day for thatching. That applied also to leaves. It was more than just practical housekeeping. Everything has its own season. He left the draughty colonnade and walked down into the orchard by the dark rushing river. Winter was on its way. Brother Fergal stood dejected, amid a swirling blizzard of leaves. Friar John was shocked to see that he was weeping.

'Your work will keep for another day,' said the friar gently, taking the rake from the old man's hand. The tears rolled down Brother Fergal's lined face and soaked into his beard. He shook his head.

'There will not be another day. I should finish my work.' He reached to take back the rake.

'And why is that?' asked Friar John. 'You have many years of work left in you.' He tried to make light of it.

Brother Fergal looked at him. His eyes were red-rimmed from weeping. His voice quavered.

'I must go away from here. Father Prior says that I must leave. He has had his orders from Friar Simon, the Visitor.'

'But why is this?' asked Friar John in confusion.

'Because I am Irish.' A tinge of anger came into the old man's voice. 'No Irish may remain in the monasteries in English lands. We are a danger to the king.' He sniffed. 'He said that I would be happier among my own kind. I said that I thought I was among my own kind.' He shook his head.

'I will speak to Father Prior,' said the younger man. 'Perhaps there has been a misunderstanding.'

'No, no,' protested the old man. 'The Visitor insisted. He is a frightening man. He hates all Irish people. He even said that in certain circumstances, it is no mortal sin to murder an Irishman. He said that I was lucky they were making provision for me at all.'

'But we are brothers, no matter what nation we come from. Before God and our holy founder, we are all brothers.' Friar John shook his head. 'I will speak to them. Have no fear. All will be well.'

All was not well. The visitor was inflexible. The prior was over-awed. He sat with his fingers laced together and eyes downcast.

'He is an old man,' said Friar John. 'He has lived all his life in this town. In pity's name, do not uproot him now.'

'It is decided,' said the Visitor. 'In himself he may be a good and holy man, but in his race he is a contamination. They are vile and treacherous people, mired in error and heresy.'

'I have never heard this before,' protested the young friar.

'You are young and probably gullible, my son,' said Friar Simon, 'and for that I shall make allowances. It would take too long to enumerate the many errors into which the Irish have strayed and the barbarous practices our Irish brothers condone in return for alms.'

'Brother Fergal is a poor man. He takes nothing for himself. He lives as our founder ordained, in the service of others.'

The Visitor froze. 'This poverty is yet another heresy. Have you forgotten that our Holy Father settled this issue? Have you forgotten that our own great teacher, Roger Bacon, was imprisoned for many years for preaching poverty? You must be careful, my son. Error is all around us. We must be on our guard. This matter is settled.'

He made the Sign of the Cross at Friar John, with the side of his hand in a rapid, chopping motion. The prior shuffled awkwardly. He cleared his throat.

'Friar Simon has agreed, out of charity, that you may accompany Brother Fergal on his journey. You will see that it is for the best.'

Friar John tried one last plea. 'Winter is coming on. Could we at least wait until spring?'

Friar Simon looked up. His eyes were like splinters of ice. 'I am not accustomed to argument, my son. I strongly suggest that you reflect on your vow of obedience and make preparations for your journey. We are building a new house in Cork, in a place called Timoleague. Brother Fergal's skills will be invaluable to our Irish brethren, I have no doubt. You are dismissed.'

Friar John stepped back. He bowed his head and turned away. He felt the cold flagstones through the worn soles of his sandals. The wind whistled through the arched cloister. He hunched his shoulders and thrust his hands into his sleeves.

He decided to speak to William Outlawe. William was a man of influence. His kinsman, Friar Roger, was a powerful man in the order, Prior of Kilmainham and sometime deputy justiciar. Perhaps he could put in a word for a poor lay-brother. Perhaps a gift of silver might fend off the danger posed by Brother Fergal to the king's loyal servants.

But William Outlawe was gone. Neither his wealth nor his fur-lined robes could keep warmth in his emaciated body. His house was in mourning. His young widow hid her grief with a black veil. The servants walked softly in the dead man's house. Friar John knelt by the bed and prayed. He forgot his own troubles as he prayed to God, out of the depths, for a pilgrim soul. The cat came purring into the darkened room and rubbed against his knee. He stood up in alarm. The cat prowled about the room and then paced out the half-opened door, flicking its tail.

∼

Petra walked down to the river through the long grass. She stood quietly amid the withered sedge and the tall, shrivelled stalks of hemlock. She watched the river. It glided at speed, swollen with winter rain. She waited in the hope of seeing a kingfisher or even an otter. In summer she was always rewarded by a flash of turquoise, but not on this occasion. The brown water swirled along the margin, bending the rushes and forcing them to bow to its will. The rushes and tall grasses streamed towards the bridge and the weir beyond. Flood debris piled against arch swallows and the water seemed to pile up also, as if it might sweep the bridge away.

She was conscious of the ground beneath her feet becoming soggy from her weight. She stepped back onto more solid ground.

She looked down at her boots. They were soaked through. The red dye had dulled to a murky brown. Her father, she reflected, would not be pleased after all the care he had taken to make them. She began to snap off the dry stalks of the hemlock as a peace offering. She resolved to build up a fire to make the house warm and cosy. She wandered upriver until she had gathered a good bundle. A bend of the river took her out of sight of the house. She stood, holding her bundle of twigs, and watched a large tree trunk gliding past. It looked like a great ship. She wondered what it would be like to ride upon its back all the way down to the sea. A voice startled her, breaking into her reverie.

'It seems to me, Adam, that we have got ourselves a poacher.'

She turned to see two men on horseback looking down at her. One was black-bearded and wore his hood thrown back to reveal a round, close-cropped head. The other, a younger man, had long, fair hair, not unlike her own. They looked at each other grimly. Their horses stamped in the wet grass. The breath rumbled in their nostrils. The bridles clinked.

Petra's mouth was dry. She trembled.

'Do you recall the penalty, Adam, for those who despoil the king's forest?'

The younger man rubbed his chin.

'Not offhand, my lord, but I can consult the lawyers. I believe it to be something quite terrible. Perhaps flaying alive. Stretched out to be devoured by weasels. I have seen something about it in good Law French.'

'Hmm,' said the dark man. 'That sounds about right.'

Petra clutched her bundle of twigs. It seemed to offer some protection.

'What are you doing here, young lady?' The dark man's voice reverberated. 'What other crimes are you about? Are you taking my fish perhaps, or setting snares for my small game?'

Petra licked her dry lips. She found her voice, shaky as it was.

'No my lord. I am merely gathering sticks for the fire.' A twinge of defiance came into her tone. 'There are plenty for all. You have all the rest of the forest.'

The men looked down at her for a long moment in silence then they burst into laughter.

'So you are not afraid. Do you not fear the might of Sir Arnaud le Poer, the great seneschal of all this land?' He swept his gauntleted hand in a wide circle. His horse stamped its hooves in sudden alarm. It stepped back in a half-circle. He grasped the reins, bringing it under control. 'What have you to say for yourself?'

Petra looked up into his coal-black eyes.

'I am the daughter of honest parents, good Christian people. We do no harm to anyone. If you are noble knights, as you seem to be, then it is your duty to protect us, not frighten us in our daily tasks.'

The men looked at each other. They smiled somewhat sheepishly.

'You speak well, young lady. We are rightly rebuked. We have offended against courtoisie. We ask your pardon. Do we not, Adam?' The dark man spoke gently.

'We do indeed,' concurred Adam. 'It was a churlish jest. We must make amends.'

'I am indeed Sir Arnaud, the seneschal. You may gather wood at any time without fear. This is my friend Adam le Blound, vain of his good looks, but generous withal.'

He punched his friend playfully on the arm. 'And who might you be?'

'I am Petra, daughter of Alain Cordwainer. At least that is what he is called now. We used to speak French when we lived in Meath.'

'I see,' replied Sir Arnaud. 'So you braved the Irish rebels and the country roads to come here to my town.'

She nodded.

'You are welcome, little Petronilla de Midia. I hope that you may prosper here.'

She tried to curtsey but the bundle of twigs prevented her. Adam smiled at her awkwardness.

'Do you dance, young lady,' he asked.

'Yes sir,' she said. 'I dance sometimes on the dancing green, when the country people come in and the pipers play. I have danced in the churchyard on Saint John's Eve, to find a husband but,' she smiled shyly, 'I have had no luck so far.'

'Well then you shall dance at my wedding. I am to be married at Easter time and there will be dancing.' He looked down at her feet and smiled. 'You must polish up your little red shoes and dance a cantilena for us at Easter.'

She wriggled her toes in her soaking shoes. The water was cold. She felt a stab of fear at the thought of mingling with the great people of Hightown, a mere shoemaker's daughter, but then she thought, 'Why not?' It was only dancing and that she could do as well as any.

'We must go and look at the bridge,' said Sir Arnaud. 'And put men down to cut away the debris.' He pulled his horse around and saluted Petra. 'I am at your service,' he said with perhaps more gallantry than was called for. He had enjoyed the encounter. Adam also saluted. He was a man who appreciated beauty, even in a lowly shoemaker's daughter.

'I shall send for you, Petronilla de Midia,' he called, looking back as they rounded a clump of willows.

She followed slowly, until she came in sight of the bridge. The drifting tree was lodged athwart one of the arches. Already men were going down on ropes, in peril of their lives, to cut it free. The plangent sound of steel on wood echoed in the gathering dusk and seemed to bounce back from the stones of the cathedral and from the pewter surface of the weir.

FOUR

Nam fas non est inter nos – locus tristicie
Dum salus nobis oritur – fons vite venie.
(This is no place of sadness, for a font of
salvation and pardon springs up for us.)
—Richard de Ledrede

THE SLEET STUCK to Friar John's heavy cloak as he walked with eyes slitted against the wind. He wrapped his sleeve around the hand that held the bridle of Alain Cordwainer's little horse. His feet nonetheless glowed from the long walk and the stout sandals his friend had provided for the journey. Brother Fergal slept under a canvas cover that had been their only shelter for many nights. It was a relief to walk, away from the old man's incessant chatter. Friar John tired of his companion's store of legends and yarns of heroes and saints. It was as if a hidden well had been tapped, or a long-concealed trove had been discovered. The sound of the Irish tongue in everyone they encountered had revived in him his childhood memories of rhymers and storytellers, of giants and fabulous voyages. Friar John pondered these fantastical tales, but there were no facts to back them up. Boulders on mountain tops were no proof of giants. Dark mountain lakes were just that, dark mountain lakes, not entrances to hell or the realm of the Little People. He began to suspect that what they said about the Irish, that they were a bestial people, might well be true. Not bestial in any sinful sense, but motivated like animals, by appetite and sentiment, by instinct rather than logic. He longed for his books and the pure reason of the great teachers.

He saw a light in the darkness ahead. He resolved to call, regardless of risk, on the charity of whosoever might dwell in that high mountain wilderness. He quickened his pace. The encrusted sleet fell in slabs from his heavy woollen cloak. The cart jolted over the stony track. The dark shape of a building loomed ahead. He called out, to warn of his approach. A door opened and a rectangle of light showed the figure of a man. Dogs barked.

The man dragged his right leg. He carried a heavy cudgel. He looked at the strange friar and from him to the cart. He threw back the canvas cover.

'*An bhfuil sé marbh?*' He jerked his thumb at the sleeping Brother Fergal.

Friar John shook his head. He knew enough Irish words to understand, but was unable to string them into speech. Brother Fergal sneezed at the inrush of cold air. He sat up and blinked.

The man spoke again in Irish and Fergal replied. They nodded. The man looked at Friar John and raised his eyes, as if in pity.

'He's telling us to come inside out of the weather. There is a shed for the animal.'

Friar John was, at first, reluctant to let go of the bridle, but the man loosed his frozen fingers and led the horse away into the darkness. There was nothing for it but to go inside.

The room was warm and lit by a turf fire in a pit in the middle of the earthen floor. The smoke gathered under the thatch and escaped through a hole in the gable. The furniture, beds and some shelving, was made of stone slabs built as part of the walls. Sawn logs served as stools by the fire.

A second man, very like the first, stood up from his stool. He gestured to them to draw in to the fire, which they were glad to do. They stood, holding their hands to the flames, until their robes began to steam, adding a new element to the fetid atmosphere of the room.

'*Gratias agimus*,' began Friar John but the man pointed to his mouth and made a gargling noise. He shrugged.

'*Níl teanga ar bith aige*,' said the first man, coming in and pushing the door to.

'No tongue,' explained Brother Fergal.

They sat at the man's invitation. The stiffness and cold began to leave their bones. He brought them two nips of a fiery liquor in wooden cups. Friar John drank. He felt the heat trickle down into his vitals, like molten lead. It burned his throat and seemed to forage down his spine to lodge deep inside him, like a live coal in the core of his exhausted body. He drank again. He sighed.

Brother Fergal dealt with the introductions. He explained that they were travelling far to the west; that they had come all the way from Kilkenny and that they appeared to have lost their way. He listened attentively to the man's reply.

'He says that we are welcome to stay as long as we need. Himself and his brother get very little company, he says.'

'Tell him that we are grateful, but that we must push on in the morning.' Friar John realized that he was impatient to be done with his journey. He longed for the peace and order of his abbey and the safety of Kilkenny's walls at night. Set apart from the conversation, he began to pray. In truth, he admitted, he prayed for their safety. He wondered if Brother Fergal might revert to type, like a wild creature reared in captivity. In the darkness he might league himself with these two Irish ruffians and cut his throat as he slept. For a moment he imagined that eyes were watching from the darkness in the corners of the room. He heard animals snuffling on the other side of the dividing wall. Poor Alain Cordwainer would be at the loss of his horse. Brother Fergal interrupted his meditations.

'He is Felim Bacach Mac Giollapatrick and this is his brother, Conal. He says that he should be the chief of his nation, but his uncle had the two of them maimed. Now they look after the uncle's sheep on this mountainside.'

Felim spat into the fire. He gave a bitter laugh and said something under his breath.

'They will get their revenge some day, he says. The uncle styles himself FitzPatrick nowadays, like the Norman lords, but he fools nobody. Felim would rather have a decent Norman lord any day than his own kin.'

'I see,' said Friar John, distractedly. There were eyes watching him from a bed of straw.

'Spideog,' said Felim, following the friar's gaze. '*Tar amach.*'

The straw rustled. A boy of about five or six years of age emerged into the light. He wore a tunic of rough woollen cloth and was barefoot. He approached cautiously and sat down by the fire. He rubbed the sleep from his dark, slanting eyes. His skin was sallow and his hair black and long. The friar imagined that he was what a Saracen, or some other heathen child might look like. The firelight gave a reddish hue to the child's skin, making him even more strange. His eyes flicked from one face to another in the firelight, like the eyes of a wary little bird.

'Spideog,' grunted Felim. '*Arán.*'

The child rose and took a loaf from one of the stone shelves. He tore it to pieces and passed it to the men. He squatted again by the fire. He tore at a piece of bread with strong, white teeth.

The men talked. Conal gave a guttural laugh as he listened eagerly to news of the outside world. He tried to form words, but lapsed again into silence. Friar John surreptitiously watched the child.

'He doesn't say much,' confided Brother Fergal. 'Our friend here says that he has little cause to speak. A quiet house. It's the *uaigneas* out here in the mountains. The loneliness.'

'I suppose so. Whose is the child anyway?'

'Ah, *sin scéal eile*, he says. Another story.' Brother Fergal stretched. 'A story for another day.' He yawned and lay down on a pile of straw. He gathered his cloak about him and in a moment he was snoring. Sods collapsed in the fire and the room became dim.

The child played a game with pebbles, tossing them and catching them on the back of his hand, one, two, three, four, five, then replacing them on the ground, one at a time. He repeated the process again and again. The fire subsided. There was nothing for it but to sleep and gather strength for the journey.

In the morning snow had drifted against the house to the height of a man. Sheep huddled in the lee of dry-stone walls. Felim's dogs sank to their bellies in the soft surface. The men looked out at an infinity of white.

'He says we will go nowhere for a good while yet,' remarked Brother Fergal. 'We will be here until after Christmas. He says we are welcome.'

Friar John felt cold dismay in the pit of his stomach. The child came and tugged at his hand. He urged him towards the turf-stack and put some sods into his hands. He pointed to the open door of the house. Friar John did as he was bid.

∽

Richard de Ledrede was a happy man. He stayed the winter in Paris. He listened to the scholars and the lawyers and he lost no opportunity to dispute with them. They were frequently in error, but he set them straight. He measured them against the plumb-line of his intellect and the rectitude of his own holiness. He carried about him the Franciscan aura of learning and authority. He was a man to be reckoned with.

His greatest joy, however, was to stand in Notre Dame and look up at the heavenly splendour of the windows. It was fitting that the Virgin should be celebrated in such a place. In the low winter sun he read the Old and New Testaments in the great rose windows. He looked up at the carving of the crowning of Mary as Queen of Heaven, over the main portal. What would it be like to have a church of his own and such windows, blazing with colour to welcome in the day? His own poor poems, which he showed to nobody, reflected his dedication to Mary and her Son. It was not vainglory to want to praise God in a church built by his own efforts. It was not arrogance to want to lead the ignorant and the deluded into the light.

He knelt and prayed, rededicating himself to his mission. He scratched the irritating mole on his shin. He thought of Rome and the papal court. He was impatient for winter to relent so that he might continue with his journey. He was impatient to reach his destiny.

෮

'God blast your mother, young Ivo,' growled Guillaume le Kyteler. 'She has secured a judgment against me in the sum of three thousand pounds.'

His feet squelched in the mud and filth of the street. He aimed a kick at a sow snuffling in offal from the shambles.

'She is not my mother,' snapped Ivo. 'I have no time for the bitch.'

'Whatever she is she, she is trying to ruin me. My brother, God rest him, lent that money to me. He would turn over in his grave to think that his daughter would set the sheriff against his own flesh and blood. What do you think she said to me? What do you think she said to me?' His voice rose with indignation. He looked as if he might explode.

Ivo knew what she had said. In fact, the passers-by in the street had stopped to enjoy the exchange. Alice's door stood open.

Guillaume had bellowed about his service to king and lord. He had spent not only money but his very blood in defending the people of the Middle Nation. No, by God, he would not pay.

'You are mistaken, sir,' she replied firmly. 'This is not a family matter. My father's debtors, and my husband's, are now mine. You either pay what you owe or I shall distrain on your land and property. The law is with me.'

'You unnatural hag,' shouted Guillaume. 'I will see you damned for usury, before you get a penny from me.' He thumped the counting-table. The markers scattered to the floor.

Alice held his gaze. He swore and turned away. He scattered the eavesdroppers at the door and stepped into the street. Alice let her breath go in a long sigh of relief.

Guillaume strode on, with Ivo hurrying to keep pace with him.

'I will speak to the sheriff about this,' growled Guillaume. 'I will speak to the seneschal himself. No, by God, I will take service with the king against the Scots. One way or another we will mend our fortunes. You shall come with me, boy. When we come back with money in our purses we will turn that bitch out into the street.'

He thumped Ivo on the shoulder. 'What do you say, my boy? Is this not a good plan?'

Already Guillaume was cheering up at the brilliance and simplicity of his scheme. The age had not yet grown so degenerate that a man could not repair his finances with sword and lance. Ivo was not so sure. It might take longer. It might take years, but some day he would see her and her snivelling brat brought to book.

∽

'It is the worst winter in my memory,' asserted Brother Fergal, 'and I can go back a long way.' He pulled his loose grey habit up to his knees and let the fire play upon his shins. His shins were white and skinny. The heat raised a maze of red and blue veins. The skin shone over bone.

'I remember when I was a boy …' He rambled off on some distant recollection of Irishtown and the great days of long ago.

Friar John was only half-listening. He found that the meaning was coming to him unbidden. The phrases of Irish he had picked up in his daily rounds were beginning to join together. He had watched ice, one starry night, crystal straws of ice on a water butt, reaching out to one another, until the entire surface was unyielding to his probing finger. His fellow friars thought he was a bit mad. He was certainly frozen, but he had seen something he had never noticed before. Ice was just something that was there on a frosty morning. It was a property of water. It hung from the thatch in a veil of icicles. He broke them off and they turned to water in his hand. He put some over the fire in Felim Bacach's copper pot. It turned to water, seethed and disappeared. Why was that? He had plenty of time to ponder the mystery.

Now he found that the Irish words had joined together to form a mesh in his head. Phrases floating isolated in his mind, reached out and linked together. He could follow the conversations and even offer some opinions. On his daily excursions with the two brothers, to carry fodder to the sheep, he discovered speech and physical well-being. He enjoyed hoisting a bundle of hay on his shoulder and trudging off into the white wilderness. He began to talk easily with Felim. He wondered where the words had come from.

'A *bandraoi*,' Felim was saying. 'I would have used her myself only I was afraid of her.'

'A maga, a witch!' said Brother Fergal. 'God between us and all harm.'

'It's true,' averred Felim. 'When she looked at me I shook with dread.'

'No, no, no, no, no,' laughed Brother Fergal. 'You are still a young man. You were overcome with lust, with carnal desire. It takes a man's reason away. I remember, years ago …' He was off again on some rambling anecdote to illustrate his point. 'Never bothered me, thank God.'

Donal laughed again, his gargling laugh. Friar John wondered if he was imprisoned with mad men.

'*Cad a duirt tú?*' he asked in Irish. They looked at him in surprise. 'Aha!' said Felim, 'so you do understand.'

Friar John made a self-deprecating gesture, holding his hands out, palm upwards.

'A little,' he said. 'But what were you saying about a witch?'

'The child's mother,' said Felim. 'We took her in. I delivered the child myself. It was no bother to me, what with lambing and all.' He looked at his hands. 'No bother at all.'

'That was a charitable thing to do,' nodded the friar. 'A true Christian thing. So what became of her? Why did she leave the child with you?'

Felim was silent. 'Where did she come from?' urged the friar. He wished that he had pen and parchment. There was a story here. 'Where did she come from?'

'From beyond the sea,' said Felim after a while. 'From some heathen country. She followed a young priest coming back from pilgrimage, I don't know. Art was his name, I believe. She was his hearth-woman, his *focaria*, as they say. They were lovers.' He blushed. 'It's not a subject for the ears of holy men.'

'It's all right,' Friar John assured him. 'I understand about the world. This is not unknown in the Church. We are men also, my son.' He stopped, realizing that he had slipped into priestly mode. Felim was ten years or more his senior. 'Felim,' he corrected, 'we are men also, Felim.'

He saw Alice kneeling before him, a penitent. She confessed to a terrible sin. On Midsummer Eve she had climbed the cathedral tower. She was only a child. She knew no better. The door should not have been left open, the steps unattended. She carried a cat. She looked down from the top, in the pale after-glow of the midsummer sunset. She saw, among the tombstones, the white arse of Canon Bibulous, rising and falling on top of a woman of the town. Canon Godfrey was his proper name. He lodged in the Common Hall, a faithful servant of the cathedral, with an unfortunate weakness for the wine of Gascony.

He enjoyed his food. In truth he was both corpulent and bibulous. He walked with some difficulty, but it was said (it was an uncharitable thing to say) that he copulated with the facility of a boar.

She saw the white arse of Canon Bibulous. She heard him grunt. She threw the cat. The creature screeched as it fell. It landed on the couple below. She watched through a slit window. The woman screamed. The Canon clambered to his feet, pulling his drawers about him and lumbering away, crossing himself and uttering pious ejaculations. She lingered over the word.

Friar John had closed his eyes. She was truly contrite. Incongruously, he had asked her about the cat. She shrugged. It was not her cat, the dark, pacing Lucifer, master of the stable yard. It was a difficult one to judge. It was not included among the categories of venial and mortal. Perhaps a reserved sin, one for the Bishop himself to adjudicate on. She was young and tearful with remorse. He raised his hand and granted her absolution. She withdrew.

It was a terrible thing to do to a man of the Church. A dreadful thing. He felt a smile twitching at the corners of his mouth. It was a story worthy of the telling, but one that must remain locked in the seal of confession.

Canon Bibulous grappling with his lesser linen, and retribution falling upon him, spitting and snarling, from Heaven. Friar John chuckled. He began to laugh. Tears came to his eyes. If only he could share the mirth with his brothers. He could see them guffawing around the refectory table, red of face, slapping each other on the back at the discomfiture of the secular churchman and, by association, his bishop. One up for the friars. Even the Blackfriars, the Domini Canes, the hounds of God, might crack a bleak smile at that one.

'What's so funny?' asked Felim, perplexed.

'Oh nothing, nothing.' The friar realized that he had been chuckling. 'Go on. Go on.'

'There came a new bishop,' Felim resumed. 'A younger man,

full of zeal. He threw her out. She took to the roads.'

'And the priest?'

'The Bishop set him to work in his fields. He broke him with penance and labour. The poor man burned marl and carried dung, but he was still a priest. They say he was a good priest, even after all that, but she ran mad for the love of him. She was whipped out of every parish and so she came here. On a winter's day just like this, we found her in the snow. We took her in.'

'Were you not afraid of the Bishop?'

'Arrah, he died not long after. They say she put a curse on him. I don't know, but he got whatever he deserved.'

'Dangerous talk, my son.' He was doing it again.

'What?' Felim expostulated. 'Up here on this mountain. Fuck the Bishop, savin' your presence. It was no Christian thing to do. Not a Christian thing at all. What do I care for a dead bishop?'

There was silence. Friar John had no ready answer. Brother Fergal shook his head sadly. He was upset by the element of confrontation.

'I remember years ago ...' He looked at the sombre faces around the fire. His voice trailed away, a story for another time.

Friar John coughed. 'Where is the boy anyway?' he asked awkwardly.

'I sent him to look after the animals. That little horse of yours is gettin' fat on our hay.' Felim tried to raise the mood. 'He's a good child, I have to say, even for a child of sin. I wish sometimes he had more of a chance in life. He has a brain in his head. This is no place for him.'

The friar sat immersed in his thoughts. He noticed the polished pebbles lying beside the fire. Idly he picked them up and tried to do what the boy had done. The pebbles spilled from the back of his hand. He tried again with less success. He formed them into a line. He made a square and placed one pebble in the middle. He made a pentangle. It occurred to him that he might pass the time until the thaw came, in teaching the boy his numbers. Perhaps by counting he could coax language from him. It would be the Christian thing.

'Don't touch his pebbles,' said Felim quietly. 'They are from his mother's grave.'

The friar replaced the pebbles as he had found them. His heart was overcome with pity and sadness. He wished again for a warm wind from the south.

FIVE

Natus est de Virgine
In praesepi adoratur
Hodie
Natus est de Virgine
Rex glorie.
(Today, the King of Glory, born of the Virgin,
  is adored in the manger.)
                    —Richard de Ledrede

PETRA SHIVERED. The wind whistled through Coal Market, ruffling the covers of the market stalls and bringing a shine to the noses of the vendors. They blew on their fingers and stamped their feet on the frost. Helene picked through the small piles of vegetables, lifting, examining and, as often as not, rejecting. Petra wished that her mother would hurry. Surely it could not take so long to pick a few roots and herbs, but Helene was more particular. After an intolerable age of arguing and haggling, she filled her basket. Alice came upon them as they were beginning their long walk home, carrying the heavy basket between them. She trod the frozen snow in heavy wooden sabots stuffed with hay. She steadied herself with a long staff.

'Ladies, ladies,' she said expansively. 'This is too much for you. Come with me and I will have a man carry your basket for you.'

Helene murmured shyly. 'It is no trouble, my lady. We are sturdy folk.'

Alice would not hear of it.

'You must come with me to my house. We must be better acquainted. You are good tenants and must take some refreshment with me on this cold morning.'

There was no arguing. Helene, in truth, was flattered that a lady of such importance would notice them. It was said that all the great people consorted to her house. This would be something to tell her husband when they got home.

Alice slipped off her sabots and left them inside the door. She tapped them with the tip of her staff.

'How do you like my Flemish klompen? I do not think your husband would approve of such peasant footwear, but they keep my feet dry.'

Helene smiled. It was not her place to comment. Alice led them into a room warmed by a crackling log fire. A cat lay curled in the inglenook, luxuriating in the heat. It opened its eyes and looked at the newcomers. It flicked the tip of its tail and went back to dreams of mice and birds and moonlit rooftops.

The room was hung with tapestries. Ivy and holly hung from the dark oak beams. A Jesse tree stood in a tub of stones. Various symbols were tied to the branches. Winter light seeped in through snow-rimmed windows. Helene looked around in wonder and admiration.

'You are welcome to my house,' said Alice softly. She took the basket from them and placed it on a low table. 'Please sit near the fire. I will send for something to warm you.'

Helene looked at Petra in mild panic. They should not be there. She felt that they were two bumpkins intruding into a palace.

'So please you, my lady, we do not wish to be any trouble to you. We really should be on our way.'

Petra held out her hands to the fire. The cat rose and stretched, forepaws extended and back arched. A wave of pleasure passed along its body, as if it were sorting every vertebra and sinew back into its proper position. It yawned and shook some ashes from its thick black fur. It came to Petra and rubbed its head against her leg. She stooped and scratched behind the creature's ears.

'He likes you,' said Alice. 'That's a good sign.' She took a long poker and thrust it into the fire. A maidservant came in with a tray bearing three cups of wine.

'I know it is early in the day,' said Alice 'but I insist.'

She opened a small purse that hung from her belt. They watched her every move, her graceful hands, the sway of her long dark hair, the gentle smile that played at her lips, the confidence that came from wealth, her exalted place and her fine house. She opened a heavy, brass-bound wooden box. Wonderful aromas filled the room.

She took the poker glowing from the fire and thrust it into the cups of wine. She sprinkled a pinch of spice into each steaming cup and handed them to her guests. She raised her cup in a toast.

'I wish you all the happiness and blessings of this holy season,' she said, taking a sip.

Helene tasted the wine. It was like nothing she had ever tasted before. It tasted of the south and sunshine. It tasted of strange countries, where small, dark men climbed exotic trees and collected spices from gorgeous flowers. It smelled of the sea and ships and gales battering at bearded Portuguese mariners, who laughed as they clung to the high rigging. It tasted of all world that she had never known, but had heard of in fable and song.

'It is the taste of love and friendship,' said Alice softly. 'We must all be friends at this blessed time.'

Petra blinked as she drank. A glow came to her cheeks. She did not want to go out into the winter cold. But they should not linger.

She looked about, admiring the tree. There were symbols made of dough, dangling from the green bough.

'You like my Jesse tree,' remarked Alice. Petra nodded. It was not her place to speak.

'Let me show you,' said Alice, taking her by the hand. She led her to the tree and pointed to the various symbols.

'This is the history of the world. All through Advent I put these images on the tree. I am no great artist, so I must explain.'

'I see the sun, the moon and the stars,' blurted Petra. 'These at least I can recognize.'

'So I am not so bad,' smiled Alice, putting her arm around the girl's shoulder. 'And this poor effort is Moses in his basket. This is the ark with all the animals. This is a broken heart, a lamp,' she pointed to each one in turn, 'a crown of stars, a ladder to Heaven, the scales of justice.'

'And this one?' Petra touched a small crouching figure on what seemed to be a milking stool.

'That one,' said Alice, 'is the Sybil. She is a witch and a seer. She asked the gods for knowledge and long life. For as many years as the grains of sand she could hold in her grasp.'

'And did they grant her wish?'

'They did,' said Alice with a wry laugh. 'But she forgot to ask that youth would remain with her. She has lived almost since the beginning of the world. Since long before the prophets. Time has wizened her, year by year. Now she has shrivelled to the size of the smallest elf. She knows everything that has been, everything that is and everything to come, but every day she cries to the gods to grant her the release of death.'

Petra shivered. 'I do not like that story. Why do you put a pagan image on your bough?'

Alice laughed lightly. 'As a warning. If you wish for something you must get guarantees.'

'How do you mean?'

Helene listened, still perturbed by the story of the Sybil.

'Well, in my business,' replied Alice, 'I have books and tally sticks. Money is my guarantee. With money I can bend people to my will.' She laughed and returned to her seat. 'My father, God be good to him, was a Fleming. He knew the value of gold and silver. He always put a Jesse tree in his house at Advent. For luck, he said. So I continue the custom. He told me the story of Jesse, the father of David and the ancestor of Our Lord.' She laughed again, a brittle, tinkling laugh. 'He showed me a book with a picture of Jesse and all his descendants. There was a tree growing from his privy parts.'

Helene flinched. Petra frowned in puzzlement.

'All the descendants stood on the branches, you see. "This is the root of Jesse," he said. In fact he said, "This is the wurzel of Jesse." I always thought of it as a root, like the ones you have in your basket.'

Helene blushed. Perhaps important people spoke with this kind of freedom, but it was not something for her daughter's ears to hear. She stood.

'We really must go, my lady,' she said, reaching for the basket. 'My husband will be hungry.'

'They are such a nuisance, husbands. But, wait. You must meet my William.' She gestured to Helene to sit again. She went out and returned presently, holding a little curly-haired boy by the hand.

'William,' she coaxed. 'Say "Bonjour", to my good friends.'

'Bonjour,' said the boy. He smiled. He had freckles across the bridge of his nose. He was missing a front tooth. He lisped. He held his mother's hand.

'Sing your song for the ladies,' said Alice. 'He has a song about a lazy miller.'

William pulled his hand away from his mother. He put his hands behind his back and wriggled his body into the correct position for singing, bending slightly to one side at the waist. He smiled. Helene's reserve melted at the charm and innocence of the child.

William began:

> *Meunier, tu dors, ton moulin, ton moulin*
> *Va trop vite,*
> *Meunier, tu dors, ton moulin, ton moulin*
> *Va trop fort.*

It seemed that the mill was in danger of bursting into flame. Petra knew the song well.

She joined in the refrain:

> *Ton moulin, ton moulin, va trop vite*
> *ton moulin, ton moulin, vas trop fort.*

Alice beat time with both hands on her knees. She glowed with pride. The refrain became faster and faster. They laughed together, trying to keep up. William stumbled over his words:

> *Ton moulin, ton moulin, tomberel, tomberel,*
> *tomberel, tomberel*
> *va trop fort.*

They laughed again.

'William,' said Alice, gathering the child in her embrace. 'I don't think our friends want to hear about shit carts at Christmas time.'

They made their thanks and prepared to leave.

'I shall send a man immediately with your basket,' said Alice. 'It is much too heavy to carry.' She would brook no argument.

Petra stepped lightly on the frozen snow. She clutched her mother's elbow, delighted with her encounter. Helene was disturbed by a vague unease. She kept her thoughts to herself.

When the serving man brought the basket it contained also a goose and a green bottle of wine.

People came to the mountain farm for Christmas. They made tracks through the snow, a spider web of footprints and hoof-prints, with the farm at the centre. They brought food and drink and greeted Felim Bacach and his brother Donal with grave courtesy. They bowed their heads to the two friars and crowded into the room for an early morning Mass. It was a great privilege to be in the house of Felim Bacach on this day and a greater one to be there for this holy sacrifice on the day of the Saviour's birth.

Friar John was touched by the respect they showed to Felim. It was obvious that they regarded him as a man of great importance. He was even more touched by their devotion. He intoned the sonorous, wonderful words and the rough bread and wine took life under his hands. The country people came forward to receive, grateful for the rare gift, far too rare in their mountain fastness.

Afterwards there was feasting and drink. There was music and dance to the pipes and tambourine. Felim fed them royally on mutton roasted whole over the fire, his uncle's mutton. But what of it? There was chicken seethed in almond milk with barley, meat pies and eggs and always the fiery mountain aqua vitae. It was plain that the people had brought most of these things so that their chieftain should not be embarrassed. He stood up to his full height, supporting himself on his cudgel. He raised his hand to forestall a lugubrious piper.

'No laments,' he commanded. 'No laments today. Today is for joy and dancing. Today is for giving thanks to our two holy guests, who have brought us this great gift. Today is for remembering who we are.' There was a growl of assent from the assembly. 'We are the servants of Patrick himself, as good as any man, be he Irish, English or Norman. We are family. We are Mac Giolla Patricks. When the good times come again, you will come with me to claim what is ours.' There was a roar of approval, of resentment of ancient wrong and the desire for revenge.

Friar John looked around at the exultant faces; people so gentle and courteous and yet so fierce when the blood was up.

There was story-telling and singing long into the night. Brother Fergal told of Saint Brendan and his wondrous voyage. He told why so few Duggans hailed from Tory Island. He chuckled. The people listened. This was a new one.

'The Fomorians, you see, were pirates. They were black men. They preyed on the first people who came to this land. When Saint Colmcille went to Tory to preach the word, they refused him a place to build his church. He asked them to sell him a piece of land the size of his cloak. They agreed. Didn't he spread his cloak on the ground and didn't it grow and grow!' He looked around, gauging the effect. His bright eyes twinkled. 'And the Fomorians stepped back and back and the cloak grew and grew.' He spread his arms wide. 'And didn't they all fall over the cliffs for fear of the saint's cloak.'

There was silence.

'Don't you see?' he queried. '*Tá na Dubh gann i dToraigh anois.* Duggan, don't you see?'

They got the joke. They looked at each other and smiled. The Blacks are scarce in Tory today. A bit contrived, reflected Friar John, but not a bad one for a convivial Christmas night. Brother Fergal chuckled at his wit and the skill of his delivery.

At last people took their leave and drifted out into the familiar darkness of their mountains. Men departing grasped Felim by the arm. 'We'll see the two days,' they promised. 'God save you,' said the people to the two friars. 'God and His Holy Mother.'

'And Patrick,' repeated Friar John in the old formula.

Felim set the dogs to clearing the scraps. He sat by the fire, staring into the flames. The boy came and squatted beside him. He resumed his pebble game. Felim took a knife from his belt. He picked a stone from the hearth surround and began to whet the blade. He inspected the edge. He tested it with his thumb. He wiped it on his leather-clad thigh, turning it this way and that. He touched it again with his thumb, whistling under his breath. He slid it back into its sheath.

'Ah, Spideog, Spideog, son of Art,' he said softly. 'Go to bed now.' He patted the child's head. The boy placed the pebbles in a line, carefully, one at a time. He melted into the shadows.

Friar John had been wondering.

'Did she die in childbirth?' he whispered.

'No,' said Felim, 'she did not, God help her. Her wits were gone, though. She sang this sad song all the time in a language I never heard before. It would make the hairs rise on the back of your neck.'

The friar nodded. Brother Fergal sniffed.

'When her time came and the child was born she went into a decline. I put the child to her and she suckled him. I thought it would bring her back, but she was astray in herself. We kept her clean and the child too, but there was no more we could do. It was winter out.'

'So she died?'

Felim lowered his voice. 'Aye, she did. One morning I went to see to her and she was cold. When I lifted the infant there was blood on him.' He wiped his hand on his chest. 'All down his breast like a little *spideog*. She had taken my knife in the night and opened her veins.' He paused. 'God grant I put it to better use some day.'

They sat in silence.

'We had a hard time of it, breaking the ground, so we made a cairn for her above on the hill. Every time we pass we add a stone to it, like the great queen in the old days. Maybe she was a queen in her own country. I like to think that she was. God help her, she got short enough shrift in ours.'

'A spideog, you say,' mused the firar.

'You would say "robin",' offered Brother Fergal. It made a kind of sense. The little bird that had perched on the Cross and had been touched by the blood of the Crucified.

'I will say a Mass for her,' said the friar, moved more than he could have imagined by the story.

They sat by the dying fire, lost in their thoughts.

In the morning Brother Fergal came to him.

'I have a gift for you,' he said, tendering a satchel. 'I had thought to bring them with me to the west, but I will go no further on this journey.'

'But brother, we have our instructions from the prior.' It sounded like a message from another world.

'Bollox to the prior,' snapped the old man. 'He didn't appreciate me when he had me. I will stay here among my own kind. I will serve these good people until I die. If we do not meet again in this world, we will meet in a better place.'

'But my dear brother…' Friar John was taken aback by the suddenness of his resolve and the vehemence of his language.

'But your vows, my friend?'

Brother Fergal snorted. 'Poverty I have no problem with. Chastity is merely theoretical. Obedience … I will obey Felim Bacach as my chieftain.' He laughed. 'But you have not looked at your gift.'

Friar John fumbled with the thong of the satchel. He looked inside: a roll of parchment, some goose feathers already pared and stripped; three ink horns with brass tops.

'Red, black and blue,' said Brother Fergal. 'You will make better use of them than anyone else. I will tell you all my secrets before you leave.' He held his hand up, silencing his friend. 'Now listen.'

They fell silent. Outside the door they heard the steady drip of water on the threshold stone.

❧

Richard de Ledrede heard the bell for mealtime, but his hunger was of a different kind. He scratched on a writing slate with a piece of chalk. He looked at the words, feeble words to express the wonder of what had happened.

Vale virgo christifera; hail to the virgin, the Christ-bearer. It was a paradox. It was his task to exalt, most especially the Mother of

God, so often denigrated by heretics. Another paradox, that God should have chosen a woman to make His plan manifest. Women, so often the snares of men's souls, vessels of impurity. In humility he reasoned that God must know better than a humble friar, however brilliant that friar might be in disputation.

Quam laudat mundi machina; praised by all the universe. A machina of the world. He thought of machinae that he had seen, ballistae, catapultae, engines for battering down city walls. Mundi machina, a lever to send the stars hurtling through the night sky and lift the sun over the eastern horizon. But a machina was also a platform on which slaves were exposed for sale. Poor wretches, naked and terrified, sold most likely for some crime or debt, or simply for being weak and defeated. We are all naked and exposed on the machina. Only the Son of Mary can purchase our freedom.

He heard the bells ring out for Christmas. His mind brought him back to the town of his birth, an undistinguished village by Emlyn Stream. He saw the chapel and heard again the Christmas bell calling the faithful to morning Mass. He remembered the ford and the burial ground on the hill where old Viking warriors stretched out their long bones. A village of five acres, four ploughs and three hogs. There was a set of stocks, rarely used, as the age had grown lax. He had come a long way and was sure that he would go further.

∼

'I want you to take the boy with you,' said Felim Bacach. 'I want him to learn about the world. There is nothing here for him, but perhaps in a great town he might find his voice. You know what I mean.'

'But he is like a son to you,' protested the friar. 'You are his family.'

Felim gestured to the surrounding hills still patched with melting snow. He swung his arm around, taking in the encircling horizon.

'Ah, no. Sure my brother has no tongue himself and I'm a poor twisted creature, talking only of revenge. It's no place for a child.'

'You do yourself an injustice. The people turn to you for advice. You decide their disputes. You are a man of parts.' Friar John scratched his head. His tonsure had grown out. His beard was rough. He could have passed for an Irishman. 'But if you are sure, I will find something for him. I will instruct him myself.'

'Make a Christian of him, too,' said Felim.

The friar had wondered about that. The boy had refused to come to hear his Mass at the cairn. He was nowhere to be seen at the Mass on Christmas Day. Only afterwards had he seen the boy climbing the hill with a stone in his hands, labouring under the weight of it.

'Spideog,' called Felim. 'Come here to me.'

The boy came out from the barn. He looked at Felim through dark, slanting eyes. He looked at Friar John.

'You will go with the holy friar,' said Felim, gently putting his hand on the boy's head. 'Do you hear me?'

The child nodded.

'You will attend to everything he tells you. When I come to see you again I want to hear that you are a scholar and a good worker. Do you hear me?'

The child nodded again. It was settled.

The horse was fat and reluctant to leave the comfort of the barn. He baulked at the shafts, but eventually surrendered to the bit. He wheezed as he took the weight of the cart. Friar John slapped the reins. Their journey began.

Spideog looked back. He saw the low farmhouse, the outlying sheds, the men who had brought him into the world and the cairn sheltering the bones of the mother he had never known. This had been his world. The clouds drifted high above the mountains. A shaft of sunlight illumined a distant peak. The world turned.

SIX

Foras procul allecia.
Assunt festa paschalia.
(Throw out that salted herring.
The Easter festival is here.)
—Richard de Ledrede

'YOU ARE my only hope,' said Friar John. 'I am in very bad odour with the prior.' He held the child by the hand. They were a forlorn pair.

Alain Cordwainer looked at his wife and daughter. Helene was moved by the sight of the neglected, wild creature, dirty of face and ragged of clothing. Petra watched with interest.

'What do you say, wife?' queried Alain. 'Can we afford another mouth to feed?'

'He could do with a wash,' observed Helene.

'What is your name, child?'

The boy looked up at Friar John.

'He has no speech,' said Friar John, shaking his head sadly. 'He was called Spideog by the people who raised him. We would say Robin.'

'Robin,' said Petra, coming forward. She held out a piece of rye bread. The boy looked again at the friar. The friar nodded. The boy snatched the bread and began to cram it into his mouth. He turned away, as if in shame.

'He is not used to people,' explained the friar. 'It's the *uaigneas* of the mountains.'

'The what?' queried Alain.

The friar realized that he had spoken in Irish. 'The loneliness,' he said softly. There was a word, *uaig*, a grave. No more lonely word than that. He pictured the cairn high on the hill.

'He needs a home,' he said simply. Helene noticed the tears in his eyes.

'You may leave him here,' she said decisively. 'Petra will look after him. My husband will teach him his trade.'

She looked at Alain for corroboration. He nodded assent. When Helene made up her mind there was no gainsaying her.

'You are good people,' said the friar. 'God will reward you. God will provide.'

He smiled. Brother Fergal had some old yarn about a saint who lived on a pillar in the ocean. Every day an angel of the Lord brought to him a *bradán*.

When he told the story in English he said 'sal moon'. Maeldún the great navigator had offered to take the saint with him and bring him back to the world of men, but the saint would have none of it. At that point an angel had appeared with the daily sal moon. Some sort of cryptic symbol, perhaps. Maybe a loaf baked in the shape of a moon. Heavily salted bread.

'No,' scoffed Brother Fergal at his query. 'A fish, a *bradán*.' They had laughed at the misunderstanding. It made the journey lighter.

'I'm sure you thought that I had stolen your horse.'

'Well,' said Alain, 'we wondered.'

'We were afraid. We were sure that you had been murdered out there by those savages,' Helene put in.

The friar smiled again. 'I was in more danger from the prior.' He imitated his superior's bleak tones. "You have absented yourself from your duties, to go gallivanting. You have lost me one of our brethren and you bring me back a heathen savage." I shall pay for all this with bread and water, but nonetheless, I am glad to be home.'

⌒

Winter slouched away at last. Grass grew and spring flowers dotted the inch-fields along the river. The children ran in the Bishop's meadow. Robin carried the shoes that Alain had made for him. They were too good to wear in the lush wet grass. He ran barefoot and paddled where the river grew shallow over drifts of shingle. Petra showed him where the fish lay under the banks. She showed him where the otters played and where the kingfisher plied his glittering trade.

Once in Watergate, some street boys jeered them. They whistled at Petra.

'Take no notice, Robin,' she said. She held her head high and walked on. The guards at the Watergate watched with amusement as the boys minced along behind her.

'Oh take no notice of them, Dummy,' they guffawed. Robin stopped. It looked as if there might be a fight. He stooped and picked up three pebbles. The boys laughed. Now they would have just cause.

Robin began to juggle. The pebbles floated in the air. They hovered on his fingertips. He caressed them. He crouched and swayed. He did not look at the boys. They stopped and watched in wonder. The guards fell silent. The pebbles floated about his head. He caught them behind his back. They ran along his outstretched arms. He turned on one foot in a slow mesmeric dance. Like a whiplash, he let a pebble go. It caught one of the leading boys between the eyes. He staggered and fell, yelling in pain. Robin continued to juggle the remaining two pebbles. He looked directly at the boys. They fell back and slunk away. The injured one got to his feet and ran.

'That was a good one,' said one of the guards to Petra.

'The little divil,' said the other.

Robin threw the stones aside and followed her into Hightown.

At Easter time she danced with the other girls at the wedding of Alice to Adam le Blound. They danced in a round on Castlemede, to the sound of flute and drum. They wore white and strewed flowers before the bride and groom.

Alice smiled upon her and called to her.

'This is my new husband, Adam the Fair. Is he not a fine man, Petra? We must find a husband for you also.'

Adam beamed with pride. He bowed to her, sweeping the tips of the grass with his bonnet.

'Aha,' he said, 'the beautiful Petronilla. I see that you have new shoes.'

She blushed and lowered her eyes.

Alice looked from one to the other. Something flickered in her eyes.

'Do you know my friend?' she asked him, clutching his elbow.

'I do indeed,' said Adam expansively. 'I had occasion to appre-hend her in the act of poaching, if I remember. Sir Arnaud and I debated whether she should be hanged or no.' He laughed again at the girl's discomfort.

'Poaching? Indeed!' Alice spoke with mock severity. 'And is she to be hanged, may I ask? Has Sir Arnaud pronounced on her in his hundred-court? We cannot have evil-doers wandering the land.'

Petra's cheeks burned. They were making fun of her.

'No she is not. I pleaded for her with Sir Arnaud. He spared her on condition that she dance at our wedding. Has she not been the most graceful dancer here today?'

Alice looked at him again.

'Except for you, my love,' he added quickly. She laughed and forgave him. 'But she does dance well in her little red shoes.'

'But why would she not,' said his new wife. 'If a cobbler's daughter cannot have good dancing shoes, then who shall?' She smiled again at Petra and patted her cheek. A pearl hung down from her elaborate, winged headdress. It swung to and fro as she spoke, nacreous-white against the darkness of her hair. A pearl of great price.

Alice moved on, greeting her guests. Petra felt a cloud passing over the sun. Not for her the feasting and merriment in the castle hall. She could only imagine the buzz of conversation, the tinkle of glass and silver, the candles casting a honeyed glow on even the plainest of faces, the minstrels carolling from the gallery. She wished. She wished. Beware of what you wish for, whispered the Sybil.

She turned homeward. She wanted to be with her family. The guard spoke to her at the Watergate.

'So you have been to the wedding. Did you dance for all the big people?'

She nodded.

'I like the shoes,' he said. 'I'd bet that you're a mighty dancer.'

She shrugged.

'Where's your little Robin today then?'

'At home.'

'A little divil, that lad.'

She had no wish to linger in idle gossip.

'So she's done it again,' he mused.

'Who has done what?' She was puzzled.

'You know. Herself. Married money. That's what she's done.'

Petra made no comment.

'As the Irish say: *Aithníon ciaróg ciaróg eile.*'

'What does that mean?'

'One cockroach an' all that. One cockroach recognizes another.'
He laughed a dry, bitter laugh.

It was an ugly phrase. She realized that she hated Alice and yet she was drawn to her. She thought about her a lot and wanted to be near her. Was it the glamour of her money and standing, or that core of iron Petra sensed in her, that courage to go after what she wanted in life? She knew that she was poor; that her parents would never amount to much in the world, although of course, she loved them and Robin also.

'Money's the thing,' said the guard absently. He scratched under his arm. 'Lay hands on it, if you can. Get a rich husband.' He laughed again, that bitter laugh. 'Should be no bother to a fine young maiden like yourself.' He leered. 'I'd marry you, if I had a penny to bless meself.'

She moved away, conscious of his eyes following her. She stopped at the bridge and looked into the water. The river was tame and shallow. She saw fish twitching in the current. In the corner of her eye she saw a flash of movement, red, iridescent green, a rainbow flash. The kingfisher. Gone. Her mood lifted. She looked up at the hill. Smoke curled from their chimney. Robin, standing in long grass, waved to her. She waved back. She was foolish to long for more. She quickened her step.

Over time, her wish began to come true. Alice sent for her to serve in her house in Hightown. It was an opportunity for a poor girl. She would learn the ways of the great people of the town. In time she would marry well and be a support to her parents as they declined into old age. She would learn all the skills proper to a lady. She would have ample opportunity to visit her parents, Alice insisted. She spoke of how satisfying it was to her to have such good tenants and how it would grieve her to lose them. They understood. They let their daughter go. Her visits were the highlights of their humble lives. The visits gradually became less frequent. They missed her greatly. Robin missed her too.

SEVEN

Da. da nobis nunc
Da clero voluere libros.
(Grant to us in these times that the
clergy may study their books.)
—Richard de Ledrede

FRIAR JOHN PEERED at the manuscript. He wondered how it had come into their library. The writing was small and crabbed. It was like reading thorns. The letters pulled at his eyes. They tired easily on this difficult text. Yet it was by the great teacher, the learned Friar Roger, a man whose work encompassed all knowledge. It should be approached with humility and a certain wariness. Was it not knowledge that had brought about the fall of man from grace and opened the door to error and sin? 'Concerning the Secret Works of Nature and of Art and the Vanity of Magic.' Friar John was wary of any mention of magic. It was heresy to engage in fortune-telling, sorcery, the casting of spells or curses. All vanity and foolishness, according to the great teacher of Oxenford. If it be vanity then there is no magic and no need for condemnation. Magic must wither in the light of true faith and true knowledge. He read on. There were things here that he had never imagined. He stopped and rubbed his eyes.

He got up from his bench and went out to walk by the river. He came to the dunghill. He looked around among the broken pots until he found a bottle. The neck was gone. He put his finger into the concave base. He peered at it through the viridian coloured glass. His finger was definitely bigger, but blurred by the flaws and imperfections in the glass. He thought about it, frowning. Perhaps if he used only the curved base. He knelt by the dunghill and tapped the bottle on a rock, chipping away the sides, until he was left with a jagged concave, convex disc of dark glass. He peered through it. He would show this to Robin when he came for instruction.

He turned the glass over. The jagged edge gashed his thumb. Blood spurted forth. He dropped the glass. It broke into glittering shards.

He went back to the abbey and washed the dirt from his hands. He wrapped his thumb in a strip of linen. It throbbed painfully. He wondered if it might be a warning; that secret knowledge should remain that way, locked in the Hebrew and Arabic of ancient scrolls.

In the morning his hand and lower arm were swollen. He looked at the gash. The flesh looked yellow. He could not write. The pain clamped about his spirits. He resolved to go to the lady Alice. She was known for the efficacy of her poultices and plasters. She could draw the evil from a wound with ointments compounded from herbs and flowers, better than any leech.

The prior granted him permission, muttering something about gallivanting again. Friar John clutched the injured hand across his breast and went out into the fine summer weather. He winced at the pain.

Richard de Ledrede saw himself as a simple man. He lived the life of a friar but he understood that money had a power that could be used for higher purposes. Money and faith constructed churches and cathedrals and, in former times, sent armies to defend the holy places in the east. He approved strongly of the arrest of every Jew in France and the confiscation of their property. It was right that a strong king should act against Jews and heretics and use their goods to further the work of God.

He wished that Pope Clement would act with similar decisiveness. Heresy and error was spreading throughout Christendom. No matter how firmly it was put down, it sprang up again like a malign weed. He cast his mind back to when he was a student, disputing with learned exegetes and clever orators. The debate was on the importance of authority, most especially that of the Pope. He challenged the chair and every speaker, speaking out of turn, disrupting trains of learned argument and mellifluous rhetoric, until both students and teachers had come to blows. At that point he had risen from his stool and walked quietly to the podium. The room fell silent. Combatants stopped in mid-blow and let go of opponents. He stood with his characteristic little smile. He spoke softly.

'You see, my dear brothers in Christ, what can happen when authority is defied.' He bowed to the moderator of the debate. He apologized for his behaviour. Some laughed at the cunning ploy, but there were those who thought it arrogant and condescending.

Nevertheless he had never flinched from defending right authority in the war against error. Wars cost lives. It is not arrogance to denounce the vile doctrines of heretics or the lewd practices of those who preferred the power of Satan to that of God. He found it hard to credit that Count Heinrich of Sayn in Germany could ride through the air on a crawfish, but he could believe that he had murdered the good priest, Konrad of Marburg, a zealous defender of the truth, bane of heretics and sorcerers. It was Konrad who had shown that those who defend suspects are equally guilty.

Firm hands were needed in a shifting world. The Pope had abandoned Rome for Avignon. The great order of the Templars had fallen under the suspicion of heresy and in his own country the mighty Longshanks was gone, to be replaced by the second Edward, a reputed sodomite, constantly in dispute with his wife and at war with the Scots. However, to his credit, Edward proposed expanding the school at Oxenford into a proper university. It behoved Richard to go back to England, make himself known to the new king and seek preferment in a place where his talents could shine to advantage.

A twinge of anxiety struck him. Perhaps the hateful Alexander de Bicknor might forestall him. He knew him to be an ambitious and influential man. His uncle was once chief falconer to the first Edward. He had wealth and ambition, but not the razor-edged intellect or zeal necessary to be the head of a great institution of learning. It would be as well to go back to England and consign to dust those inhibitions and feelings of inferiority he had once felt as a village boy in the presence of his proud and privileged neighbours. He remembered an occasion when the same Alexander had galloped through the ford, laughing and splashing the boys who fished there on a summer's day. He knew his hatred of Alexander de Bicknor stemmed from that childish prank.

❧

Friar John laid his swollen arm on the table. Petra touched it gently. The flesh was yellow and felt like putty. She undid the dirty linen bandage. She made a soft clucking sound with her tongue.

'If you wish, I can leave it for another day until your mistress returns.'

'No, not at all. She has taught me much of her art. I will wash this and put a poultice on it to draw out the evil. You must come back to me every day until the blood is pure again.'

He watched as she poured brown liquid into a bowl of water. The drops divided into amber arabesques. She stirred the lovely shapes away and dabbed at the wound. The water stung the raw flesh. He gasped. The pain radiated through all his limbs even to his privy parts. His knees became weak and wobbly.

'O Jhesu,' he groaned through clenched teeth.

'I am sorry,' she murmured, smiling gently. 'It will not be so bad the next time.'

He watched fearfully as she dabbed again.

'Be brave,' she mocked, as if talking to a child. 'If it hurts, it is doing its work.'

He sat quietly, enduring the pain like a stoic. He was quite proud of himself actually. The pain receded.

She applied a poultice that she scooped with a wooden spatula from an earthenware jar. She held his hand in hers. He enjoyed the sensation. No woman had touched him so tenderly since his mother had said farewell to him as he left to join the abbey. He did not want the moment to end.

She bound his hand in clean gauze and tied a napkin around his shoulder to serve as a sling. His hand felt warm again.

'Keep it up as much as you can,' she advised. 'Come back to me tomorrow.'

He asked after her parents. He had not seen them for a long time. He wanted to linger. He detected a slight hesitation.

'They are well,' she replied, her eyes downcast as she adjusted his hand in the sling.

'Do you see them often?'

'As often as I can. I am kept busy here, of course. I have charge of young William much of the time. He is a sweet boy.'

'Good. Good,' murmured Friar John. 'You have a fine position here. I am sure they are grateful to the lady Alice.'

'They are dutiful tenants,' she replied.

He searched around for something to prolong the conversation.

'Young Robin learns well,' he began.

She smiled a smile of pure happiness.

'Yes. My father is so pleased with him. In fact he made these shoes for me. He brought them as a present.'

She raised her hem to show him. They were light summer sandals with straps criss-crossing halfway up the calf of her leg. He looked away. She turned them this way and that.

'I do love nice shoes,' she said, like a child.

The friar coughed.

'I meant with his studies. But I am glad that he is a good apprentice. I have taught him to read and cipher. He writes well, so I know he understands what he reads. It is a great pity that ... '

'I know,' she agreed. 'But it will come some day.'

'Please God,' he said. 'Please God.'

∾

Alice and her husband paused by a little chapel overlooking the great monastery of Kells. It was like a walled city in miniature. The abbey church gleamed in sunlight, beside the tumbling King's River.

'What a place!' exclaimed Adam. 'I would give a lot to possess this.'

'Would you sell your soul to be lord of all this?' she asked lightly.

Adam shook his head. She noticed that his long blond hair, of which he was so proud, was thinning at the crown.

He laughed awkwardly. 'Too great a price,' he replied, leaning forward to pat his horse's neck. 'Good boy. Good boy,' he said soothingly. She urged her mount close to him so that their knees touched. She was breeched like a man, in dark leather with a split surcoat. She rode astride, like a man, a matter that caused no little comment. She could arouse him with the slightest touch. He shifted awkwardly in his saddle. She nudged him again with her knee.

He looked around. He could see the monks bending to the harvest in the distant fields. Cattle grazed placidly by the river. He wanted to take her there and then, in among the gorse or up against the sun-warmed chapel wall. He swallowed. She read his mind.

'Adam, my love,' she said softly. 'There is something that I must say to you.'

He waited. He could feel something between them, like a charge of energy in the atmosphere before a lightning storm. Energy that must be released in crashing thunder and a blaze of fire. He felt perspiration cooling on his well-trimmed moustache.

'I know that you are a man of an amorous disposition. I am sure that you have had your hand in many a placket.' He grinned sheepishly. Guilty as charged. He waited, wondering where all this was leading. It was hardly the preliminary to a lusty tussle against a lichen-clad chapel wall. An inventory of his infidelities perhaps, as a preliminary to more demands, more lavish gifts. He had signed over many a property into her name in trust for the boy, William. He had invested heavily in her business ventures, but it was all worth it when she disrobed and came to his bed, an ivory statue in the candlelight, a tiger between the sheets.

'You know when we are lovers together and what you like me to do?'

He nodded. Things were looking brighter again. He knew very well indeed.

'What I just wanted to say is this.' She paused. 'If you ever lay a finger on the girl, Petronilla, I will bite off your organ of generation.'

She dug in her spurs and was gone from him, galloping down towards the river, swinging left along the monastery wall, making for the mill near the bridge. She turned and waved back to him.

He sat watching her dwindle into the distance. She could see into the hidden recesses of his mind. It was futile to dissemble. He had looked at Petronilla as she went about her tasks in the Kilkenny house. He could see how her shoulder blades moved under her light blouse. They were like the wings of the pert, black-headed gulls that sauntered upriver to perch on the wall by the New Quay, waiting for scraps from the fishermen. He watched how they swooped down to alight and fold their wings away, their organs of flight. He was well and truly rumbled and he knew it. Organ of generation. There was no sign of any such generation between himself and his dark, fascinating and sometimes unnerving lady wife. He followed glumly, wondering what it would take to buy his way back into her favours.

The miller watched them passing by. He paused in his work, standing, up to his thighs in the water. He held one of the confiscated quern stones in his hands. He used the stones to reinforce the weir. It was obvious to him that there had been an argument. She rode in silence, but Master Adam was gesticulating and nattering away as usual.

The miller would have loved to catch what they were saying. Their attitudes said a lot. Somebody should tell him, he reflected, pushing the stone into the pile under the water. He knew that at night it would disappear again. He was like the giant in the old story, who pushed a great rock up a hill only to have it roll down again as soon as he got it to the top. The Abbot sent his servants to search for querns and grinding stones to protect his suit of mill. The people resented this. They knew that the stones were put into the weir. They came in the night, like otters and pulled them out again. The Abbot sent men to search for them and the process began again. In the meantime the people had to bring their corn to the miller and pay their tenth part to the Abbot.

'Somebody should tell him,' he remarked to a man standing by the water's edge. The man carried a sack of grain on his shoulder. He was not for letting go of it. He would watch the whole process, grumbling that he was being cheated again, grumbling about monks and lords, taxes and purveyances and the waste of money on war with the Scots. He grumbled about the miller wasting his time with quern stones.

'Tell who what?' he growled. The sack was heavy on his shoulder.

'That fool, Master Adam. Before he gives all his land away.'

'Why would he give his land away?' The man was curious.

'Because he is a love-thrall to a witch.' The miller laughed. He waded out of the water and stood, letting the sunshine dry his legs. He was in the mood for a chat. It was true what people said: 'From alehouse, from mill and from convent the news travels.' Not to mention the bawdy house. Or was it the forge? Gossip travels anyway, wherever it may start from.

The man swung the sack to the ground. He retained a grip on it with one hand.

'A witch? Why would you say that now?'

'Well,' conceded the miller, 'I don't mean that kind of a witch. Not one of the heretic witches. Oh good God, no! But you know yourself.'

The man did not know.

'You know. You know. A woman gets her claws into a man, gives him what he thinks he wants and takes every brass farthing. He thinks she loves him. He follows her around like a trained monkey. That kind of witchcraft.'

He hoisted his tunic and pissed elaborately into the mill race. He groaned.

The man was puzzled. 'So he gives everything to a woman, because he thinks he loves her. She makes him a slave.' He shook his head. It was a comical idea. He scratched his poll with his hand. No woman would ever do that to him.

'They have their ways, women,' said the miller sagely. He sat on the grass verge and began to pull on his breeches. 'They use their charms and before you know it's… Pouf! You're a pauper.' He laughed at the cruel beauty of love.

'Damn near a pauper anyway,' grumbled the man. 'Don't get me started.'

'The only way to break that spell,' confided the miller. He nudged the man in the ribs with his elbow. 'The only way to break that spell is to make a jakes of her shoe. Somebody should tell him that.' He guffawed and nudged the man again. 'That would put a stop to her gallop.'

He reached for the sack. The man drew it back.

'Aren't you goin' to wash your hands?'

It was the miller's turn to be puzzled.

'Wash your hands,' repeated the man. 'After you visit the latrine, you wash your hands.' That was what his wife always said. She insisted on it, said it was a safeguard against pestilence and infection. He always did as she directed. He frowned. Maybe he was one of those love-thralls. He smiled for the first time.

The miller looked at him strangely.

'Begod, but you're the comical man,' he remarked, but nevertheless he stooped and washed his hands in the flowing water. 'Here give us that sack.'

He lifted the hard-won grain and hefted it. 'Hmm,' he mused, gauging it thoughtfully. 'Now mind you, I'm not spreading any scandal. I'm not accusing, but I hear they have some queer parties out there in Outer Farm.'

'That was no love gift, was it,' replied the man. 'She took that from her uncle for a debt.'

'That's as may be.' The miller shrugged. 'One way or t'other, she gets what she wants.'

He carried the sack into the mill, with the man following close on his heels. He climbed the ladder and poured the grain into the hopper. He set the millstone in motion. He released the grain.

Water thundered in the mill race. The great machine creaked and protested. The rough flour emerged.

'I thought everyone knew that,' he said absently. 'A man must be master in his own house.'

He shifted his weight and scratched his crotch. He looked at the man guiltily and wiped his hand on his tunic before scooping the flour into the sack, not forgetting to set aside a generous portion for the Lord Abbot of Kells and maybe a pinch or two for himself.

∾

'I think you may do away with the bandage,' said Petronilla. She had grown used to the name, little Petra, as she had grown taller and grown also into womanhood, a woman of gentleness and quiet grace.

Friar John flexed his thumb gingerly. It still throbbed a little when he lowered it, but it had begun to itch, a sign of life returning, she said.

'You will always have a scar,' she added. 'Don't scratch it or the poison will return.'

The skin was red and shiny surrounding the gash, but it was mending. He was wary of bending his thumb, feeling pressure building up at the joint. He was anxious to return to his writing. There were many important events to be chronicled.

There was a parliament in the offing to hear the case against Sir Arnaud for the murder of a certain John de Bonneville.

There was the matter of the Templar Knights and the destruction of their order. The king of France, at a stroke, had seized their hundreds of properties and was in the process of rifling every chest and cupboard in a frantic search for their fabled wealth. He leaned his considerable weight on the Pope, now a virtual prisoner in Avignon.

There was the scandal of the king of England and his Gascon favourite, Gaveston, a man who attracted the particular hatred of the king's own loyal and not-so-loyal barons. At least the barons could agree on something.

Even in Ireland, the ripples of mighty events were felt. The Knights Hospitallers of the Order of Saint John of Jerusalem, favourites of the king, had slipped adroitly into the place of the disgraced

Templars. Heresy was in the air again and the hunting dogs of God, the Blackfriars, walked with a definite swagger.

She was still holding his hand. 'You will always have that scar,' she said again, touching the area of the wound. 'It is a memory of the hurt.' She smiled and his heart turned over inside his breast.

'You will be able to strut, like Sir Arnaud and his rowdy knights, showing your scar and talking of valour.'

He liked the way she teased. Perhaps he had missed his vocation. He saw himself in the thick of the melée, lance couched in its rest, his eyes measuring his opponent through the slit in his helmet. Not a chance.

'My battles are against error and superstition,' he replied. It sounded pompous. He had almost said 'against the Evil One himself' in order to impress. Friar John, soldier of the Lord.

She let it pass. She crumpled the discarded bandage and threw it in the fire.

'Tell me about all those boxes and jars.' His gaze ran around the well-stocked shelves.

Petronilla shrugged. 'My mistress collects all manner of salves and herbs. She forbids me to touch some of them, aconite for instance, and belladonna. Only the most skilled may use them. This one is delphinium, used for lice.'

'Ah yes. Brother Fergal of our abbey, showed me how to make blue ink with a pinch of alum and the juice of the leaves.'

'Oh,' she sounded impressed. 'I didn't know that.' She ran her finger along the shelf. 'Beeswax, of course. Royal jelly for salves and unguents. This one is sulphur, for disorders of the skin.'

'Sulphur, I see. Do you think I might beg a scruple or two of sulphur? There is a process that I have read about, which involves sulphur.'

She paused for a moment, frowning. 'I don't know. My mistress is away hunting. Perhaps we should wait until she returns. It came all the way from a fiery mountain in Italy, she told me.' She saw his disappointed expression. 'Well, maybe a little.'

She took a clump of yellow crystal from the shelf, lemon yellow as befitted its country of origin. 'She won't mind as it is for you.'

He looked closely at the strange crystals and slipped the lump into a pocket in his sleeve.

She was interrupted by the sound of William shouting outside in the garden.

'No, it's mine,' he was screaming, in a flaring rage. 'It's mine.'

Petronilla looked through the window. The rough glass distorted the shapes of Robin and William fighting over a ball. They had been hurling, a game learned from the Irish. Robin raised his stick as if to strike the younger boy.

'No, Robin,' screamed Petronilla. She ran from the room. There would be hell to pay if anything happened to William. She saw William clutching the ball defiantly. He waved his stick in an arc in front of him, keeping Robin at a distance. Robin grinned and jabbed at William, goading him to attack.

'It's mine,' the child yelled again. 'Tell him to go away.'

It was, of course, true. Everything belonged to William, or would come to him. He liked to let people know it.

'Robin,' said Petronilla, 'leave it be.'

Robin grinned, a grin of pure mischief. His white teeth gleamed. He threw the stick in the air, making it spin against the sky. They watched it spin. He caught it as it fell and cast it aside. The cat scampered to avoid it, levitated to the top of a high wall and sat watching, in fear of attack.

Friar John watched the scene through the window. He found that by swaying slightly from side to side, the ridges in the glass caused everything to flicker and move, even the wary cat on his lofty refuge. He became aware of Petronilla watching him from the doorway.

'Is everything all right?' she enquired, puzzled by his odd movements.

'Oh yes, yes,' he replied in some confusion. 'I was just, just, em.

Just going, actually. You have been kind. I will pray for you. I will take Robin away and give him some errands. Keep him out of trouble.'

She thanked him. She had tasks to do before her mistress returned. She had William to placate and to feed. In the absence of his playmate, she would have to find something to entertain him for the afternoon. She had a lot on her hands.

EIGHT

Tenens libram et pondera
nobis remittat scelera.
(May He who hold the scales and weights
   forgive us our wrong-doings.)
                              —Richard de Ledrede

THE PARLIAMENT CAME to town like a travelling circus. Tents and pavilions made a portable village on the Castle Mede. The great people, the lord justiciar, the king's right-hand man in Ireland, lodged in the castle with Sir Arnaud. It was a convenient arrangement, as he was to adjudicate on the charge of murder levied against his host.

The Anglo-Norman lords came from all over to argue about levies and taxes and to settle disputes among themselves and with their Irish neighbours. Scribes and lawyers grappled with feudal allegiances and bewildering patronymics and titles: James Fitz Maurice, Maurice Fitz Thomas, Thomas Fitz Gerald Fitz Maurice, ancient lineages receding into the past like an infinity of mirrors.

Alice gave a special dinner for her cousin-in-law, Roger Outlawe, Prior of Kilmainham, more soldier than churchman, more politician than monk. Her husband, the prior observed, was a wishy-washy fellow very much down in himself, a bit of a skull at the feast. The prior was civil to him but he knew where the power lay in that household.

Alice, looking around at the scene of merriment and good cheer, reflected that there were people worth cultivating at her table. Moreover, it might be an idea to expand her premises and entertain revellers and diners for hard cash. People of substance would pay to dine at the house of so prominent a citizen. She glowed in the candlelight.

Petronilla served at table. She wondered if her mistress had brought these important people in order to find her a husband.

The boy, William, sang his song about the miller. The guests beat time on the table top. Faster and faster:

> Tomberel, tomberel, tomberel, tomberel,
> tomberel, tomberel,
> va trop fort.

He bowed to the company, acknowledging their applause.

Robin astonished them with feats of dexterity. The room fell silent. His eyes were lined with kohl, like those of the Saracen women. Naked from the waist up, his body was green with chalk that Alice herself had applied, stroking his swarthy skin with soft, persuasive hands. He wore a hood and breeches of otter skin.

His dance elicited confused responses from both men and women, arousing both sexes by his ambiguous beauty. He was a creature of the wild, a spirit of the woods. Five steel balls floated at his fingertips. They glowed like stars in the candle-light. They formed an orrery about his head. Eyes followed him as he swayed to the music of a flute. Petronilla, seeing the hunger in the eyes of his audience, feared for him.

Adam le Blound stared into his cup. The song about the miller still beat in his head, 'Tomberel, tomberel', a song about dung. He thought of the foul-mouthed, drunken miller at Kells and how he had spoken when Adam had paused one time to water his horse. He could still see the weal on the man's fat, ugly face, where the whip had caught him. It gave him some satisfaction, but the man's words had gone deep: 'make a jakes of her shoe'.

He had done it. In the dead of night he had taken one of her high riding boots and used it as a privy. He threw it into the river. There was, as usual, hell to pay. She beat the servants and searched the house. She screamed in fury. He tried to placate her, promising to send for the cordwainer as soon as they returned to town.

'This is witchcraft,' she hissed, with a wild light in her eyes. 'Someone is out to injure me.'

He was free. He realized that he had never liked her and now he no longer loved her, whatever that might mean. He considered his state. His wealth and property had leached away. His manhood, his organ of generation, lay limp and flaccid to her touch and now she no longer came to his bed. His stomach churned with the fear that some watcher might have seen him in his foul and shameful deed. Some eyes, spying from the darkness, might have seen him by the river in the fitful light of the moon, a time when witches walk abroad. Perhaps she already knew. He suspected that she had gone elsewhere for her carnal pleasure. He beckoned to the slattern, Petronilla, for more wine.

∾

Sir Arnaud was acquitted by a jury of his well-fed peers. They threw the charges out. In generosity, he had offered to pay compensation after the Irish fashion, an *éiric* assessed on the value of the man and the degree of provocation. De Bonneville's family refused it, preferring to nurse their resentment and a grudge to be passed down the generations like a legacy, an infection of the blood, to be purged at some time in the future. Sir Arnaud was too well connected. Only God or the Devil himself could dislodge him.

~

Darkness was closing in on Paris. The great crowd dispersed. The king and the mighty prelates went back to their palaces, the curse of de Molay, the last of the Templars, still sounding in their ears. A pile of ash and glowing cinder, human charcoal, smoked at the base of the two charred stakes. The island was silent. A world had come to an end.

Richard de Ledrede stood in contemplation. He looked up at the dark bulk of Notre Dame. No light shone through leaded windows. No bell rang. No holy chant echoed in the evening air. He prayed to the Virgin.

He felt peace descend upon him. Out of this healing fire a new world would come. Obstinate heresy had been defeated and a new spring was on the way. At the cost of a few old and broken knights, the true authority of Pope and king had been reasserted. The cold March breeze whipped away the stench of burnt flesh. He felt invigorated, and renewed with courage to fight always for the truth, at whatever cost.

~

Friar John paused in the street. A troop of horsemen advanced from the direction of the Watergate. Their hooves rang on the stones of Coal Market. People stopped in surprise to see Irish hobbelars riding armed and bareback, in an English town. At their head rode their chieftain, a striking man on a fine, prancing stallion.

One of their number turned aside on spotting the friar. He threw his leg over the horse's crupper and slid to the ground. He was a wild and dangerous-looking customer.

Friar John stepped back. The Irishman threw his arms about him and lifted him off his feet. He set him down and thumped him heartily on the back.

'*An é nach naithníonn tú mé?*' he bellowed. 'Is it how you don't know me?'

The friar gazed at him in surprise.

'Felim Bacach,' he said, taking the man by the hand. 'Felim Bacach.'

'In the flesh,' said Felim, speaking in English, 'and heartily glad am I to see you.'

'What are you doing here in Kilkenny?'

Felim gestured to the troop of horsemen, as they diverted to the right, into the High Street. 'I ride now with a new chieftain,' he replied. 'Maurice Mac Thomáis, Fitz Thomas to you. A decent man, a Norman, but a man who knows how to live like a proper Irishman.'

'I see,' nodded the friar. 'So you have learned the English tongue in his household.'

'I slip in and out of it,' said Felim, 'when it suits. But tell me, what is the news of little Spideog? Does he prosper in the world?'

The friar beamed. 'He is the cleverest creature that ever I saw. He reads and writes as well as myself. He can cipher and do the mathematics better than any and he can draw like an angel.'

Felim was pleased. 'Aye, but can he look after himself?'

'That he can,' replied Friar John. 'He is apprenticed to an honest tradesman.'

'No,' said Felim, shaking his head. 'That's not what I meant. Can he defend himself in a fight? It's hard for him being as he is.'

'Oh, indeed he can,' the friar assured him. 'He can defend himself all right.'

He did not elaborate. Felim was even more pleased. 'I will come to see him before we leave. You have done well, my friend.'

He grasped the friar's hand.

'And what of your brother? Does he ride with you?'

'Ah no,' said Felim. 'He remains on the mountain. He feels at home there now.'

'And you, my son? Why did you leave? Are you reconciled with your uncle?'

Despite his limp, Felim sprang nimbly off his good leg and remounted his horse.

'I am indeed, my friend. I am indeed.'

'That is well,' said Friar John looking up at him. 'There should be no animosity between kinsmen.'

Felim nodded humbly. 'Indeed there should not,' he agreed.

'You have done a Christian thing, my son,' said the friar, patting the horse's neck.

'That I have,' said Felim. He laughed suddenly, an uproarious guffaw of mirth. 'And I got fifteen pound for his head in the castle above in Dublin.' He dug in his heels and trotted away to catch up on his fellows.

∾

The cot men found Adam, floating face down in the New Quay. They dragged him out, covered in streamers of green weed and smeared with black mud. They laid him on the river bank. They went sadly to pound on the door of la bele Aliz. She came out in her nightgown, with a robe thrown over her shoulders. She looked down at her husband's corpse and shivered. She stooped and touched his cold face. She brushed weeds from his long blond hair. The cot men stood awkwardly, with their hats in their hands. They looked from one to another. There was fish to be unloaded.

She had to use influence and copious alms to have him buried in consecrated ground.

∾

Friar John exhaled deeply, emptying his lungs several times before taking a deep breath. He was like a man preparing to dive into the depths of the sea. He held his breath and plunged into the miasma of the tanner's lean-to. The saltpetre grew like white fur on the limestone wall. He kept his lips shut, but already he imagined that he could taste the foul air on his tongue. Flies buzzed around a pile of fresh hides. Their music hummed under the slated roof. A tanner whistled as he scraped the hair from a part-cured cowhide.

'Good day to you, Friar John,' he called cheerily. Friar John mumbled a greeting through pursed lips. It cost him some precious air. He scraped rapidly, gathering the white salt into an earthen jar. His knife grated on the stones. He exhaled in a long gasp of despair. He was forced to take another breath of the indescribably foul air. The tanner gathered the naked hide and lowered it into an evil-smelling vat of mingled urine and dog shit gathered from the streets of Irishtown. He was in the mood for a chat.

Friar John felt the atmosphere settle on his tongue. He was desperate for a breath of the relatively clean air of the outer yard. He looked into the jar. He had a goodly supply. He stepped out from the lean-to. The tanner put aside his work. He took off his leather apron and hung it on a nail. He wiped his hands on his shirt. The friar wondered why he bothered with an apron. His garments were soaked in the vile witches' brew. The miasma followed him like a cloud.

Friar John wiped his lips with the back of his hand. He felt that he had only made matters worse. He wanted to go back home and duck his head in the rainwater butt. He wanted to hang his woollen cassock in the breeze of the cloister and let the wind carry away the smell that impregnated it.

'You'll be wanting your usual pinch of alum, I take it,' began the tanner. He was a kindly man. He liked to think that he was furthering the cause of learning. The old brother had come to him for many years to beg a lambskin or a calfskin. He was a great man for a chat, a warrant to talk, what with stories of giants and saints and the Little People. He had a good one about the people away to the north of Dublin, who stole Saint Patrick's goat.

'Did Brother Fergal ever tell you the one about the saint and the goat?' It was worth telling again.

The friar nodded. He had heard it many a time, how the saint took a great lep from his island and how his footprint can be seen in the rock to this day. Didn't he demand his goat back and didn't the people deny that they had it? It was true up to a point, because the goat was eaten.

The butcher from next door joined them.

'God save you, Friar John,' he said. He lent his ear to the story.

'The dirty liars,' went on the tanner. 'And didn't the goat inside in their bellies hear them and didn't he give a great maa out of him?'

'What was that?' asked the butcher. He loved a yarn. He was, in his own way, an artist. Whenever he put a carcass to hang on the row of hooks outside his shop, he made little nicks in the outer membrane. As the days went by and the wind and sun did their work, the nicks widened and stretched to form pleasing floral patterns, a florilegium of shoulder, brisket and haunch. He knew by the ripeness of the blossoms when the meat was ready. He also had come for saltpetre to add to his steeping corned beef, the best corned beef in Kilkenny.

He folded his arms as the tanner, out of consideration, began the story again. The tanner fumbled in a satchel and took out a lump of dark bread. He tore a piece off and offered it to the friar.

'No, thank you,' declined the friar, raising his hand. 'Fasting.'

The tanner took no offence. The ways of the friars were inscrutable. They lived by denying themselves all the simple pleasures of life, God's gifts to men in a hard and cruel world. He spoke with his mouth full. He chuckled at the humour of the story. 'So the good saint put a curse on them. It is a fact that the women of that nation grow beards, like any goat.'

The butcher laughed. 'By the Lord, that would be a sight to see.' He apologized for the oath. 'That would be a sight.'

Helene, the cordwainer's wife, appeared at the gate of the yard. She stood awkwardly, shifting her weight from one foot to the other.

The tanner went to speak to her. He towered over her, bending his good ear and nodding. It seemed to Friar John that she was tired and anxious. She clenched a fold of her apron in both hands.

'Ah the poor woman,' said the butcher gently. 'She has a lot to put up with.'

Friar John reflected that he had sorely neglected his friends. He vowed to make amends.

'Her husband has took to the drink. Not a happy man.' The butcher shook his head. 'Not a happy man at all.'

The tanner was nodding. 'Wednesday, then,' the two onlookers heard him say. Helene went away. Her shoulders drooped. The butcher took a deep breath and went into the shadow of the lean-to. The tanner went back to his work, thinking of bearded women.

Friar John went back to his book, cradling his jar of saltpetre. Words revolved in his head: *De Secretis Operibus Naturae Artisque*, by the great teacher Bacon. A foolish thought. Was the great teacher led to saltpetre through his own name? The friar stepped quickly, anxious to be in time for midday prayers and lunch thereafter. His mouth watered in the hope of bacon and cabbage. Lofty studies, even the secret works of nature, must yield occasionally to the needs of the inner man. Even Aquinas, in the blinding effulgence of his mighty intellect, took time out to enjoy a good meal.

∾

The parliament concluded with a High Mass and *Te Deum*, sung in the cathedral by the choir of canons, deep bass and tenor and the piping soprano of the altar boys.

The Bishop, not long for this world, sat bent over on Saint Canice's stone seat. The great lords in their finery knelt and received the Body of Christ, accepting that in the final analysis, the Church was the power. Every office, every title, every law was ultimately subordinate to the Pope and his bishops and through them, to God.

On the ground, however, in the workaday world, the sword and lance resolved most questions. It was a balancing act, weighing king and noble against the awesome power of the keeper of the keys to Heaven and Hell.

Alice took her turn in the queue. Followed by her maidservant and her son, she stood in the aisle with hands joined in reverence. She noticed the old bishop parked on the slab of stone. It would have been a kindness to have given him a cushion. She wondered if he would be sending to her for a stoup of turpentine to bathe his haemorrhoids. She saw Sir Arnaud and his scrawny wife, the lady Agnes. She wondered what he saw in her. In another life she and he would have made a great partnership. He caught her eye in a flicker of recognition. He held her gaze just a fraction of a second too long. She watched the sanctuary lamp sway gently from side to side. It hung from a chain that disappeared up into the darkness of the rafters. There was a joint on the chain from which sprang three smaller chains of gold to support the bowl of the lamp. She looked at the little bead of red light in the glass. She remembered how Walter, her father, had pointed to the lamp with his long staff.

'You see those three chains holding the bowl? Those three golden chains?'

'Yes father,' she had nodded.

'Well, the lamp is the world. We all live in that bowl of light. Those chains are the three great laws that hold up our world and keep it level. They are the law of God, the law of Fealty and the law of Hospitality. Now what are they again?'

She repeated the formula, 'God, Fealty and Hospitality.'

He nodded. 'And what would happen to the bowl if we were to break even one of those chains?'

'Everything would fall out,' she said brightly.

'And we would be spilled into the exterior darkness,' he concluded gravely, leaning on his staff. 'Into exterior darkness.'

The idea frightened her. She felt demons plucking at her

garments, seeking, even in the hallowed precincts of the cathedral, to drag her down into the abyss. She prayed for the soul of Walter.

She prayed also for the soul of her departed Adam, a man who had once loved life, loved music and dance, falconry and sport of every kind. Maybe he had stepped on a stray sod. Maybe he had crossed some malevolent person or fallen victim to evil bait, laid by a witch, a *sortilegia*. Perhaps the Little People had led him astray. It occurred to her that the cot men had forgotten, in the drama of his death, to pay their farthings for discharging their catch. She thought she might let it go.

She knelt to receive. Canon Bibulous proffered the Host. She saw his pudgy fingers, mottled like beef sausages. She lowered her eyes. His belly loomed over her like a cliff. She heard a rumble from within. The canon was in need of his breakfast. She opened her lips.

'… *custodiat animam tuam in vitam aeternam,*' he intoned.

'*Amen,*' she whispered. It was comforting.

∽

Richard de Ledrede fancied that he was becoming a wandering scholar. In his middle years, he had not, as yet, found a position suitable to his ability. He had briefly met the king and queen. He had sensed the animosity between them, barely concealed to avoid public scandal. He had seen the open hatred between the king's favourites, the De Spensers, father and son, and the queen's favourite, rumoured to be more than a favourite, Mortimer, the great Earl of March. It was obvious to Richard that some terrible clash was on the way. The reverses suffered by the king's barons in Scotland might well be enough to turn the world upside-down. In a way he was relieved that they had sent him back to the papal court at Avignon. He was to stay there and do the king's bidding until such time as a place might be secured for him, worthy of his manifest ability. He had been brushed off and he knew it. He was tired from travelling.

The mole on his leg was troubling him. It had grown larger. He offered his disappointment and discomfort as a sacrifice to God. He scratched the mole. Blood came away on his fingernails.

∾

There was an insolent air about the woman that had always got under his skin. Canon Bibulous stood at the western doorway in order to ingratiate himself with the great lords and the powerful burgesses, as they filed out of the cathedral. He had made his manners to the seneschal and his lady and to the justiciar from Dublin. Like everyone else, he knew that there was no lasting in the Bishop. There would be a vacancy there before very long. He wheezed a little, unused to exertion, but he hoped that his speed would pay off.

'God shield you, Canon Godfrey,' said Alice with a little curtsey.

He condescended with a slight nod. His eyes took in her fine clothes, her lithe figure, all too evident under costly silk, her long staff, surely not necessary to a young woman. He noticed her maid-servant, a comely young woman. He sniffed. The Devil plucked at the fringes of his thoughts, venery and lust. In the delicate political situation in which he found himself, tupping young women in the sacred precincts of the churchyard might not be the wisest course for His Grace, the prospective new Bishop of Ossory.

The maidservant, of course, did not presume to speak. The boy, William, scampered ahead. He wanted to go to where young pages and squires were holding their masters' horses.

The canon's eyes slid after the two women. She had taken her maid-servant's elbow. She pointed with the staff to the top of the tower. Their shoulders touched. It was obvious to Canon Bibulous that they were laughing. They looked back and giggled. They were giggling at him. The scales fell from his rheumy eyes. At last he knew.

William stood with the other boys, watching the knights. They particularly admired the lord Butler from Gowran. His men were the best equipped and the most arrogant. The boys liked that. The knights sat on their horses in the full panoply of feudal magnificence, dressed to kill. Butler's horse was a paragon, but not, the boys argued, as impressive as that of Sir Arnaud. Sir Arnaud's horse wore new German armour on its neck and withers. When it flexed its neck the interlocking plates flexed also, sliding over one another in the most ingenious manner.

''Tis like a crawfish,' blurted one of the boys. He was correct. They gazed and admired. They argued as to who was the better man, Butler or Sir Arnaud.

Sir Arnaud handed his lady and her maids into their carriage. He nodded with cold civility to Butler. He directed his squire to lead the horse after him and called the reeve and several leading burgesses to follow.

'Let us walk, gentlemen, and inspect our walls.' This with a pointed nod in the direction of the departing Butlers. Butler's knights clattered away up Vicar Street, in the direction of the Great Bridge. Some of the boys ran after them, breathless from trying to keep pace. William trudged homewards. He would have liked to run with the urchins of the street, but he knew that he was a special child and could not do so.

Sir Arnaud walked briskly, pointing out places where the walls should be raised.

'Costs money, sire,' said the reeve dubiously.

'Well then, raise it,' replied Sir Arnaud. 'Who knows when an enemy might descend upon us?'

His companions looked at one another and raised their eyebrows. They strode up the narrow street to Black Freren Gate.

'Another six feet here,' he said. 'More building. More building.'

'Expensive,' murmured the reeve.

'It must be done. Who knows when the Irish might come down? Or even the Scots.'

His companions looked at one another again in surprise. One of them made a circular motion at his temple, with his index finger. They smirked like schoolboys.

'I will take back that key from the Blackfriars. You can never trust the friars.'

'But sire,' the reeve protested. 'They have enjoyed that privilege since the time of the great Marshal. They will not be happy.'

'Let them offer it up, then. I will not have my men dying on the walls or river bank only to have some conniving friar open the back door to the enemy.' Sir Arnaud was not a great friend of the friars or of the Church in general. He would protect Hightown to the end, but the Bishop might look after his own.

He led them along the sconce of James's Street.

'Shabby, shabby,' he muttered.

They went out by James's Gate and onto the Fair Green. He indicated the low hovels that clung to the outside of the wall, like barnacles on the keel of a ship.

'Have these removed,' he commanded.

The reeve wondered where he might send the poor people.

'Send them down to Irishtown. Let the Bishop look after them.' Sir Arnaud dismissed the dilemma.

He took them out by Watkin's Gate, appraising the towers along the wall. He seemed reasonably satisfied. They turned east and re-entered by Patrick's Gate. Perspiring and footsore, they fetched up at the castle. He led them to the top of the northern turret and pointed to the river.

'This is our weak point. We cannot rely on the river. We need a wall.'

The reeve blanched at the thought of the expense. He raised his concerns.

'Tax everything,' said Sir Arnaud. 'There are enough goods coming through those gates to pay for twenty walls.'

'But the land, my lord. The lady Alice owns much of the river frontage. Have we funds enough?'

The seneschal snorted. 'Nobody has funds enough for Dame Alice, God wot. I shall speak to her myself. We can come to some understanding. Now, gentlemen, that you know my mind, let us take meat together and some light refreshment.'

They were glad of the respite, but appalled at the thought of the work ahead. They wondered why Sir Arnaud was so anxious about the walls. Time would tell.

∾

Friar John was a gifted teacher. He preferred to demonstrate rather than tell. He permitted Robin to take part in the transcription of manuscripts, working at an upright desk, with the page held secure by a dangling weight.

Friar John showed him the mystery of the Arabic numbers and how, with a mere ten symbols, he might measure the universe.

'The greatest of these is zero. There is no finger for zero. Zero means "nothing". It is an absence, a void, but look.' He joined his forefinger and thumb to form zero, a gesture of exactitude, of precision.

'But with zero, one becomes ten.' He wrote the digit and added a zero. 'It becomes ten. It becomes a hundred.' He wrote another zero, pleased with the light of understanding in Robin's eyes. 'It becomes a thousand, ten thousand, one hundred thousand.' He wrote more zeroes, forming a necklace across the scrap of parchment. 'As far as the furthest stars, a million, million miles and more. The Roman Emperor could enslave the world. He could even crucify our Blessed Lord, but he had no zero. He could neither multiply nor divide. Now let me show you something. I will explain the notion of proportion.'

They had the scriptorium to themselves in the quiet of the dying afternoon. He took down three jars from a shelf of books.

'This one is sulphur. Some call it brimstone.' He lifted a pinch of the ground-up sulphur on the tip of a quill and placed it on the flagged floor. 'The great Roger decrees that we mix one pound of this with two pounds of charcoal.' He took two pinches of fine-ground charcoal and placed it with the sulphur. 'Now, six pounds of saltpetre.' He explained the source of the various compounds and their many uses. He added six quill-tips of the white powder and mixed all together. 'Now, obviously we have not used nine pounds of the ingredients, but each stands in relation to the other in proportion to what it says in the book.' Robin nodded. 'Now hand me a taper.'

It was time for a practical demonstration.

He touched the flame to the little pile of powder. There was a bright flash and a loud crackle. Black smoke spurted from the small conflagration. They stared at each other in astonishment. Robin grinned. An acrid smell pervaded the room. Friar John was dismayed. There was a bad scorch mark on the flagstone, not to mention the drips of candle wax. He had got a fright.

'So you see,' he said, retrieving his dignity, 'the importance of proportion.' He sneezed. Robin nodded. He gestured to his teacher to do it again, this time with more powder. Friar John was not so sure. He frowned, deep in thought. A true philosopher would never shy away from knowledge. He scratched his chin.

'Well, maybe. If we place the mixture in a container we will protect the floor.' It was an excellent solution. He took down an empty earthen jar and let Robin add the various powders, watching carefully and counting aloud. Robin stirred the mixture.

'I have an idea,' said the friar. He snapped a candle in half and pulled out the wick. 'It might be as well to stand back a little and introduce the flame from a distance.' It was a sensible suggestion. He put one end of the wick into the powder, poking it in firmly. He touched a taper to the other end and stood back. The first bell rang for vespers. They looked at each other in gleeful anticipation. They watched the flame creeping along the wick. The bell rang again.

The prior sat in his sedilla. He joined his hands together and closed his eyes. He let the sound of the Latin plainsong flow over him. There was nowhere else he would wish to be, other than in chapel with his dear brothers, singing praise to the Lord. It was the closest thing to Heaven on this earth.

A shattering peal of thunder startled him from his meditations. A blinding flash of lightning lit the tall lancet windows. They left off their chanting and ran to see what had happened. Smoke came from the direction of the scriptorium. It must have been a fireball or a direct strike from a bolt of lighting. A thunder-stone.

The place was in chaos. Pages from precious manuscripts lay everywhere. Some priceless volumes were smouldering. The writing desks were tossed about, as if a riot had taken place. Coloured inks spattered the walls. The monks coughed in the choking smoke. There was brimstone in the room, as if Satan himself had been there.

They found the two natural philosophers unconscious and bleeding, but mercifully still alive. The pair lay under a heavy table that seemed to have saved them when the lightning struck. They lifted them gently and bore them to the infirmary.

༄

The reeve rubbed his eyes. He turned to his clerk.

'A farthing here; a ha'penny there,' he said, jabbing a finger at the list on the table in front of him. Increasing tolls would not garner him the love of the burghers of Kilkenny. These murage levies had remained fixed since the days of William Marshal himself. 'You know how it works, like cheese-paring or clipping a coin, not that I condone such practices, of course. A little and often. They'll grumble, but they will pay.'

The clerk understood. He took the list and dipped his quill in the ink-horn. He began to make the adjustments. A sack of wool, two pence. That could bear another farthing. He wrote in the margin 2 ¼d; a horse-load of cloth and other divers and minute articles coming within the walls, ½d. Add one farthing. He wrote ¾d. One thousand salted herrings went from a ha'penny to three farthings. Every lamprey during Lent, three farthings. He shivered. The lamprey, succubus of the fishy world. If he had his way he would levy a pound sterling. With its rasping teeth it fastened itself to nobler fish, a nightmare creature of river and sea. God spare us from the lamprey and demons that fasten themselves to Christian folk. Make it 1d. One hundred woolfells, skins of goats, stags, hinds, bucks, does, up to 1¼d and one hundred skins of kids, hares, rabbits, foxes, cats and squirrels up to ¾d. There would be many an argument as to whether the skin was that of a goat or a kid.

Linen, cloth of gold, samite and baudekyn. The list went on. If they can afford cloth of gold or baudekyn, they can afford another farthing. The seneschal would be glad of every farthing, that little speck of silver with a rather handsome Edward, Rex and Dominus on the face and a long cross on the obverse, God and Caesar together. Whether struck in London, Lincoln or York, nobody refused a farthing. Even the Irish accepted the image of their Dominus, although they rejected his claim. A hogshead of wine. Worth every penny. A hogshead of honey, even more so.

Each hundredweight of avoirdupois, 1d, no matter what it might consist of, a catch-all tax. In a way, mused the clerk, the reeve and myself are the first into the breach. He felt quite proud.

❧

'What have you done this time, Friar John?' queried Petronilla. She looked at the poor, scorched friar. One of his eyes was still puffy. His beard was singed, as were his hands. The absence of eyebrows gave him a vaguely comical expression of perpetual surprise.

The friar looked sheepish. 'A little mishap, I fear. Robin and I …'

She was startled. 'Robin? Is he injured also?'

'He is well,' he reassured her. 'He is resting in the infirmary.' He coughed. 'In fact he is enjoying the attention, as one favoured by God. One who survived the thunder-stone.'

'Lightning?'

He lowered his eyes. The prior gave thanks daily that his beloved brother and his pupil had been spared by divine favour. He assured Friar John that his survival was a singular mark of God's love and that he would repair the scriptorium without delay, in thanksgiving.

'In a way,' he muttered.

She took his battered hands in her own and inspected them. It was all worth it for this, the fire, the brimstone, the thunder, the flying furniture, the smouldering parchments. A man might go to Hell itself for the touch of this woman's hand. But Hell would exact its dues, when the prior found out what had really happened. In the meantime, the bruises, the singeing, the thought of penance to come and long days on bread and water, were all worth it. His heart sang.

She touched his forehead with a cooling salve. The infirmarian had no such salves and no such skill. He closed his eyes. She anointed his eyelids.

'They will grow back, your eyelashes and eyebrows.'

He opened his eyes. Her face was close to his, as she inspected her work. He looked into her blue irises, not only blue, but a universe of many colours, all combining in blue. It was a wonder, like seeing into the depths of the ocean, with all its many strange and sapless plants.

He bethought himself of his vows, of his work in the world, of the Judgment to come and the day of even greater reckoning with the prior. It was all nothing compared to the happiness that flowed through him. A dark thought intruded, the confession of poor Adam le Blound and the sordid thing he had done against his wife. It was nonsense, he had assured the humiliated and conscience-stricken man. The great Bacon himself had laboured to show that magic and witchcraft were merely the products of ignorance and superstition.

Reason and natural philosophy always show that there is an explanation. Witchcraft and magic are only to impress children and the gullible. Reason and the truth will be revealed.

'But what if there are things beyond reason?' the poor man had asked.

'Then we must place our trust in God,' he had advised.

'But what if reason and your natural philosophy discover something that conflicts with the revealed word of God? Suppose, just suppose that there are people on the moon. They cannot be descended from Adam. What then?'

The first part of the question was one for the schoolmen, grave and knowledgeable philosophers. He had smiled gently at the second part. He made light of it.

'Then we must sail thither in some curious ship and bring them the news that we are indeed saved.'

But Adam was not comforted. He was free of her spell, but she was still Alice and he was penniless.

'There is no witchcraft,' Friar John had insisted. 'Put your mind at ease.'

Now he was not so sure.

'Have you been to see your parents?' he asked, mindful again of his pastoral duties. She looked away, fumbling with the lid of a jar.

'I have been much occupied here,' she replied. 'My mistress needs me.'

'You should visit them more often,' he advised. 'They long greatly to see you.'

She nodded, biting her lip. In truth she did not enjoy her visits. There was always friction in the house. Alain neglected his trade and his apprentice, Robin, was an incorrigible truant. Helene was tired of pleading with tradesmen for a few more days' credit. Petronilla felt guilty. She knew that her absence was the cause of the dissension. They were pining for their daughter, in their different ways.

'My mistress says that they will always have a roof over their heads. As long as I am in her service they are safe in that regard. She says that I must make my way in the world and that my best chance is to stay in serve… to stay with her. She has great things in store for me, she says.'

Live horse and you'll get grass, reflected the friar. The lady Alice liked to get her value.

'She says that she will find me a good husband.'

'Aye,' he murmured. He drummed his fingertips on the table. He winced. He had forgotten that they were scorched and blistered. A husband. He resented the man already.

Whatever about a husband for Petronilla, he reflected, Alice had no great trouble in finding another for herself. In many ways it was the perfect match. Richard de Valle was a man of substance. He preferred to live on his lands around Clonmel, making infrequent visits to his wife in Kilkenny. They came together like sun and moon at a time of eclipse, for a brief embrace, only to part again to their own separate orbits. A marriage made in Heaven indeed.

'You should go to see them.'

She lowered her head. There were tears in her eyes. Startling blue sapphires, lapis lazuli. 'O Jhesu!' he exclaimed inwardly. It was time to go.

'I will see them before Christmas,' she promised. 'We will spend Christmas and Twelfth Night at Outer Farm.'

He realized that he was jealous. He could see her there, amid feasting and music. There would be green boughs on the walls, ivy and holly. There would be gleemen and dancing, while he would sit at a bare board with bread and water.

'You will be pleased to know that she has been reconciled with her stepson.' He had heard about that. It was a Christian thing, in this season of good will. He had heard how young Ivo, son of William Outlawe, had been knighted on the bloody field of Bannockburn and how Guillaume le Kyteler had fallen, crashing among the foemen, bellowing to the last. The glum and surly boy was now Sir Ivo, a knight in the service of the lord Butler of Gowran. Friar John was indeed pleased. God is good.

He took his leave and murmured many prayers, as he trudged slowly back to the abbey, to shrift and retribution.

∾

From years of watching her father and from her own experience in banking, Alice had developed a wry sense of humour. She smiled when she saw one of her clients crossing the street to avoid meeting her. She knew that she would reel him in, in time, struggling and squirming on the hook. Like a spider, she sat at the centre of her web, feeling for the slightest 'thrum' as a fly drifted against a far-flung filament. It was almost too easy. Money flowed to her door, or rather to William's door. The boy showed promise. He could pluck an apple from the orchard, peel it and eat it and then sell the peel to a street urchin for some service or maybe a rare bird's egg. He could sell the stone from a peach, having enjoyed the fruit, explaining that the boy could grow his own peach tree and in the long run make a greater profit than William himself. Everything she did was for William and for the children that someday he would have. The Kyteler line would go on down through the centuries, bankers to kings and princes, greater than the bankers of Flanders or Milan, greater even than the merchants of Hansa. It was a dream to be nurtured and cherished.

'Butterfingers,' she thought, looking at the bundle of Templar notes, now just a fistful of useless, crumbling paper. She was at the loss of a considerable sum of money but there was a lesson to be learned. The mighty Templars had lost everything. They had lost the

Temple and Jerusalem itself. They had let Cyprus slip and all their lands, their towns, villages, demesnes and granges, to the greedy and cash-strapped kings of France and England. They had lost even their order and their freedom. They were taken in the night, dragged to prison and to the stake. Men who had endured long night watches and bloody battles against the Saracen foe, had failed to notice the enemy creeping up behind them. They had cost Alice Kyteler money. Butterfingers! They deserved everything they got.

Outer Farm could well support the Christmas revels. Sir Guillaume had built it up, before losing it to his niece. It was a large house with a tower and walled bawn. There was a village on the estate and large open fields. It pleased Alice to observe the well-kept fields and expanse of forest land. She registered the cattle still grazing in the open, in mild December weather. It was as if autumn would last forever, a propitious sign. She noted the stacks of straw in the haggard and the barn crammed with hay. She would give a handsome gift to Galrussyn, the steward, and his wife.

It was said that everything she touched, turned to gold.

She set up her Jesse bough in the hall and gave orders for holly to be brought indoors. She gave ribbons of sarcenet to Petronilla to bind into wreaths of greenery. She checked the pantries and cold room for meat, game, hares, venison, beef, guinea fowl, pork, mutton. She checked her cellar for ale and wine, red wine of Gascony and the sweet Malmsey of Malvasia, that jewel set in the brimming ocean. She appointed Henry the Smith as Lord of Misrule for twelve days and Galrussyn as Master of the Revels. A fire crackled in the fireplace of the hall. Flames danced on glassware and burnished pewter. She was pleased with what she saw.

∽

Friar John passed Christmas in silence and labour. He ate bread and drank only water. He worked every spare moment in the scriptorium, making good the damage caused by his experiment. He copied page after page, but the secret works of nature and of art were no longer open to his enquiring gaze. Robin was forbidden to enter the grounds of the abbey. Friar John was forbidden under pain of mortal sin to enter the house and inn of Alice Kyteler, or to have speech with her or her maidservant, Petronilla de Midia.

He scraped with his knife. He rubbed the parchment with pumice and dusted with chalk. He mixed new inks and scratched with his quill. His sandaled feet were cold. His belly rumbled. He ached for the touch of a gentle hand. The cuts and burns on his fingers mended, but his heart was bruised.

NINE

Lumen stelle praefulgidum
Ne declinent in devium.
(With the light of the star shining before them,
   may they not stray into error.)
            —Richard de Ledrede

ALICE GAVE HER a cloak of red velvet and a pair of sleeves, silk with threads of silver. She wore the cloak to morning Mass, but the sleeves would be too grand in front of the villagers. They might accuse her of vanity. They walked as a family to the chapel and smiled upon the country people. They brought gifts for the humble priest, for his woman and for his children, marchpane, conserves, almond bread, a loaf of sugar and a guinea fowl. The priest bowed in gratitude. Sir Ivo, tall and strong, as a knight should be, handed him the basket. The hungry man's eyes gleamed with happiness and gratitude.

Petronilla wondered if Sir Ivo might be the man. She sneaked glances at him throughout the Mass. He was handsome, with the confidence of one who had carved out a place for himself with his sword. She hardly dared to hope.

Their guests arrived for dinner. The revels began. Henry the Smith wore a cap of maintenance with an ostrich feather, as befits a monarch. He wore a velvet doublet and buskins of white baudekyn silk. He called in the huntsman to salute the feast.

The huntsman entered with bow and quiver. He was dressed entirely in green.

'Let us have a blast of venery,' called Henry with a wink to all the company. 'Let the hunt begin.'

The huntsman blew a long 'halloo' and they fell to feasting. There was wine and also possets of sack with nutmeg and cinnamon. Crab apples from the fire, sizzled in ale. The odour of game and garlic-scented beef filled the hall. There was laughter and cheer. Alice presided over it all, glowing like a queen. Petronilla savoured the sweetness of liquor and cinnamon. She felt that she had come into her rightful place.

An Irish harper crouched over his instrument. He was an odd-looking fellow with straggling hair. 'Jing, jing, jing,' he strummed. He sang some gibberish song in a strange tongue. He left off as the servants came in to clear the boards and move the benches back to the wall. The hounds foraged among the rushes. The company sat back.

The huntsman returned. This time he carried a net containing a cat and a fox. The fox's eyes darted about. The cat was tense as a drawn bow. The hounds went wild. The huntsman released the two captives in front of the fire. The hounds fell upon the hapless pair. The huntsman urged them on, blowing a whoop, whoop, whoop, on his horn. There was laughter and excitement as the animals surged about the hall. Wine was spilled on costly finery. Ladies leapt onto the benches to avoid the snarling, snapping, biting fury of the hounds and the flurry of the panicked quarry, but eventually it was over. The hounds snuffled over the tattered victims and played tug o' war with the remnants.

After the excitement of the sport died down, a troop of minstrels culled from the village struck up for dancing. Petronilla watched the huntsman ushering his hounds out of the hall. She saw their mouths flecked with foam and blood. She recalled how Alice had told her about her first wedding and how her husband had provided sport and sustenance for all the town.

A bear, chained to a stake had seen off every hound and cur in Kilkenny. Everyone was there, even the friars. William Outlawe knew how to entertain.

Petronilla had taxed Friar John about this.

'I thought that Saint Francis was kind to animals. Why were the friars watching such a spectacle?'

'Ah,' he responded, shaking his head. 'I was not there to see such cruelty. They were Blackfriars, I'll be bound. They're hunters in their own way. Never cross the Blackfriars.' He left it at that.

She wondered momentarily how Friar John was enjoying Christmas. The friars were reputed to enjoy their victuals on holy feast days. He had not returned for his final treatment. Like most men, he had little care of his health.

She danced opposite Sir Ivo. The lines advanced towards each other. They skipped. They clapped and retreated, Crusaders and Saracens clashing in a mighty battle. Sir Ivo had a crescent scar stretching from the corner of his right eye, slicing across his cheek and curving under his ear. If Sir Ivo had moved even a fraction of an inch, if his adversary, some rebel Scot, had even sneezed, the blade might have severed his jugular and her gallant knight would have expired in a fountain of gore in a muddy field. It was too terrible to think about, but it was the chosen profession of noble men. She danced towards him again. He smiled.

Two huntsmen duelled with hunting horns from either end of the room. Each one excelled the other. They challenged from distant hills. They galloped together, leaping over hedge and fosse. They drew apart, their challenges and ripostes fading again beyond the woods, elfin woodsmen departing. They went away. Silence.

The listeners applauded. They had been transported out of

themselves. They had run with both hounds and stag. They had flitted through the mysterious greenwood where stories begin. Her fell of hair prickled on her scalp.

Sir Ivo bowed. His sleeves were slashed with scarlet silk. He doffed his bonnet.

'Is it not curious that we use this word "venery" for hunting the stag and for the amorous pursuits of Venus?' A smile played about his lips.

She felt herself blushing. She was not used to the banter of courtship. This language of the court and of love was unknown to her. She could dance with natural grace, swaying to the music of the drum and pipe, but she was not skilled in the art of advance and retreat.

The minstrels began again, saving her from further blushes. They played a soft cantilena. The dancers joined hands and moved in a circle. Sir Ivo watched her. Candles glowed. Petronilla sparkled.

The guests drifted away to bed. Alice sat on a rug in front of the fire. She played the pebble game with Robin, her new favourite. He had abandoned his trade and was banished from the abbey. Robin always won. Petronilla sat quietly, watching them. Sir Ivo lounged on a bench. He smiled his contented, slightly mocking, smile. He nursed a cup of warm wine.

'No, Robin,' interjected Alice, stalling the click of pebbles and the rapid movement of his hands. 'Now you must play it my way.'

She opened the purse that always hung from her girdle. She spilled out some keys, coins, a perfume bottle and five yellow bones. She picked out the bones and tossed them. She caught all five on the back of her hand.

She invited the two watchers to join in the game. Petronilla moved closer. She relished the warmth of the fire. Sir Ivo declined.

'I always win with these,' smiled Alice.

'What bones are they?' Sir Ivo was intrigued. 'Rabbit? I am not very fond of rabbits. I lost a good horse to a rabbit warren.' Of recent provenance, the rabbits had bred well. 'They breed like ...' he shrugged, 'like rabbits.' He chuckled at his wit.

Alice flicked the bones and gathered them, one, two, three, four, five.

'No,' she said. 'These are the fingers of an Irish thief. They will pick no more.' She laughed.

Sir Ivo sat forward. 'An Irish thief?'

She nodded, engrossed in her game.

'My uncle, your good friend Guillaume, hanged them on Gibbetmede. They hung there for months and months, like two black poppets. My friends dared me to go there at the full moon. On my own.' She picked and tossed. 'And bring back proof.' She tossed and picked. 'I found a hand in the long grass under the gibbet.' She passed the bones to Petronilla. Petronilla paused. She touched one with her forefinger and drew back.

'In the long grass, nourished by the juices of Irishmen.' She laughed again, daring them to react. Sir Ivo looked amused.

'The scavenger crows overlooked them.' It was a small triumph over her friends, a joke that had stood her in good stead whenever she wanted to shock. Even the Irishmen had grinned at the joke.

'At midnight?' queried Sir Ivo. 'I never realized I had a mother of such courage.'

She snorted at the idea. 'Nor I, that I had so valiant a son.' She laughed again. 'But not so precious as my son William.'

Sir Ivo smiled again. 'It is enough for me to be here and in your good graces. I will remember this night and your strange story.'

Robin gathered the bones and jiggled them in his hand. He tossed them on the rug. They fell in the pattern of a pentagon. Petronilla wiped her fingers on her costly sleeve. She clasped her hands around her knees and looked into the fire.

In the bright sharp days after Christmas they walked by the river. Sir Ivo flew his falcon at a heron, a silent sentinel among the reeds. Petronilla was glad that the heron beat off its assailant with a few flaps of its slate-grey wings. Sir Ivo whistled the bird home. It perched on his gauntlet, fidgeting, anxious to be off again.

'What a thing it must be to fly,' said Sir Ivo. 'What would you give to be able to fly, mother?'

'I am told that it can be done,' replied Alice. 'They say that some heretics can fly, the Scobaces, the Poor Men.'

'That would be flying in the face of God,' said the young man solemnly.

'My son is so serious, Petronilla. Perhaps he should have been a soldier monk.'

Sir Ivo wound the bird's jesses loosely around his wrist. He looked about, hoping to see some lapwing.

The wind nipped at their faces, with a promise of frost. It was time to return to the house. They dined again to the music of the minstrels. They played with dice and told old stories. William Payn sang in a strong baritone, a sad song of love:

> For her love in sleep I slake,
> For her love all night I wake,
> For her love mourning I make
> More than any man.
> Blow northern wind.
> Send thou me my sweeting.
> Blow northern wind. Blow, blow, blow.

Sir Ivo applauded, looking directly at Petronilla.

~

The reeve's clerk had a good Christmas. He stuffed a goose, pricked it all over and set it over the fire. The fat dripped and sizzled, threatening to set his house on fire. Although a man in minor orders, he did not go to Mass. In truth, he was incapable of going anywhere. From early morning he celebrated the coming of the Saviour, with draught after draught of good wine. He attended to his goose. He dozed and snored. He woke to drink. The fire died down, but he carved the goose and feasted on the half-raw flesh. There was enough to keep him going for a week.

He revelled in the alehouses. No dancing girls there, but good companionship and warmth. He bought generously and pounded his tankard on the board for ale and more ale for his good friends.

He stopped to relieve himself in a narrow alleyway. He walked homeward, thinking of the remains of the goose, dry and hard, still hanging over a neglected hearth. He placed one foot carefully in front of the other. They should do something about these streets. He would mention it to the reeve. His other foot refused to touch the ground. He tried again. He wobbled backwards. He tried again. The ground shrank away from his reach. He was bewitched. The wayward leg waved from side to side. It was a mystery. He laughed aloud and fell backwards. The reeve's officers found him, still laughing and struggling, like an upturned beetle.

'These streets are a disgrace,' he whined as they took him away.

The disgrace, however, was his. They searched his house and found the source of his sudden prosperity, a bag of farthings and ha'pennies, a groat, even two shillings, an abundance of pennies. The reeve sent him to the dungeons under the castle, pending the return of the seneschal. Perhaps he should have sent him to the Bishop's gaol, but that was at the other end of the town and the weather was harsh. Anyway it was a matter touching on the defence of the town, a civil matter, nothing to do with the Church.

༄

Sir Arnaud came to Outer Farm, meagrely attended by a page and a single knight. His title and the force of his reputation were enough to protect him in English land. They came, all three, for Twelfth

Night and the Epiphany, riding through snow, bearing gifts, like the Magi. They were made welcome. He gave Alice the first salmon of the year and a coat of dusted sable. She stroked the dark fur in delight. The skins had come a long way, from Norway or Tartary, to protect her from the cold.

Sir Ivo was wary at first, awkward to be in the same house as his lord's great rival. In the way of hospitality and in seeming deference to his new-found mother, he put aside enmity. It was the last day of Christmas. Normal business would resume soon enough.

The holly leaves were sere and coated with fine dust. The Jesse tree had shrivelled. Brown needles lay on the ground beneath it. The knick-knacks and symbols looked cheap and gaudy. The jokes and pranks of Henry the Smith, Lord of Misrule, had grown tedious. The Master of the Revels was a pain in the arse. Sir Ivo was prepared to wait for the one last entertainment, maybe try his luck with the handsome serving girl and depart in the morning, snow or no snow.

However, Henry spared no effort in his final presentation, a masque, with music.

There came first the preliminary clowns and tumblers, village boys, not very skilled, but their incompetence an integral part of the act. Annota Lange and the lady Eva appeared, dressed as Turkish women of the harem. They raised the temperature with a sinuous dance. Helena and John Galrussyn appeared as an Irishman and his wife, to much hilarity. John played the oaf to perfection.

King Robert of Scotland and his villainous brother were booed and pelted with crusts. Sir Arnaud applauded. There was a gross farce in which a straggle of Waldensians, riding broomsticks, capered about the hall. They clutched their broomsticks, making obscene gestures with them and prodding the person in front in the backside in imitation of the lewd practices common among that sect.

Two drunken 'Templars', in white shirts daubed with red, bared their backsides and mimed the notorious obscene kiss of peace.

The 'Pope', wearing a crown of three tundishes and brandishing a fiery cross, pursued them about the hall and put them to flight.

Sir Arnaud leaned back in his seat and laughed. He took a posset-cup of cream and old sack and drained it. He looked for Alice, but she was gone.

Some morrismen and a man wearing antlers danced in a ring. The man with the antlers swayed and staggered. He fell to the ground. His legs jerked convulsively. He expired. He could get three years' penance for that, mused Sir Arnaud. The drink was clouding his vision and his reason.

There was a flash and a puff of white smoke. Sir Arnaud blinked. The onlookers gasped. The stag man had come back to life. He danced again. He juggled five steel balls. He was naked to the waist. Sir Arnaud could see his face and the black rims around his eyes. He was fascinated. If he could give this young man to the sodomite king his fortunes would be secure.

There was another flash and more smoke. The stag man was still dancing, but behind him stood Diana the huntress, attended by a fair wood nymph. Diana wore a light tunic draped over one shoulder. Her left breast was bare. She carried a bow and quiver. Her arms were long and white. A coiled golden snake twisted about her upper arm. She drew back her bow, aiming an arrow at the stag. The hall was silent. Sir Arnaud swallowed. There was a clap of thunder, lightning and more smoke, wafting up to the rafters, escaping under the eaves. When the smoke subsided, the vision was gone. The onlookers applauded wildly. The revels were at an end.

❧

Petronilla sat on a stool beside her bed. She took the garland of leaves from her head. She shivered in her light Grecian costume. She began to comb her long, fair hair. The candle flickered in a draught. She scratched at a red spot on her arm. She was not too sure about her bed and the creatures that lurked within it. She found another spot and scratched.

'I have a salve for that,' said a soft voice behind her. Petronilla turned, startled to see Alice standing in the entrance to her low chamber. The heavy curtain fell to behind her. She wore her warm sable coat. It descended almost to her ankles. She carried a silver cup, warming it in both hands. Steam curled from it, a wraith in the candlelight.

'Drink this,' said Alice proferring the cup. 'It is cold in here.'

It was indeed. Petronilla sipped the sweet liquor. It warmed her insides, but her feet were cold on the strewn rushes. She scratched again.

'Use this,' said Alice, taking a jar of unguent from the deep pocket of her coat. She opened the jar and put a dab of the contents on the spot, red and raw from Petronilla's scratching. She rubbed gently. Petronilla felt the irritation cool immediately as the astringent worked its way through the broken skin. Alice dabbed again on a second spot. Her fingers massaged, firm but gentle.

Petronilla put her head back. The fumes from the cup made her head swim. She drank again. A languorous warmth pervaded her whole frame. Her fingers and even her toes tingled. She put her head to one side, inviting, surrendering. Her hair cascaded about her shoulders. She felt her mistress's hands anointing her neck and kneading her shoulders, the thumbs working at the base of her skull. She groaned with pleasure.

Alice whispered. 'You will fly tonight. He will come to you.' Her voice was low and hoarse. She laid Petronilla on the bed, lowering her gently, slipping the wood-nymph costume from her shoulders. She anointed her white throat, her breasts, her soft belly. She touched her where no one had ever touched her before. Petronilla closed her eyes, surrendering completely to the probing, caressing fingers.

'He will come to you,' whispered Alice.

Petronilla opened her eyes. She saw her mistress's hands. They were the skeletal hands of the thief. Her head spun. The candle flame whirled about the room. It made a smear of light in the gloom. She tried to stop it, to fix her eyes upon it, to hold it in one place, but if spun again every time, a girdle of fire.

Figures swirled about her, the company of Twelfth Night, gibbering and laughing, Alice, bare-breasted, the huntress, the heretic Scobaces on their staves, the stag, a fox.

'The truth,' said the Blackfriar. 'Tell me the truth.' His face was hidden in the shadow of his cowl. 'I command you to tell me the truth.' His voice was low and icy.

Her hair streamed behind her as she flew through the darkness. She perched on a horn of the crescent moon. The stars made circles about her head. Smoke swirled and coiled about her. She lay on the margin of a great mere. The wind whistled in the withered reeds. She felt her heart beating. It rang in her ear, tang, tang, tang, like a blacksmith's hammer. The crescent moon stood, a lonely stylite, on the pillar of its own reflection. A fox slunk towards her, snuffling at her naked helplessness. The huntress drew back her bow. The fox mounted her prostrate form. The huntress loosed her arrow. Petronilla felt it pierce her vital organs. She felt the hot seed of the fox inside her.

'The truth,' bellowed the boar. Foam flecked his lips. His eyes were red and watery. 'I command you in the name of Our Lord Jesus Christ, to tell the truth.' He passed a candle before her face. Her skin burned. Darkness closed about her.

Robin found her wandering naked in the snow. He wrapped her in her red velvet cloak and carried her to her chamber. He massaged her frozen feet and put them inside his shirt, until the warmth began to return. He drew the covers about her and watched over her through the night.

Sir Arnaud came to Alice's bed. She had been waiting for him. They made love urgently, with a desperate violence. She had waited years for him. She had dreamt so often of his coal-black eyes, his strong arms, his powerful body. At last she had him in her power. She was warm and safe. She plucked at the black hairs on his chest. The fire-light glowed like a halo around him.

'Will you not leave your scraggy wife for me? We could have everything, the two of us together.'

He chuckled, a low reverberation inside his chest.

'Why would I do that?' he asked. 'My wife is an heiress in her own right. I need her money.'

'So that we can be together all the time.'

He laughed a deep rumbling laugh.

'You want too much. You have a husband.'

'I know how to manage a husband,' she replied. 'God knows, I know that much.'

He pondered a while.

'There are many reasons. It would not be politic. Besides I am beholden to your husband for his support.'

'Leave her.' She realized that she was pleading. 'I can take care of my husband.'

He shook his head. 'My wife has powerful friends. It would not be politic to offend them. It would cause great scandal.'

'You are the power. You may do whatever you wish.'

He shook his head. 'There are many powers in this world besides money and beauty. You understand little. We can be together like this if we are discreet. I am the power in this country, but I am merely a small flea on the back of my lords De Spenser. They are but fleas on the arse of the king.'

'I will have you,' she murmured, moving close to him, 'I always get what I want.'

She put her knee across his thigh and rubbed against him, but he was preoccupied.

'That boy,' he said, musing. 'Your pot-boy, the juggler.'

'Robin?'

'Where did you find him?'

She shrugged. 'He is a foster-brother to my maid, Petronilla. The good friar, John, brought him back from the mountains. They called him Spideog among the Irish.'

'I see.' He laced his fingers together across his chest. 'Spideog?'

'A robin, or so the friar told me. He was raised by a wild Irishman. Some tragedy. I don't recall. He was suckled by a shepherd's bitch.'

Sir Arnaud grunted. 'A bitch! Will you sell him to me?'

She was startled. 'Robin? You want me to sell Robin to you?'

He nodded. 'He is exactly suited to the king's taste. He could be one of the king's favourites. It could be to your advantage.'

'No,' she replied. 'I could never sell Robin to a sodomite, no matter what it might gain me. The king is well supplied, by all accounts. Robin is more than a pot-boy. He has many strange skills. He deserves better.'

'It is no matter. It was just a thought. A business proposition.'

A log fell in the fire. She watched him covertly.

'However,' she said, after a long silence.

He turned his head to her, waiting. The lady Alice was known for her business acumen.

'However,' she repeated, propping herself on one elbow. 'If you will leave your wife, I will give him to you as a gift. The king may use him however he wishes.'

Her free hand plucked at the hairs on his chest. Sir Arnaud shook his head.

'You ask too much, Dame Alice. You cannot have everything in this life. I will leave you with your familiar and you leave me with my wife.'

He turned towards her, but she turned away.

There were scraps of food on the table in the hall, bread and cheese, mustard and brawn. There were hoof prints in the snow, as of one departing early. The northern wind blew across a frozen landscape.

TEN

Cerne mundi naufragium.
(Behold the shipwreck of the world.)
　　　　—Richard de Ledrede

THE WIND SET IN from the north. Although the light returned,
the biting cold kept spring at bay. Richard de Ledrede petitioned the
Pope for advancement. He wrote to Queen Isabella, asking her to
use her influence with the king. Richard received no reply.

The Pope had nothing to offer him. He received a blessing and
admonitions to be patient. The school of Paris turned him from the
door. They had grown tired of his querulous brilliance. In despera-
tion, he wrote to Hugh De Spenser, favourite of the king. It humiliated him that he had to go, cap in hand, to this depraved and corrupt
young man, a man who shared the king's bed as freely as he shared
his treasure.

His heart sank at the reply. There was a vacant see. The king
would be pleased to recommend his servant, Richard de Ledrede, to
the chapter of the diocese of Ossory, for election as bishop. The king
required him to go again to Avignon, footsore and feeble though
he was, to be consecrated by Pope John, the twenty-second of that

name to occupy the seat of Peter. The De Spensers owned the town of Kilkenny in Ireland, a prosperous and commodious town, populated by industrious and loyal subjects of King Edward. The lord De Spenser would write also to his seneschal, Sir Arnaud, a good and pious man, instructing him to make his new bishop welcome and to assist him in every way.

Ireland! A place of heretics and barbarous practices; a place where they eat their offspring; where feudal custom and the true religion had fallen by the wayside and lycanthropes make the night hideous. Hibernia, named for winter itself. The bile of disappointment rose in his gorge. He wrote a letter of gratitude, as any beggar might. He prepared, yet again, to set out on his journey.

❧

Alain Cordouanier, master craftsman, coughed a long rasping cough. He leaned forward and spat into the embers of a failing fire.

'There is no need for that kind of talk,' he grumbled.

'Look at him,' scolded Helene. 'He is nothing more than a drunken sot.'

Petronilla regarded her father. His chin was dusted with a white stubble. He had once been so proud of his appearance, shaving every second day with a sharp blade. His cheeks were gaunt. His bench was abandoned, his tools scattered about the floor, knife and hammer, templates for the shoes of fashionable men and women.

'No need for that,' he grumbled again, filled with the bitterness of failure, a beggar living in the house of the woman who had stolen his greatest treasure. He coughed again and spat.

Helene sighed. She wrung her hands. The world had darkened about her.

'So you are with child.'

Petronilla nodded. Helene looked away from her. 'Do you know the father? Are you so completely whored that you do not know your child's father? Are you whore to the public in that bawdy house?'

Petronilla shook her head. 'No. I am not a whore. My child's father is a noble knight. I know that he will come back for me.' It hurt her still that Sir Ivo had left without a word. 'I know that he will return.'

'A noble knight!' Alain's spirits revived. 'Well, then.' All would be well. Tomorrow he would go back to work. He would set up his neglected bench, whet his knives and lay his tools out within handy reach. Saint Hugh would look after him. He could go himself to the tanner and choose the finest of leather to make shoes for the wedding. This was something to celebrate. He would go to the alehouse at the bottom of the hill, beside the Great Bridge, to drink his daughter's health and that of the infant to come. The landlord would be pleased to extend credit to him, on foot of his good fortune. Alain would attract a better type of client to his poor premises, gentlemen and knights. Pages and squires would hold their horses outside to impress the passers-by.

Alain rose and kissed his daughter. He stumbled to the door. They heard him coughing as the cold air hit his lungs.

Petronilla lowered her eyes. Her mother put her arms around her. She tugged the velvet cloak tighter around her, protecting her, as she had so often done before.

'You could come home,' she murmured. 'If you were to come home, he would be well again.'

'I cannot. I must wait for him in my mistress's house. He will not come for me to the house of a cobbler.' Her eyes glistened.

Her mother held her close. 'You must send for me when your time comes.'

Petronilla nodded. 'I promise,' she mumbled.

She lifted a basket of bread, cheese, a little meat and some dried fruits, onto the bench. She touched some of the scattered tools, as if to put them in order. She let her hand fall by her side. She shook her head.

There were two guards at the Watergate, Herebert and a taciturn companion. They stamped their feet and blew on their knuckles. Petronilla clutched her cloak about her. The guards studied her closely. Her pregnancy was becoming obvious.

'I thought I saw a star in the east,' said Herebert. 'Did you see it, lady? The star in the east?' They smirked at each other.

Petronilla put her head down, quickening her step.

She saw the sandaled feet and the fringe of his grey robe just before she bumped against him.

'Petronilla!' exclaimed Friar John. 'I was not sure that it was you. I mean …' He was overcome with confusion. He studiously looked away from her growing waistline. 'Are you well?'

'I am not so bad,' she replied, 'considering.'

He nodded. She noted that he too had changed. His face was lined and gaunt. His beard was streaked with grey. His eyes were sunken and intense.

'But you?' she queried. 'Have you been ill?'

He shook his head. 'Not quite,' he replied, with a wan smile. 'I have been paying the price for delving into secret knowledge, things perhaps better left unknown.'

'Your hand? You never came back to me.' She took his hand in hers and touched the scar. The hand was thin. She could see the sinews and blue veins, like the hand of an old man. 'You need feeding. Will you come with me to the inn? We can sit and talk in the private apartments. I can give you something to put some flesh on your bones.' She spoke lightly, to conceal her concern.

He slowly withdrew his hand. He lowered his head.

'Alas, I am forbidden,' he began. 'I am forbidden to enter alehouses and inns.' He spoke in general terms. 'I am under penance for the damage I have caused. I am forbidden to teach. What of my young friend, Robin? He is denied permission to enter the abbey.'

'He is well,' she assured him. 'He is my true friend in this time of difficulty.'

The friar nodded. 'The child's father? Does he acknowledge you?'

She looked away, biting her lip.

'If he does not,' said the friar, with cold intensity, 'if he does not, he deserves Hell fire.'

She looked into his eyes, startled at the violence of his language. She saw there a hunger of the soul, not one that might be slaked by victuals and wine. She understood.

'I must leave you now, good Friar John,' she said gently.

'If he does not acknowledge you,' his voice faltered, 'and the child that is to come, he deserves no luck.'

A silence descended between them. The guards, at some distance, were observing the encounter.

'You must send the child to me for Baptism,' said the friar. 'No, I mean bring the child yourself.' He was already anticipating an awkwardness with the prior. He raised his hand and blessed her.

'That's a good one,' said Herebert to his companion. 'I must try that sometime.' It would be cheaper than paying good money for the support of his several bastards. 'Here, take my blessing for your supper, my child.' His companion put his head to one side, considering the ruse. It was worth a try.

They leaned on their halberds, bored and chilled by the wind. It seemed to pick up with renewed ferocity under the archway. It would be nice to be permitted to shut the gate and oblige travellers to knock politely.

'You know, the Flemings destroyed the French cavalry with these things.' Herebert stamped the shaft of his halberd on the ground. The sound rang on the frosty earth, echoing in the gateway. His companion grunted. He longed for some excitement, some incident to break the monotony of their day.

'Goes right through chain mail.' Herebert assumed a defensive stance, grounding the halberd and bracing it with his foot.

They lapsed into silence. Lascivious talk of friars and women palled. They accepted that the good friar was an unlikely candidate for paternity. He and the woman had gone their separate ways, the woman to Kyteler's Inn and Friar John to his prayers.

That would be the place to be, a fire in the taproom and a mug of good ale. The inn was yet another of the lady Alice's astute business ventures. Everything she touched turned to gold.

'You know,' remarked Herebert, after a contemplative silence. He had stood in contemplative silence at that gate, at Troy Gate and at the Great Bridge, for many a year. He had seen it all. He remembered when the friar had brought the cobbler's family into the town, late one evening, and how he had joked with him about being late for vespers.

'You know,' he began again, 'they say the both of them are witches. Herself and her mistress. They say that's why they have so much money. Like the Templars. They use supernatural powers. That's a fact.' He liked the word 'supernatural'. It had a ring to it, a word that might fall from the lips of a scholar, even a bishop. 'Infernal powers,' he added for good measure.

'She can put a spell on me any day,' leered his companion.

'No, I'm serious. You don't get that kind of money by honest means.' Herebert had cracked it.

'Bollocks,' scoffed his companion. 'She opened her legs for two rich husbands and saw them both buried. There's no magic in that.' He knew that to his cost. 'Now she's workin' on a third one. She has a bank stuffed with tally sticks. She's friends with the seneschal and all the quality. She's no sortilegia.' Two could play the big-words game.

'A what?'

'Sortilegia. A fortune-teller, a magician, a what-have-you, a witch.' Herebert was impressed. He had met his match.

'Well, fuck me,' he said, in admiration. 'A scholar!'

'She would, you know. If you had land and houses; maybe a castle or two; cattle; a forest full of game; riparian rights. Do you know what that means? She'd fuck you then, all right.'

Herebert looked down Watergate Street. There was no French chivalry charging to their doom on the point of his halberd. There was not a sinner to be seen. A bell rang for curfew. It was time to knock off. They heaved the heavy gates on their protesting hinges. They manhandled the great locking bar into place. They shivered in the sudden absence of wind. They handed over their responsibilities to the night sentry.

'If you weren't such an ugly, pot-bellied ignoramus, without two pence to bless yourself.'

Herebert laughed. 'Maybe you have a point. What about a warm ale?'

With the main gate secure, and with two rivers to embrace it, the great one and the lesser, both swollen with unseasonal rain, the town was safe from brigands and marauding Irish. With the cathedral bell echoing from on high, it was safe also from witches and demons that fly by night. It was time for two honest men to put their feet up and discuss weighty matters over a comforting cup or two.

∽

The northern wind wafted the Scottish army to Ireland in bleak and blustery weather. Edward de Bruis, chafing under the dominance of his brother, and an Anglo-Norman himself, came to make war and dispossess his counterparts in Ireland, the people of the Third Nation. With a tincture of Irish blood, and a whisper of a connection to the ancient kings of Ireland, the merest cobweb of a claim in the dusty traditions of that island, he came with six thousand veterans to carve out his own kingdom. He came to seize a rich and bountiful land, a land that had, for generations, fed the armies of the English king and subsidised his wars against the Scots.

He arrived to flooded fields and cattle murrain. Carcasses of sheep littered the mountainsides. The early corn was lodged and useless. The so-called Irish allies were half-hearted and surly. They hung back, waiting to see how things might turn out. The people were already hungry. He was obliged, to his chagrin and humiliation, to send to his brother, Robert, for supplies.

He marched south, swatting aside all opposition. Plundering and burning all that he found in his path, he forced the Moyry Pass and took Dundalk. This town he burned, making a great slaughter of its people. At Ardee he set fire to a church crammed with women and children. He would be king of Ireland and his new subjects would look upon him with respect.

Butler of Gowran, the king's new justiciar, raised the feudal host of Leinster and Munster to drive the insolent invader back into the sea. He joined with The Red Earl of Ulster, harrying the Scottish rearguard, driving the army back northwards, until they clung by their fingernails to the very margin of the island.

The two armies eyed each other across the swollen Bann. The Scots ravaged as far as the Foyle. They fed on meagre rations and promises from the perennially disaffected Irish chiefs. Some 'sea scummars' from the Western Isles ferried them across the Foyle. They disappeared into the forests and mountain wilderness of the west.

Butler led his army south again to protect the English towns. The harvest failed and winter set in.

Bruce, as he had come to be known, intrigued with the Irish chiefs, setting one against the other with contradictory promises. He showed his battle prowess against the English of Connaught. Like Hannibal of old, he wandered the country, leaving havoc in his wake, widows and starving children, gibbets bending under their burden of hanged men.

The English lords were no match for the Scots. They had grown soft from years of peace and prosperity, and had lost the ability to work together against a common enemy. They had no stomach for a winter campaign against this agile foe, and quarrelled amongst themselves.

In brutal January weather, Butler and Sir Arnaud, along with some Normans of Munster, brought the Scots to battle at the great motte of Ardschull. This was their best chance to crush the invader. They made no effort to hide their mutual dislike. A confused and indecisive battle ensued in blinding sleet and snow. Few casualties resulted. Bruce withdrew northwards again, claiming victory, but with an army maimed by disease and starvation. Sir Arnaud returned to Kilkenny to see out the winter.

∾

Helene was turned away from the door.

'I shall see to things here,' declared Alice. 'Your daughter is in good hands.'

Helene felt black hatred rising from deep within. Her voice trembled with rage.

'You have stolen my child,' she shrieked, attempting to strike.

Alice caught her by the wrists, holding her fast.

'You are not needed here. Go away.'

She pushed the older woman backwards, causing her to stumble in the gutter. She fell. 'Remember your position. Your daughter and her child will want for nothing.'

'But this is my only child,' pleaded Helene, getting to her knees. 'And my grandchild.'

Alice stood half-concealed by the door. Costly rings glittered on the fingers of her right hand. 'Mine also,' she whispered. The door closed.

Helene knelt in the mire, bereft of everything. She called down silent curses on the head of Alice Kyteler.

It was a girl. She was called Basilia. Alice took the infant to Friar John for christening. She stared defiantly at the curious gazes of the friars.

'She is Basilia,' she commanded.

Friar John poured the water. He said the prayers. He drove out all demons with holy chrism. He absolved the infant of Original Sin.

'Her father was born on the first day of the year, Saint Basil's birthday.'

'Her father?' queried the friar. He raised his eyebrows. He held the child in his arms, soothing her whimpering. 'Now, now, now,' he murmured.

'Yes, her father.' Alice held his gaze, declining to elaborate.

The friar looked down at the infant. He nodded. 'Basilia, then, and may good fortune attend her.'

Alice reached out. 'Give her here,' she said, taking Basilia in her robe of white lace. Friar John let her go. He tucked a fold of lace under the infant's chin. 'It is a cold world for such a small creature.'

Alice turned away. He watched her leave without a backward glance.

∾

Petronilla looked at her daughter with lacklustre eyes. The father had never returned. Her mother had failed her in her time of need. The days were grey. At any time the murdering Scots might descend on the town with rapine and fire. She had little to look forward to.

She sat on the edge of a carp pond. Her seat was a slab of black stone. She liked to come there away from the hubbub of the inn. She looked at the white flecks in the stone. It seemed as if all the creatures that writhe and scurry under stones were subsumed into the rock in one cataclysmic instant. Friar John would have an explanation, but he came no more to see her.

The infant mewled. Her lips puckered like a little bird's beak. Petronilla wondered about the night of the child's conception. Was this a human child or a creature sent to torment her, a child of the fox with the darting eyes? Had she been penetrated by the Devil himself? No, no. Sir Ivo was no devil. He was a traitor who rejected his own child. If Basilia were a devil's child, she reasoned, Dame Alice would not dote upon her so much. Unless – unless! A witch would recognize a child of the Devil. It was hopeless. She looked at the tumbling river. She could resolve it all now, very simply. There was a drowned calf lodged in driftwood at the lower bridge. Its belly was swollen almost to bursting. Its eyes were open. Hungry people looked down at it, but made no effort to retrieve it from the flood. The calf looked up at them.

She could go into the water, let it close over them both, surrender to the authority of the river and go to join the calf, offering a spectacle to the people on the bridge, a momentary wonder to enliven their turgid lives. A drowned woman in a red cloak, her fair hair streaming with the current and a baby clutched to her breast. It was the makings of a ballad, a sad song for minstrel and jongleur.

She looked again at her daughter. The little hands waved in the air. The mouth pecked. She touched one cold little hand. Perfect fingernails. The fingers closed tight on her thumb. She was surprised by the strength of the grip. She tugged. The infant gripped harder. Petronilla smiled.

'Basilia,' she murmured, pulling her cloak about the two of them. 'Basilia.' She put the infant to her breast. A carp flicked on the surface of the pond with a slight 'plop'.

Petronilla rocked back and forth as the baby fed. She hummed a plaintive melody as the cold wind plucked at her cloak:

> *Syne the time I knew you first*
> *You were my joy and my trust.*
> *Why so unkende, alas?*
> *Why so unkende to me?*

The reeve's clerk cursed the wind and the weather. He cursed the gyves on his ankles and the overseer with his whip. He cursed Sir Arnaud and his seneschal's court. They had no right to send a man in holy orders to work with common criminals. They had no right to try him in the first place. There was still law in the land. They said that they would not hang him, out of respect for the Church. They had even laughed when Sir Arnaud pronounced sentence – fifty lashes and a year in the Black Quarry. May God strike him down!

He had pointed all this out to the overseer. There was a mistake. The overseer felled him with a blow that knocked out two of his teeth.

'Take it up with the Bishop,' he laughed. He delighted in tormenting the clerk. It pleased him to see a man of higher social standing than himself struggling to lift a heavy splitting-maul with his skinny arms. He laughed in glee at the clerk's ineptitude when trying to drive a metal spike into a cleft in the rock. He might well hit his own foot or miss the spike altogether, sending a shuddering jolt through the sledgehammer to shake his feeble frame. He reserved a special animus for this supposedly learned man, who would betray his fellow citizens to the Scots for the price of a fat Christmas goose. The overseer enjoyed his work. The clerk cursed his own folly. His goose was well and truly cooked.

Robin drew her as she sat nursing the child. His pen scratched on the parchment as he drew her looking down at her baby. Her eyes were large and pensive, her fair hair partly covered with a white wimple. He draped her in a cloak lined with blue and edged with cloth of gold. Her dress, he coloured with red ink stolen from Friar John's scriptorium. He salved any qualms he had about the theft with a resolve to give the picture to the good friar as an image of the Virgin, for inclusion in one of his books.

Robin regarded the finished work. He could not bear to part with it. He blew on the ink. He waved the parchment gently, allowing it to dry. He brought it to Petronilla. He knelt beside her as she studied the drawing. She smiled at him and touched his hand.

'God bless your hands, Robin,' she said quietly. 'In this I will live forever.'

He rolled the parchment carefully and left her there, rocking her baby and crooning. The sight of her awakened in him some deep memory.

෴

Friar John riffled through sheets of notes. He peered at old pieces of parchment that he had used as aids to memory when he began his annals. He had often written in haste when something occurred to him. He scratched out letters or let blobs of ink fall from his quill. Some of the sheets had been scraped over and rubbed with pumice, trivial matters jotted down, dates, lists. The shadows of those former notes lurked behind the later writing. Something was tapping at the back of his mind. He could almost see the words.

Brother Fergal used to tell a story of a monk who kept a cock, a cat and a fly as his helpers. The cock woke him before dawn for matins. The cat drove the nibbling mice from his cell. The sagacious fly kept track of the letters as the holy man read his book. There was the familiar blot. Brother Fergal had chided him. It had prompted the story. The monk, in a moment of absent-mindedness, had shut the book on the faithful fly. The fly remained on the page ever after, at the point where its life's work had ended, a dark blot reminding the monk to consider others before attending to his own desires. Friar John could not recall what had happened to the cat and the cockerel. No doubt they had stepped warily around their master for quite some time.

He studied the entry: 'At Pentecost died Michael, Bishop of Ossory, who was succeeded by William FitzJohn, consecrated at Kilkenny on the Sunday within the octave of the Epiphany.' They took their time, he mused. These things cannot be rushed.

Behind the note he could descry what he had been looking for, faint brown letters, almost obliterated by chalk and pumice. Something of no great importance, not worthy to stand forth in the finished version. Obliterated, its letters scraped away.

He moved a blob of glass along the line of text. The letters grew and swam out of shape. It was a piece of the window that he had destroyed, with the help of Robin and the saltpetre. The glass had flowed downwards as it hardened from the furnace and had taken on this strange property of making things bigger. He said nothing to the prior about this.

He had written the words himself, about two years before the death of the Bishop: 'On Saint Basil's Day.' There it was. He traced the faded letters with his finger. 'On Saint Basil's birthday, born to William Outlawe and his wife, Alice, a son, William.' He remembered why he had noted it. The boy was born on the first day of the first month of the new century, exactly thirteen hundred years after the birth of Our Lord.

He put down the glass. A cold dismay settled upon him. Petronilla had debauched a boy, a mere child, one who had been in her care. He had been wrong all the time. He realized that he was a fool in the ways of the world. He trembled.

The prior found him, still seated at his desk, with his head in his hands. He was touched by Friar John's devotion to his work and to prayer.

'My dear brother,' he said, tapping him gently on the shoulder. Friar John looked up in surprise. The prior was shocked by his appearance.

'I have been too harsh with you, my friend. I have made you ill.'

Friar John shook his head.

'I am gravely at fault and I humbly ask your forgiveness,' said the prior gently.

Friar John nodded assent. 'You have done penance enough. I beg that you will come with me now and take some nourishment.'

The food tasted like ashes. A light had gone out in Friar John's world. 'Basilia.' It was a mockery to a saint who had battled all his life against the monstrous crime of heresy. Friar John resolved that never again would he be taken for a fool.

ELEVEN

In ulnis eum tu gessisti
Sinu matris confuisti.
(You rocked him in your arms and
warmed him at your breast.)
—Richard de Ledrede

EDWARD BRUCE CONSIDERED his options. He was a king by his own hand, but not by the will of those he sought to rule. He was a king without a capital, having been repulsed from Dublin. He had neither mangonel nor trebuchet to batter the walls of any town worth the taking. He was a fugitive in his new kingdom, excommunicated and damned by the Pope himself. The Irish shied away from one who carried on his shoulders the curse of interdict. Behind him stretched a via dolorosa of shattered villages and smoking farms. He was learning the folly of going up against a king anointed by God.

The great Mortimer, the new Keeper of Ireland, dogged his heels. The feudal lords put aside their animosities to combine against the Scots. His men were gaunt and tired, his horses bony and ill-shod.

He heard that scream again. He turned his horse and rode back along the straggling line. The men looked at him, leaden-eyed, as he splashed past them. It was raining.

Some women were huddled in an open cart. It jolted and swayed. On the floor of the cart, on a bed of empty grain sacks, there lay a washerwoman in labour. At every jolt she screamed. The stubborn infant refused to come out into the world. The attendant women looked at Bruce in despair. All their skill was defeated by the rain and the motion of the cart.

Bruce raised his hand. The column halted. He called to those in front to turn back and bivouac for the night. He ordered that a tent be set up for the washerwoman. He sent provisions and fuel for a fire. He waited. The washerwoman screamed.

'But sire,' protested his lieutenant, 'this is a vile and worthless woman, justly punished for her sin. We must move on. Mortimer will compass us on all sides.'

Bruce looked into his cup of wine. He grimaced.

'Mortimer has no stomach for a winter war. He thinks of the queen's warm bed. He will not stay in Ireland.'

The lieutenant shrugged. He tried again but Bruce stayed him with a raised hand. The assembled lords fell silent, each one thinking of wives and the comforts of home. They shivered at the woman's screams. Bruce spoke softly.

'Even if we are to die here tonight, we wait until that woman is delivered of her bairn.'

There was a profound silence in the darkened camp and then it came, the cry of an infant thrust into a world of sorrow, a squawk of protest, infinitesimal in the darkness. A child had come to save them. Bruce smiled and raised his cup. In that moment he became their king.

There was no Christmas at Outer Farm that year. Outer Farm was a blackened shell, all animals and gear gone to the Scottish horde. The village was deserted. Wolves were reported in the district. It would not have been decent, even had it been possible, to feast and revel in the presence of famine.

Alice gave the inn over to entertaining her husband and his retinue, a group of gentlemen of mature years, uncomfortable in the suits of mail they felt obliged to wear on their journey. They had long passed the days of battle and melée, but in troubled times it behoved a man to keep his weapons close at hand. They clattered, two by two, into the stable yard, bringing news from the outside world. Their weary mounts snorted plumes of breath in the frosty air.

They ate well and drank moderately. They conversed at length about the affairs of state. They spoke of the feud between the king and the De Spensers on the one hand and the queen and her avowed lover, Mortimer, on the other. The kingdom hung in a precarious balance. They spoke of the renewed vigour of the Scots. Like a horse getting its second wind, the Scottish host moved swiftly and at will throughout the devastated land. There were reports of even worse famine in Ulster. And cannibalism. The rumours were horrendous. Graves were no longer sacrosanct. The brains of the corpses were being boiled in the very skulls.

'Nonsense!' interjected Alice. All conversation halted. The men at table turned to look at her. She was resplendent in a gown of peacock eyes. How many proud birds had been plundered of their finery to adorn this wealthy woman? Richard de Valle noticed the attention his wife attracted.

'Nonsense!' she repeated. 'Pay no heed to these rumours. The people in that part of the world eat meat in Lent. That is all. Stories always get out of hand.'

The men looked at one another, uncertain how to take her. There was no denying that in her own case rumour ran riot. Wealth in the midst of famine is bound to attract envy and resentment.

'Then they are justly punished by the Scots,' said Richard soberly. He addressed himself to his plate.

'Anyway,' continued Alice, with a tinkling laugh, 'if I were to cook a man's brains, I should use a cooking pot. Are there no pots in Ulster?'

There was some uneasy laughter. Richard pushed his plate aside. He was impatient to be back in his own home, eating from his own plate and sitting by his own fireside. Like any dormouse or squirrel, he resented being disturbed in mid-winter and turned out of his comfortable nest.

He also resented being a minor player in the drama that always seemed to surround his wife. He was bored with her talk of the seneschal and how Sir Arnaud hobnobbed with royalty; how he would lead the chivalry of Leinster to destroy the upstart Bruce.

Rich montrews of chicken and ginger did not agree with him. He recoiled from blancmangers of meat, anise, sugar, almonds and pepper. Every damned thing, as long as it came from afar. There was pepper in everything, as if people had never eaten properly until the Venetians had discovered the accursed spice. There was nothing wrong with game taken in his own forest and roasted over his own fire. He noticed that she was growing stout. Under that magnificent gown there lay a goodly layer of fat. Her rich necklace could not distract from the fold under her chin, a sign of prosperity and excess. Soon, he mused, she would be so fat that only a Turk could admire her. Perhaps she should go to that country, not as a pilgrim, but as a gourmand. Heartburn rose in his gorge. He shuddered. He was tired of her wit and the conversation bordering on scandal.

'The new bishop has written to Sir Arnaud.' She was laughing at the absurdity of it. Sir Arnaud again. Always Sir Arnaud. 'He demands that Sir Arnaud deliver up to him the reeve's clerk. He maintains that though he be only in minor orders, he enjoys the full protection of the Church.' She laughed at the drama and the absurd comedy of it all.

'What does the great Sir Arnaud say to this?' growled her husband. This was news. Perhaps the seneschal had met a worthy opponent.

She held his stare for a moment. She read his mind.

'I could hardly report what he said. Not in polite company.' She bestowed a smile on the table at large and especially on Richard. 'In effect he said that no scrofulous, renegade, English peasant would tell him how to run his town. He had half a mind to cut his balls off and feed them to his hounds.' She looked around, enjoying the effect. Sir Arnaud had said a great deal more, which, to tell, might reveal too great an intimacy with the seneschal's deeper feelings.

Richard looked around the table. His knights were eating and drinking in an awkward silence. The few ladies present kept their eyes down. Young Sir Ivo, the stepson, reached for the pepper. Might as well be scattering gold dust. Sir Ivo caught his eye. A flicker of a smile played on his lips, an instant of understanding. Sir Ivo sprinkled the pepper.

Petronilla kept to her room. As long as Sir Ivo stayed, she would not come downstairs. She played with her daughter and sang old songs to her. She was glad of young William's company. He seemed devoted to Basilia. He carried her about and talked to her. He dandled her on his knee. He spoke gently to Petronilla.

She was even more glad of his company after Robin left. William was growing up. He showed a natural aptitude for business, combining something of his father's elegant graciousness with his mother's relentless pursuit of profit. Petronilla thought, at times, that he should spend more time with boys of his own age and class. He should be learning to ride and manage arms. William however, preferred the counting-house. He esteemed the snap of a tally stick above the shattering of lances. 'There are fools enough to make war,' he maintained. 'I can buy them if needs be.' In the final analysis everyone and everything has a price. He said it often enough.

'You should be outside, looking for a wealthy bride,' she chided.

'I will not have to look. I can have any girl I want in this town, but not yet.' He took Basilia by both hands and walked her about the room. He lifted her almost to the ceiling beams.

'There's my girl,' he laughed, swinging her around. The child screeched and dribbled down at him. He lowered her gently and wiped his cheek with his sleeve. He gave her to her mother. Petronilla was glad to have a friend.

❧

Robin travelled westward through an empty landscape. There was no sound of a bell giving shape to the day. No cattle lowed. Only the crows were in voice. They swayed in the treetops, a raucous assembly.

He followed the sun, keeping it at his back in the morning and striding towards it as it fell below the rim of the world. He supported his steps with the shaft of a spear that he had picked up in a deserted farmhouse. He dug roots from abandoned fields and gnawed on them as he walked. He snared a rabbit and made a fire. He heard the blood-chilling howl of wolves at night. He kept his spear always by his side. He slept fitfully in ruined cottages or clefts in the rocks. The moon grew with each passing night and waned again to a sliver of gold in the sky.

Frost persisted for much of the day but he was beginning to notice growth. There was a dusting of green on the trees. The crows were busy in the topmost branches. The land belonged to the crows. Mountains rose above the horizon. He stepped towards them every day. He forded freezing streams and followed the valley of a great river. He stood at a weir and caught a salmon in mid-flight. He flipped it onto the grass.

'Can you use that thing?' said a voice. The man spoke in Irish. Robin knew the voice. 'Can you use that spear?' asked Felim Bacach again.

Robin nodded. Felim Bacach sat easily on his horse. He still rode bareback.

'Ah, Spideog,' he exclaimed. 'You have grown. Where are you bound for?'

Robin shrugged. He pointed to the distant line of mountains.

'I see,' said Felim, slipping from the horse. 'Let us eat this fine fish and then we will travel together.'

He took out his knife and gutted the salmon, setting the roe aside on a flat stone. He struck fire while Robin gathered sticks. He spitted the salmon on a willow twig and set it over the fire. He grunted with satisfaction.

He told the story of the famous warrior, Finn, who stole the first taste of the Salmon of Knowledge from the druid, Aengus. Aengus had spent all his life at a bend of the river Boyne, near the tombs of the ancient kings, waiting for that fish. When at last he caught it, he set young Finn to cook it over a fire. He told him on no account to taste it. All the knowledge in the world would go to whoever was first to taste that miraculous fish.

'And didn't there rise a blister on the skin of the fish?' Felim found himself lapsing into Brother Fergal's narrative style. 'Just like that one there.' He poked his finger at a blister on the broiling skin. He drew back dramatically and put the finger in his mouth. He looked at Robin. Robin smiled. He understood. Felim was pleased. Perhaps he had a natural talent for storytelling.

'Y'know, all those years living with my brother and yourself, I had to do all the talking. Maybe I talk too much.'

Robin put his head to one side as if to say that Felim might have a point. Felim lifted a piece of sizzling roe on the tip of his knife and passed it to Robin.

'I am going now to collect my brother and the mountain people.

We are going to kill Scotsmen. Will you come with me?'

Robin licked his fingers. He chewed. It was a chance to see the world, to gain knowledge. He nodded assent. Felim Bacach put out his hand. Robin became a soldier.

∼

Bishop Richard de Ledrede climbed the winding stairs to the top of the tower. He lighted his way with a horn lantern. His leg pained him, but it was of no great importance. He knelt and prayed in the darkness. He watched the passage of the stars overhead. He thought of Simeon, the Stylite, a man who lived on a pillar for most of his life, a man so close to God both corporeally and spiritually that he allowed his own mother to die at the foot of his pillar, rather than give in to her pleading.

Bishop Ledrede scratched at the bandage covering the suppurating sore on his calf. Saint Simeon spent the last twenty years of his life standing on one leg. It enhanced his mortification and his piety. It undoubtedly gave him more influence with God. It was not a choice open to Richard, Bishop of Ossory. He had work to do on the ground.

He watched as light crept into the eastern horizon. The grey of dawn took on a warmer tinge. He thought, as he always did, of the Resurrection. A grey and pallid corpse, inert in a tomb. A pulse begins. A warm pink suffuses the corpse. The chest begins to rise and fall as the Spirit returns from darkness. The limbs stir. He is risen. It is a miracle. Richard prayed in gratitude that he was there to see the day and to be trusted with God's work.

He saw the orb of the sun creeping above the mist. It glinted on the curve of the river and the long diagonal of the castle weir. The dark bulk of the seneschal's castle rose out of the river mist. There were problems in that quarter, and danger. There were voices muttering against him. '*Uisce faoi thalamh*,' one of his canons had advised him, an expression used by the Irish. It put him in mind of the river Mole of his boyhood. That river cut a cleft through flinty chalk, sometimes diving below ground, like any mole, only to emerge as Emlyn stream and retreat, after running some distance in the sunlight, to the infernal regions. The sneering Bicknor laughed when he splashed him at the ford. Richard de Ledrede never forgot an injury or a slight. Bicknor wasn't his match in intellect, but now, by a grotesque caprice of fortune, he was Metropolitan Archbishop of Dublin and king's justiciar. Worse still, he was Richard de Ledrede's superior in all matters relating to Church lands and Church law. He was in league with the De Spensers and, consequently, with the defiant seneschal, Arnaud le Poer. They were combining to do him down. 'Uisce faoi thalamh' indeed.

Smoke was rising from chimneys, forming a pall over the town. He surveyed the battlemented walls peeping above the mist, Hightown and Irishtown, like twin yolks of the one egg. He had an aversion to eggs. Once upon a time, he climbed to the swaying top of a high beech tree to steal an egg from a crow's nest. It was a swaying city of crows. The citizens went wild. They swarmed in the air above him in raucous protest. They swooped at his head. He popped the egg into his mouth and beat them off. He looked down at his companions, dwindled to homunculi, far below him in every way. Their white faces looked up. He was master of the high places. He swung down from branch to branch until he had nothing to cling to but the smooth bole and a few low-sprouting twigs. He could still feel the tug on his ankle that sent him plunging the last few feet, into the nettles and leaf mould. Alarmed by the jolt, he bit down on the egg. His mouth filled with the revolting mess, a half-formed chick, with head, beak and limbs, almost a scaldy. He retched in disgust where he lay.

How they had laughed. It was Bicknor, of course, almost falling from his pony with mirth. Afraid or unable to climb the tree himself, he contrived to deprive Richard of his just reward. His oafish companions fell about, pointing and cackling. They thumped one another on the back and hooted with laughter. He envied the boys their easy fellowship, even as he was still spitting out the intolerable residue. Even the crows enjoyed the joke. He was forced to smile, to pay the price of inclusion, but some day, some day … Richard could never eat another egg. The sight of an egg reminded him that he was different from the others.

He surveyed the roof of his cathedral. There were loose slates around the bell tower. The cathedral was a poor stunted thing. It lacked one arm of the cruciform. It could use a spire. It was begun by Irish monks, he was given to understand, and further cobbled together by Englishmen born in Ireland, almost as bad as the natives. He determined to take matters immediately into his own hands. He would build. He would beautify his church until it was a jewel of the Christian world.

He felt the strength of righteousness flowing through his veins. There were many things amiss in Ireland. It was a soft and soggy land where men were infected with indolence and error, but he would show the way.

A mad woman had accosted him in the street with a preposterous bargain. Something about a witch. If there were witches lurking down there in the smoky town, spreading their vile heresies, he was the man to root them out and purify all of Ossory, if needs be, with holy fire. He bore in his hands an awesome power. He could open the gates of Paradise to his faithful flock and cast into Hell all those who walked in error and darkness.

In the meantime there was work of a temporal nature to be done. He would install a great eastern window, with scenes glorifying the life of Christ and His Holy Mother. He would bring craftsmen and masons to Kilkenny and workers skilled in the art of glass-making. The faithful could come to his cathedral and admire his work. They could gaze upon the life of their Saviour and feel the burdens lifted from their shoulders.

He would by-pass his archbishop and write directly to the king. He would write to the Pope himself about the flouting of Church law in the diocese. He snuffed out the lantern. It occurred to him that he would direct that a lantern be placed in a window of the tower every night, to reassure the people that God and His poor servant Richard were watching over them.

He sat in Chapter with his canons and chaplains, outlining to them the work that lay ahead. They looked at one another in apprehension. It sounded as if their life of ease and dignity was about to change.

'I shall require your dedication to the tasks facing us. Matters have been allowed to drift. Laxity and error have been tolerated.' Bishop Ledrede allowed his gaze to travel around the room. The clergymen listened in silence, with the exaggerated attention of the guilty. He seemed to see into their inner thoughts. He divined guilt in some who were unaware of their wrongdoing. They felt guilt rising in their throats and had to restrain the urge to blurt out some admission, in order to avoid worse condemnation. They said nothing, in the hope that someone else might speak and, like a lightning rod, deflect the Bishop's wintry displeasure.

Canon Godfrey could smell his own sweat. It trickled down his brow and into his eyes. He wiped it away. It prickled at the back of his neck. He wiped again. The Bishop's voice went on, bleak and penetrating as the wind whistling in the keyhole.

'To avoid any misunderstanding I shall henceforth speak in English. I have heard some of you speaking Latin. It was not edifying. As for your French ...' He let the sentence trail away. 'Anyway,' he smiled, 'we must use the tools that are to hand.'

He coughed. He made them feel like bumpkins, people of an inferior nation, Englishmen of a lesser breed. His accent grated on their ears.

'So we are agreed then.' It was not a question. There was no demur. He looked around again.

'Good. I am gratified by your assent. In order to achieve my objective of bringing good governance to my diocese, I shall require the following: any of you who receive temporalities from parishes in which you do not reside, will divert these funds to the cathedral.'

This was too much. Canon Godfrey coughed.

'But, my lord bishop, how shall we live?'

Bishop Ledrede eyed him directly. Here was a fat goose ripe for the plucking, a bibulous parasite. He did not like this canon. He would break him and then make use of him. He ran his thumb down the margin of a list.

'My dear brother in Christ,' he began softly, 'I note that you enjoy the income of three parishes. You have been granted an opportunity to do great service to Holy Church. As you reside in Common Hall, your material needs are already provided for. Think of the lilies of the field. As God has provided for you, in His loving mercy, it will be a source of great joy to you to pay Him back in a small way, by helping to beautify His cathedral.'

Canon Godfrey lowered his head. There must be a way …

'In consequence, the stone of these parish churches will be used as a contribution to the building of the new choir.'

'But what of the people?' squawked Canon Godfrey. 'It would be dereliction of duty to deprive them of their churches.'

The Bishop cleared his throat, a staccato warning to the querulous priest.

'They have managed without your ministrations for many years, as I understand it. I have every confidence that they will continue to manage. And furthermore …'

Canon Godfrey subsided in his chair like a deflated bladder. There must be some higher authority who could forestall this sacrilege. His mind raced. There is always somebody higher up the ladder. At the very least there must be some way of pulling a few rungs out from under this arrogant Englishman. In the meantime, woe betide anyone who crossed his path.

'And furthermore, any priest who maintains a focaria, shall put her out on the road, along with any children he may have had with the aforesaid focaria.' He indicated to his secretary to note it down. The secretary scratched rapidly with his quill. It was written. It was now law. The secretary looked up at his master, with his pen at the ready. He had the eyes of a terrier waiting to go among vermin. He dipped his quill in the ink-horn and tapped it on the rim.

'There is, however, some good news. The lords De Spenser, mindful of the rights of Holy Church and anxious to avoid any disagreement with Her, in their present exigencies, have instructed their vassal, the seneschal, to release into my care, the wretched embezzling clerk. Have the creature brought before me a month from this day.'

The secretary wrote. The canons looked at one another in surprise. This was indeed a turnaround by Sir Arnaud. Perhaps in Bishop Ledrede they had found a champion to stand up for their rights.

'I want it to be clearly understood.' He grasped the arms of his chair and leaned forward. 'Clearly understood that I will tolerate no attack on the Church, either by the civil power or by heretics and sorcerers. I will not hesitate to use both fire and interdict. I will deny Christian burial to all such and command that they be cast upon the dunghill like a dead dog. A dead dog, I tell you. This is regrettable but if it must be done, out of love of God and all Christian souls, then it will be done.'

'Like an hunde,' wrote the secretary. He looked at the terrible words. Fear gripped his heart.

Canon Godfrey also felt the fear, but there was one small compensation. There was no money. The Scots had taken everything. The farms were destroyed, stripped of all gear and livestock. The Bishop could whistle for his money.

TWELVE

Vigent ubique spolia
Livor et incendia.
(Rapine, hatred and arson flourish all around us.)
—Richard de Ledrede

ALICE JOINED Petronilla on the seat by the fishpond. It was the first warm day of the year. Cherry blossom floated on the water. The petals had turned from white to mucky brown. Alice wore sombre widows' weeds.

'I hope the wind did not take them too soon,' she remarked, following Petronilla's abstracted gaze. 'The cherry blossom. I hope the wind has not stolen our crop.'

She laid down her staff. Petronilla nodded. She looked around for Basilia. William was holding the child's hand. The pair stood watching the fishermen at the New Quay.

'Be careful, William,' called Alice. 'I fell in there once, when I was Basilia's age.' She laughed at the memory. 'I wore weeds then as well.'

She twitched aside her black veil. 'My father laughed. I remember it clearly.' The sun fell on her upturned face. 'Oh how he laughed.' She regarded Petronilla with a sidelong look. 'Why so sad?' she queried.

'My father is dying,' replied Petronilla. 'I should be with him.'

'No,' said Alice, patting the back of her hand. 'You are needed here. Your parents will want for nothing. Your father is dying. That is sad. People die. I have lost three husbands. It is sad, but I survive. I grieve but I must look to the future. So must you.'

In fact she had taken her latest bereavement with quiet resignation. Richard de Valle had expired from some disorder of the bowel. He had expired on his privy, a merciful release from his suffering. Strange and marvellous diseases were abroad in the land. She had sent him a variety of nostrums and remedies culled from ancient lore, but his case was hopeless. He had expected such an outcome for most of his life, obsessed with salts and purgatives and constantly grumbling about the food. She was glad that she had not been there to tidy up. She took her bereavement with resignation, but she took also her inheritance.

'I should be with him,' said Petronilla again.

'There is disease abroad. I do not want any disease brought into this house. You are responsible for my grand-daughter. Basilia, Basilia,' she called.

The child came running over to them. Alice took her on her knee and bounced her up and down. 'To see a fine lady on a white horse,' she sang. Basilia's little teeth chattered to the movement. She tried to sing along, but the words jounced on her tongue. 'Bell on her toes,' she managed, but Alice quickened the pace. Basilia became alarmed. She began to whimper. Alice stopped suddenly.

'Now go and play with William,' she ordered, putting the child down. 'I wish to talk to your mother.'

Basilia sniffed. She recovered her good spirits. She took the staff and, sitting astride it, she galloped around the orchard, pursued by William.

Petronilla called her back.

'Don't do that,' she reprimanded. 'That is no game for a young lady.'

She took the staff from the protesting child. Basilia wailed. William took her to see the horses in the stable yard. They spoke to the ancient Lucifer and the latest of his line. The cats basked in the sunlight, enjoying the easy life. They purred at Basilia's touch.

'You are strict with her,' said Alice.

Petronilla pondered. 'I do not want her to end up like me. I want her to be a lady, to have a future.'

'But you are a lady,' Alice protested. 'Why do you think so many men frequent my inn? They come to see the beautiful Petronilla.'

'I am a curiosity. That's all. They whisper and nudge one another and laugh into their ale.' She said it with bitterness.

Alice swept the tip of her staff in the gravel with her characteristic motion. She described a semi-circle, enclosing them where they sat.

'They come to see the witches,' she said lightly. 'They drink their ale and wine and hope to be transported to a place of debauchery and excitement. I let them believe it. I tell them that I bathed last night in the waters of the Devil's Bit and they believe me. I tell no lie. Look there.' She pointed her staff at the river. 'It flows past my garden. The river was born in the Devil's Bit. It was born on the same night as the great Irish king, Conn, the Hundred Fighter, or so Friar John told me. All stories for children. Men are fools anyway.' She laughed again, a short derisive chuckle. 'They would sell their souls for a glimpse of either one of us taking a bath. Like the Elders of Babylon.'

She smiled at the thought of the lecherous old men, hooshing each other up onto the wall to watch Susanna at her ablutions. 'It is the only witchcraft. We can make them do anything we like.'

She continued to swing the tip of her staff. They sat in a crescent moon. 'All the wealth of Kilkenny town,' she crooned. 'When you roll up your sleeve, or pour from a jug of ale, they look at you. They look at your hands and the soft place inside the crook of your arm. They look at your pretty shoes. I see the shutters come down on their eyes, trying to hide what they are thinking. They are never so obvious as when they try to hide what is in their minds. They are bewitched.'

'But Susanna was the one accused,' retorted Petronilla.

Alice became still. She waited.

'Susanna was an honest wife. They look at me as they would look at a harlot. Where is the father of my daughter? Why cannot I walk in the street without insult?'

'Hold their gaze. You will see fear and doubt in their eyes. They will shy away. It always works. If anyone says anything or challenges you, just ask "Why?" It is the most powerful word.'

'Why then did Sir Ivo not come for me? Why did he not acknowledge his daughter?'

Alice swung the staff again, back and forth, back and forth.

'Because,' she replied quietly, 'because he is not Basilia's father. William is.'

The words hit Petronilla like a blow. She heard a roaring sound in her head. She stood up, clutching her elbows, as if to protect herself from an attacker.

'William! But he is only a boy. Sir Ivo … ?'

'Sir Ivo would have taken you merely for sport, but I forbade him. I kept you pure and clean from the start. I kept my goat of a husband away from you. I wanted you myself, from the first time I saw you outside the counting house. You were sitting on your father's cart. I thought that I had never seen anyone so beautiful. When I got to know you I wanted you for my bed, but I kept you for William. I gave you to him instead.'

Petronilla was numb. 'You gave me?'

She felt sick. She heard Alice's voice from far away.

'It was time. I wanted it to be perfect for him. I told you that you would fly that night.'

Petronilla swayed. She sat down again. She remembered Alice's hands and the sweet-smelling ointment.

'You used me,' she accused. 'You gave me to your son.' Her head was clearing. 'You drugged me and gave me as a plaything to your son.'

Alice shrugged. 'It was time for him. You have not been the loser. You have Basilia. You live in comfort here as my friend. Is it so bad?'

'I must leave this house. I must take my daughter and go.' She stood and walked to the river wall. She thought of the drowned calf. She looked into the remorselees stream.

Alice's voice sounded behind her. It struck her with the sting of a whip-lash.

'You will not. Basilia is mine. You will not take her to live with a drunken sot and a mad woman. I will turn them out if you try to take her away. Your mother may shout all she likes in the street, but she will not have my grand-daughter.'

She came and stood at the river wall. Petronilla turned away. She had no words to describe the turmoil inside her.

'It is not so bad,' reasoned Alice. Her voice was gentle again. 'Is it so bad in these terrible days, to have a warm bed and a roof over your head? Your child is safe, with people who love her. William is devoted to you. Long after I am gone from this world, there will be an honoured place here for you. You are my most precious friend.' She looked downriver to the looming castle. 'We have the protection of one of the most powerful men in Ireland. Is that not good?' She put an arm around Petronilla's shoulder and rocked her gently, cajoling. 'Are we not friends?'

Petronilla felt defeat flooding through her veins. She was weary. She wanted to sleep. She lowered her head onto Alice's shoulder. She closed her eyes.

❧

Felim Bacach walked among the ruins of the farmhouse. The sun shone down on him through a lattice of blackened rafters. A lark shrilled overhead. Everything was destroyed. The flocks were gone. The hay garth was empty. Even the stack of hard-won turf had been taken from the gable wall.

Two shrivelled corpses hung from a twisted tree. His brother had died without protest. The font of Brother Fergal's stories was stopped. Felim Bacach would bury them and then he would take revenge.

'Mactíre,' he said aloud. 'I will hunt this wolf down so that my brother may sleep easy.'

He looked up the hill. Robin was standing where the cairn had once stood. The landscape looked awry. Felim struggled up the hill. Not for the first time he cursed the uncle who had lamed him.

Robin knelt down. He felt among the stones. He picked up a long bone, a femur. He held it in his hands, staring at it for a long time. He looked up at Felim Bacach, a dark figure against the light. He squinted his eyes.

'This was my mother,' he said. His voice was hoarse and rasping.

Felim Bacach removed his hat. He knelt down on one knee. 'May God be praised,' he said, crossing himself. 'May God be praised this day.'

Reverently he took the bone from Robin's hands and placed it back among the stones.

'Let us bring my brother and the poor old man to lie here,' he said gently. 'It is a good place.'

It was fitting. They worked through the dying afternoon, bringing the corpses to the hill and gathering the scattered stones. They piled the stones up until the cairn resumed its former height. The landscape looked right again. Robin took five pebbles from his purse and set them on the topmost stone.

'Farewell,' he said, turning away. 'Farewell, Mother.'

Felim Bacach scratched his head. He replaced his hat. He shouted. 'Mactíre. Táimíd ag teacht.' His voice echoed in the valley below. 'ag teacht, ag teacht, acht acht, acht.' The hills took up the cry, 'Mactíre, Mactíre, we are coming.'

Bishop Ledrede regarded the spavined wretch standing before him. There was a certain cockiness about the ragged creature. The Bishop placed his fingertips together, forming a steeple. He tapped his forefingers against his lips, deep in thought.

'You are a clerk in holy orders, I understand,' he began.

'I am, my lord bishop,' replied the prisoner.

'And you have been punished by the seneschal, Sir Arnaud.' He sucked in his breath. 'Hmm.'

'I have been most cruelly used, my lord bishop. Most cruelly,' the prisoner whined. 'It is an affront to God and to His Holy …'

The Bishop stilled him with a raised hand.

'Your sins are manifold, my son.'

'A few pennies, my lord bishop,' the prisoner whined again. 'A few pence to celebrate the birth of Our Divine Saviour.' He dropped to his knees.

The Bishop sighed. 'Be quiet.' He nodded to his secretary. 'Item,' he directed.

The quill scratched on parchment.

'Item. You stole from your fellow citizens.'

The prisoner bowed his head.

'Item. You exposed your town to danger from the ravening Scots.'

The prisoner looked up, surprised.

'Item. You brought scandal by public drunkenness.'

The prisoner lowered his head again.

'And finally …'

The prisoner waited. He trembled.

'You have been the occasion of dissension between the civil power and Holy Church.' He drew in a long, slow breath. 'You are a vile and worthless creature. I would not contaminate my gaol with you.'

The prisoner looked up. He saw a glimmer of hope. There was none in the Bishop's lapidary eyes.

'Consign him to the pillory by the Great Bridge. Let the crows and the water rats deal with him.' The prisoner's bowels let go.

'Remove him,' ordered the Bishop.

Two guards took the prisoner under the armpits and dragged him screaming from the room. He left a wet trail on the polished flagstones. The Bishop rubbed his forehead. He exhaled in disgust. He turned to the secretary.

'Furthermore, I direct that the seneschal, the aforementioned Sir Arnaud le Poer, appear before me one month from this day, to accept a suitable penance for the wrong done to God and Holy Church.'

'Oh shit!' thought the secretary, but he wrote what the Bishop instructed. Sir Arnaud must come and kneel before the Bishop of Ossory, on the flagstones of the Chapter house.

Canon Bibulous closed his eyes. He needed a drink. He longed for the good old days, before zealots and thieves had begun to disturb the tranquillity of his Christian life, before a man was forced to take sides in a war to the death.

'Canon Godfrey,' he heard the Bishop say. 'You will take my letter to the seneschal and await his reply.' Canon Bibulous felt the sweat trickle between his shoulder blades and prickle under his arms.

The secretary closed the ink-horn with a snap.

❦

'We will go to MacPheorais,' said Felim Bacach, 'and sell our services to him. He is raising a great host against the Scots. He can call upon twenty thousand armoured knights and forty thousand foot.'

'MacPheorais?' queried Robin.

'John de Bermingham,' explained Felim, 'the greatest of all the English knights of Leinster.'

'But I thought you said that FitzThomas was the greatest of all the English knights,' Robin argued.

'By God, Spideog,' replied Felim, 'since you found your tongue, you've become a terrible man for the questions.'

'I have a lot to learn,' said Robin evenly.

'Indeed you have. FitzThomas is a Munster man and a great one. He lives like an Irishman and may be our king some day, but he is not in this war just now. MacPheorais will teach you about war. We will go to MacPheorais.'

There was no argument. Robin was eager to learn. He wanted to come face to face with those who had disturbed his mother's bones.

～

Helene, wife of the cordwainer, rooted about in the scattered tools, until she found what she was looking for, a crescent-shaped paring knife. The edge was dull. There were specks of rust dappling the blade. She found the whetstone amid the clutter of rasps, gimlets, pincers and hammers. She whetted the stone and put an edge on the knife. She tested it on a scrap of leather. Sadly she regarded the clutter, the debris of her life with Alain and her daughter. She wondered about Robin and where he might be. They were once a family. She remembered how Petra used to take the boy to marvel at the otters playing in the river. The otters made a slide of wet mud. They lay in the water on their backs, juggling with shining pebbles. He had particularly loved the otters.

She looked at Alain asleep in a corner of the room. He was thin and pale. He coughed, even in his sleep. They had been robbed of everything. A thief must pay the price.

She put a cup of water and some bread beside him, in case he should wake. She went out into the late summer sunshine. She went down the hill and over the bridge into Irishtown. A corn cart was rumbling through the gate. She paused to let it pass. She watched some boys tormenting the scarecrow figure in the pillory. Their laughter carried on the balmy air. The harvest was good and the farmers were taking advantage of the weather, for fear that the Scots might be tempted to move south again.

She wandered around the market in Hightown and, as darkness began to fall, she went back into Irishtown. She lurked about the cathedral, hoping that she might catch sight of the Bishop. There were new foundations and piles of masonry and lime. The evening was warm. She loitered.

In the pillory, the reeve's clerk prayed for death. Sometimes, in the night, a charitable soul brought him a drink of water. He had no idea who it might be. He tried not to drink the water as it merely prolonged his suffering, but still he drank. Eyeless as he was, he could not see his benefactor. He wondered who it might be that would dare to defy the Bishop.

He heard a shuffling of feet in the dirt. He tried to speak, but his tongue was dry. He felt someone holding his fingers. Oh, thank God! An angel had come to set him free, to lift him to Paradise. God had taken pity on him. He felt a blade sawing at the skin of his wrist. He was almost beyond pain. He heard, rather than felt, the blade chopping at tendons and prising the bones apart. He knew that his hand had fallen away. His arm slipped through the hole of the pillory, to hang by his side. The dregs of life seeped from the severed limb and gathered in a pool at his feet. He was free.

❧

By the light of a gibbous moon, Friar John anointed the reeve's clerk and absolved him of his sins. He put down the flask of water. He knelt and wept beside the pillory. His mind was in despair. There was no kindness left in the world. The Devil, he concluded, was winning. For the price of a fat goose, this poor soul had endured beatings and slavery. He had endured mockery and condemnation, starvation, mutilation by brute beasts and even more brutish man. God had washed His hands of the world.

He looked up at the stars. What is the point of it all? The moon hung behind the cathedral. A pinpoint of light shone from a high window of the tower. Friar John was not reassured by the thought that God and Richard de Ledrede, His implacable servant, were watching over Kilkenny town.

❧

Alice heard the murmur of voices outside her door. She blinked at the sunlight. She slipped from her bed, shivering in the morning chill. She went downstairs in her night attire, to see what was afoot. She threw her sable coat over her shoulders and opened the door. The people shrank back. The voices stilled. They watched to see her reaction. She looked from one to another, but they avoided her gaze. She saw what was attracting their attention. A bloody hand hung from the iron door knocker, on a loop of waxed hempen thread.

For the second time in her life Alice felt fear. She drew in a sharp breath.

'What is this nonsense? Who is responsible for this?' She had a fair idea.

Nobody spoke. She noticed that some of them had their thumbs clenched between their fore and middle fingers, a protection against sorcery, the evil eye and all the malice that lurks invisible in the air. She tore the hand free and threw it to a slouching dog. The animal snatched the hand and scurried away.

'Get away, all of you, before I blast you,' she said with nonchalant contempt. The people fell back, muttering to one another. She went back inside and slammed the door. The knocker jolted and echoed through the awakening house.

She stood with her back to the door. Her heart pounded. She

had seen their looks of fear and horror. She had seen the glee behind their eyes. She felt sick.

She went out into the yard and drew a bucket of water from the well. The windlass squealed. She washed her face and hands and swilled the water onto the dusty cobblestones. She sat on the rim of the well, struggling to regain her composure.

❧

Friar John reviewed his annals. He had fallen behind. It was a chronicle of feuds and treachery, of struggles between lords both great and small and the intense rivalries between clergy, regular and secular. He wondered what difference his poor efforts would make. Some day he would die and the feuds and wars would go on, with no one bothering to record them. He wrote:

'William FitzJohn, Bishop of Ossory, is translated to the Archbishopric of Cashel, in whose place is substituted Friar Richard de Ledrede, who was consecrated by the Pope at Avignon, where the Roman court then abode, on the eighth Kalends of May.'

The summer had passed since he had last written. Perhaps he needed a cockerel to wake him and a fly to keep him to his task. What was the point? The fly had fallen victim to its own diligence.

He wondered if the suspension of his penance entailed permission to visit the house of Alice, the daughter of his old friend. It was not very likely. He would have liked to write about the child, Petra, and how she came to Kilkenny on a luminous summer's evening, when the town glowed in heavenly light. He would like to write about how she had filled his whole being with a warm glow; how she had made him believe in a better world. But she too had fallen into a sink of depravity. He could no longer sit with her and talk of the world. He could no longer feel her soft touch on his hand, as she confided in him her hopes for the future.

He looked at the scar on his thumb. There was still a tenderness around it. He picked up his pen. He could write about how she still haunted his dreams and how he awoke in joy, only to feel the greyness of reality creeping back. He dipped his pen in the ink-horn and wrote: 'In this year Bishop Ledrede began the building of a new choir in the cathedral.' He was building and building, like a man demented, but it was no longer Petra's resplendent City of God. There was evil abroad in the streets of Kilkenny town.

THIRTEEN

Rupta fila sunt sagene
Hostis stricta sunt habene
Inferni patent spolia.
(The net is torn asunder, the enemy reined
in; the spoils of Hell lie open to plunder.)
—Richard de Ledrede

JOHN DE BERMINGHAM did not, in fact, command a great host of the chivalry of Leinster. He brought with him his family, their liegemen and their levies. He brought some good friends, notable among them Hugh de Turpilton, Milo de Verdun, Richard de Tuit and a gathering of the burghers of Drogheda. There was also a rout of slack-jawed peasants, butchers and tradesmen, armed only with the tools of their occupations, a ragged regiment. They put de Bermingham in mind of a poem that poked fun at the butchers of Drogheda: 'Flies hem followath. They swallowath eneugh.' There would be butchery and flies aplenty in the days to come.

He was glad to have with him Lord Butler of Gowran, a hard man on his great armoured warhorse. Butler brought a contingent of Anglo-Norman allies from the south, one of them Sir Ivo Outlawe of Kilkenny. Most importantly, the Archbishop of Armagh imparted his blessing to the departing army, but he stayed prudently within the walls of Drogheda. Amid this assorted crew rode the hobbelar, Felim Bacach Mac Giolla Phádraig, accompanied by a light-stepping wood kerne whom he addressed as Spideog.

They marched to stake everything on one last battle with the Scots and their Ulster friends. De Bermingham, Mac Pheorais, whatever they chose to call him, knew the land. He decided to assault the enemy near the Hill of Faughart, before the Scots might dig pit-falls for his cavalry or line the ditches with sharpened stakes. It was there that Bruce had insolently crowned himself king of Ireland and there de Bermingham was determined to humble him.

'No, no,' said Robin, 'that was the other one. That was the saint who drove the black men off the island of Tory.'

'No,' argued Felim Bacach. 'It was Saint Brigid that had the cloak. Didn't it grow and grow, until she had the whole of the Curragh of Kildare?' He held a piece of meat on a stick over the fire. He drew the meat back and bit a chunk out of it. He offered the remainder to Robin.

'Jhesu Spideog, but you're an argumentative man. Are we not on Saint Brigid's own ground? Everyone knows that story.'

Robin shrugged, deferring to Felim's superior knowledge. He chewed on the meat.

'Is that the sea?' he asked, pointing to the glint of light in the distance. 'How big is it?'

'Oh, big enough,' said Felim. He knew little about the sea, but felt a duty to enlighten the younger man. 'If you go down to the harbour after we finish our bit o' business here, you will see boats the like o' which you've never seen before, boats that go all over the world. They go to Araby and France and even The Land of the Lakes; anywhere you want to go to.'

Robin was entranced. He walked to the low wall surrounding the churchyard and looked down. He saw a scrawl of river straggling towards the bay and beyond the bay, an expanse of water stretching to the horizon. To his left loomed the mountain barrier, brown and purple with, here and there, a slash of green. There were gaps in the mountain wall, through which at any time might come the Scots, hardened by years of war and privation and eager for blood. A stab of fear ran through his belly. He knew that he might die there on the saint's holy hill. It would be a pity to die without ever experiencing the sea.

'She took her father's sword and picked the jewels out of it to feed the poor.'

'Who did?' Robin turned again to the fire.

'Saint Brigid,' said Felim patiently. '*Muire na nGael*, the Virgin of Ireland. Her father was angry. By God, I would be angry myself.' He checked himself. 'I suppose it's different for saints. I have little knowledge of saints.' He chuckled. 'Did you ever hear how she turned her bath water to ale and gave it to a poor man to pay a debt?'

Robin shook his head.

Felim laughed. 'I've drunk a drop of ale in my time, but I wouldn't be too happy about that, with all due respect.'

Robin opened his satchel. He took out the rolled parchment and straightened it out. Felim looked at the picture of Petronilla.

'Is this Saint Brigid?' he asked. He touched the border of the gown, an intricate pattern of gold. He peered closely at the gentle face. Robin shook his head.

'Ah yes, of course, the child. It's the Virgin Mary.'

Robin shook his head again.

'If I die tomorrow,' he began, 'I want you to take this back to her. Go to the house of the lady Alice, in Kilkenny town, and ask for Petronilla.'

'Aha!' exclaimed Felim. 'You have a lady love, just like the knights and the minstrels in the stories. Be careful, son. That can only lead to trouble. Get your leg across her, by all means, but never give your heart away.'

He punched Robin playfully on the shoulder. Robin shook his head again.

'It is not like that. She is a good person.' He was not accustomed to banter. He rolled the parchment and put it away again. Felim saw his sudden anger.

'I have no doubt she is. I will do as you ask. But have no fear. You may bring it yourself. We should have little trouble with these Scots. I'll tell you one thing.'

Robin sat cross-legged by the fire and inspected his boots. He probed at a gap where the upper had come away from the cleat. The leather was too weak and soggy to hold the thread.

'What might that be?'

'If you look sharp whenever we win this battle, you'll get yourself a decent pair of boots.' He chuckled. 'Assuming of course, the Scots have a pair between the whole blasted lot of them.'

'Supposing I die?'

'Then you won't be worried about boots, will you?'

He looked up at the birds circling overhead, jackdaws and choughs, ravens and crows.

'Can you see The Bau?' he asked, pointing upwards.

'The what?'

'One of those is The Bau, the *Bean Sidhe*. If you see The Bau, it means that you'll die. You're finished.'

Robin looked up at the circling birds. They all looked the same to him.

∾

Edward Bruce came south at great speed. A fine rain was falling. The ground was soft underfoot. In a sudden thrust he seized the heights of Faughart and, by nightfall, he was looking down at the camp fires of his dislodged opponents on the long scarp sloping to the sea. He took counsel with his leading knights and his Irish allies.

'We have the advantage here on this hill. This is my lucky hill. You recall how I became a king on this very spot.'

They recalled well enough and also the three long years of marching and slaughter, the winters and the hunger they had endured in his company. They had little to show for it but promises of land and riches. Their king was excommunicated and doomed to hellfire. Their Irish allies were shifty and grudging. The expected reinforcements from Scotland had not arrived. It was raining as usual. A cold wind set in from the east.

'This is no conquering army before us. It is a gathering of the country, with a few poor knights trying to make a name for themselves. Tomorrow they come up against a real king, not some mincing fop, who cannot control his own wife.' He laughed. 'Tomorrow they will see what Scottish men are made of.'

His words warmed them. They would ride with him to their deaths or to victory and lawful spoils.

He gave the order of battle, dividing his forces into three columns, one to smash the enemy knights in the centre and two to encircle them and the Irish foot soldiers. The Irish, he pointed out, would lose no time in scampering for the woods. He knew the Irish well. As for his own Irish allies, he directed them to remain on the hill and protect the rear. This they were not loath to do. They had no experience of the melée and the shock of heavy cavalry. They preferred to fight and flee, fight and flee again, draining the strength of any advancing army, using the bogs and forests as their first line of defence.

In the morning the king awoke to the chink of armour, the rasping of blades on grindstones and the snorting of warhorses. This was his natural milieu. A great joy came over him. He permitted his squire to buckle him into his armour. He mounted his horse and settled his helmet. He took his lance and shield, a blue lion on a white field. The lion's tongue was red as blood. With a great roar, the cavalry of the latest king of Ireland moved forward into battle.

The English knights took the full force of the Scottish charge, in a cataclysm of steel and blood, of floundering horses and heads rolling in the mud. De Bermingham sent forward his foot soldiers in a counter-surge, to work among the fallen knights and wreak havoc among the Scottish infantry. His archers rained arrows upon the Irish on the hill and the advancing second column. The third column went astray somewhere over to the right of the hill.

Bruce was everywhere, rallying his troops and dealing out death with a flanged iron mace. He called his friends to him in a desperate charge and drove the English army back. He pressed hard, certain that the enemy would crack. De Bermingham gave the order to fall back, to regroup and gather breath. It smacked of defeat.

Bruce paused on the side of the hill. The weak October sun showed him the field of victory, strewn with the bodies of friend and enemy alike. The trees wore their autumn glory. There was a melancholy beauty about it all, but most of all, there was the exhilaration of carrying the day and being alive to tell the tale. He spurred to some knights who had gathered under a tree to take refreshment. Dismounting, he removed his sweaty helmet, and felt a welcome breeze on his brow. He took some wine. The knights were pointing to the retreating English army. They were too exhausted to cheer.

Bruce looked up. Already the birds were spiralling down to pick over the field of corpses. His eye caught a large kite, high overhead. It kept aloof from the other scavengers, turning in a steady circle over the hill and the Scottish army.

He wandered away from the company of knights and walked about, noting the arms of those who had fallen in his service; poor Gilbert Harper, his most loyal friend. Gilbert had insisted on carrying Bruce's other shield, his arms of Carrick, to confuse the enemy. There lay Mowbray, his life blood pooling around him. There lay MacRory of the Isles and MacDonnell of Argyle, good friends both, lying far from home, prey to the carrion birds. He placed his shield, a red chevron on a white field, over the face of 'Gib' Harper. It would protect his eyes from stabbing beaks until burial parties could be sent out.

Suddenly tired and saddened by the slaughter, he sat down on a rock. He watched the kite, a black arrowhead against the clouds. He rested his elbows on his knees. His surcoat was stained and torn. He was a sorry sight, but a king nonetheless. No one would shake him now.

A cloud of gnats and little golden flies swirled about him, drinking of his sweat. They irritated him, but there was a beauty to them in the weak autumn sunshine. A long-legged harvestman floated in the air, its wings a blur, its flight a dance of indecisiveness. A wasp followed it like a malevolent shadow. The wasp struck, folding the harvestman in a lethal embrace. It carried the spindly insect away. Bruce mused that in the kingdom of the beasts and insects, as in the world of men, there are those who prate and gesticulate, making ineffectual noise and there are those who strike. He frowned. A flash of colour caught the corner of his eye.

He watched a figure approaching up the slope, a man dressed in a yellow fool's coat. The man was dancing and swaying, capering and bowing, yet all the while keeping five shining balls circling above him in the air. Bruce smiled. Here was a clown, seizing his opportunity to secure a place at court. It was amusing that a fool should be the first to pay allegiance. He would reward such enterprise. He beckoned to the juggler.

The knights, watching from the shelter of the tree, saw the juggler performing in front of the king. The fellow crouched low, as was only appropriate. His toes peeped from his shabby boots. The knights laughed. The shining balls flowed along the clown's arm, over his shoulder and down the other outstretched arm. They rose in a glittering arc, over the juggler's head. He leaned forward and the orbs floated above his fingertips. The knights saw the king sitting up. He was laughing too. They saw the juggler turning away, flexing his lithe body like a bent bow. They saw the flash as a ball struck the king's unprotected forehead. They heard the smack of the impact. The king toppled forward. Men rushed from the bushes and stood over him.

Before the knights could even get to their feet, there was a savage roar and the king's severed head was held aloft in a bloody hand. At the same time, the main body of the English army on the slope below, turned about and charged up the hill. Bruce's knights took to their horses and fell back in confusion. They left the body of their king in the hands of his enemies, a shameful thing. Their cause was lost.

'And there was not done, from the beginning of the world, even the destruction of the Fomorians,' Friar John was to write, 'a deed that was better for the people of Ireland, than that deed. For there came death and loss of people in Ireland for the space of three years and one half and people undoubtedly used to eat each other throughout the land.'

The Bau had had her fill.

FOURTEEN

Nam calidis et frigidis – siccis et ydropicis
Contractis – paraliticis, rupturis, apostematis
Leprosis, demoniacis-desperatis et mortuis
Cunctis sucurrit morbidis – empericum est hoc medicis.
(It is the true physician, healer of every ailment, a cure for the
fevered and the chilled; the withered and the dropsical; for cripples
and the paralysed; the broken and the swollen; for lepers and
those possessed; for the despairing and even the dead.)
—Richard de Ledrede

SIR ARNAUD WAS furious. His enemy, Butler, was glorying in his part
in the destruction of Edward Bruce. It was said that Sir Arnaud was
afraid to march against the Scots. It was whispered that he preferred
to stay safe and warm, in the bed of Lady Alice. He had seen them
sniggering behind their hands. It was also whispered that his wife, a
good and virtuous woman, had turned away from him.

He prepared to depart for England to mend his fortunes and
his reputation. It would be a strange paradox. His liege-lord was
Hugh De Spenser, the most reviled and hated man in the realm.
The depravity and corruption of the De Spenser had earned him

the implacable hatred of the queen and her paramour, Mortimer. Sir Arnaud knew that he would have to tread carefully in the court of the sodomite king. He had one card only to play. His friend, Alice, had money. The king was always in need of cash.

A page came into the hall. He coughed. Sir Arnaud turned from his contemplation of the fire.

'What is it, young man?'

'There is a priest here, sire, with a message from the Bishop.'

'What does he want now? Does he want me to hand over my castle and my town? Does he want money for his infernal building?'

'I do not know, sire,' said the boy. 'He is waiting outside.'

'Oh, send him in, in God's name. Send him in.'

He kicked a log in the fireplace. It rolled forward onto the hearthstone. The sparks flew.

∽

The boys worked in the armoury, polishing and oiling the tools of war. The page shook a hood and coif of mail in a bag of sand. He gasped as he shook. It weighed a stone, almost too much for his young arms. It sounded like a bag of money. He liked the sound. He liked also the fact that he was going to England with the seneschal. He wanted to get a good shine up on the mail.

'You should have seen it,' he said to the squire. 'A big, fat priest.' He paused for breath.

The squire was envious. He had not been chosen for the great adventure. He had never travelled on a ship. He had never even seen Dublin. Life was passing him by. He probably would never see the king and the great assemblies of noble knights. He scrubbed at the horse armour, the chanfron mask, the plated crinet for the neck. He used linen, powdered chalk and the juice of lemons. He sniffed at a half-lemon. It smelt of the south, of sunshine and troubadours. There would be castles with pennants flying from turrets and ladies casting silken scarves from lofty windows. It was not fair. Just because the page's uncle was to marry Sir Arnaud's lady friend.

'What about the big, fat priest?'

The page put down the bag of sand. He drew breath. He opened the bag and took out the coif mail. It shone like silver. The squire examined it closely. He put it back into the sand. He closed the bag and twisted the neck into two ears.

'Give it another go,' he ordered. It was a small revenge.

'But I was telling you about the priest,' the page protested. He had not wind enough for two tasks.

'Well, go on then,' said the squire grudgingly.

'This big, fat priest came into the hall. He was this big.' He spread his arms wide. 'Sir Arnaud was standing by the fire. "What can I do for you, good Canon Godfrey?" he says, all polite. "The Bishop desires that you read this letter and that you favour him with a reply," says the priest. His eyes were going all around the hall. I think he was looking for the best escape route. Sir Arnaud turns around, like this.'

The page became Sir Arnaud. He plucked an imaginary letter from the imaginary Canon Bibulous. He frowned. He growled, just like his lord. He put one hand on his hip and perused the invisible missive.

' "Hmm," says he. "I see." He paced about. I could smell the priest from where I was standing. "I see," he says again.'

The page stroked his imaginary beard, deep in thought.

' "Penance," he says. "And a fine." The priest was shaking. "Well you may tell the good Bishop that there will be no penance and no fine either, not to him or to God." He throws the letter in the fire and turns on the priest. He draws his sword and knocks him down with the flat of it. He kicks him in his fat arse. He kicks him all the way to the door and belts him with his sword. The priest was squealing like a pig. "And you may tell your master that if I have any more insolence from him, I will chop his bollocks off and burn them before his eyes. Do I make myself clear?" He gives him an almighty boot and then he turns to me. "Now, young Wat," he says, all polite again, "would you be so kind as to show his reverence to the gate?"'

The page gave a courtly bow, sweeping the ground with his bonnet. The squire was amazed.

'I'm sorry I missed that,' he said, with open envy. Young Wat had all the luck.

'I can tell you, the priest went out that gate like a rabbit,' laughed Wat. 'That's the last Sir Arnaud will hear from that quarter.'

'He was never one for diplomacy. Was he?' The squire went back to polishing the crinet. He was pleased with his work. He could see his face in the scales. His nose was enlarged. He moved back and forth. He laughed at the changes in his features.

'Look at this,' he said, inviting Wat to try it. 'They call this the crawfish,' he explained. He flexed the heavy plates, letting one slip over the other. 'All the knights use them nowadays.'

'I knew that,' said Wat. He was something of an expert. 'He used this when he rode against Bruce.'

They argued about that battle and the chances that had been lost.

'He missed the big one, though. Didn't he? Now he has to go to England to explain himself to the king.' He scrubbed again, improving the shine. 'And you're going with him.' He sniffed.

'I am,' said Wat, pleased with his luck and pleased with life. He whistled. He took the shining mail from the bag and shook the sand from it. It shone like a pile of silver coin. It jingled like harness bells on a lady's horse. A fine lady on a white horse.

'When I'm a knight,' grumbled the squire, 'you won't find me in a shithole like this place. Oh no. France is the place for me, or Spain. I will sell my lance to some independent company. I might even take the Cross and fight against the Saracens.'

'That's all gone,' scoffed the younger boy. 'Don't you know anything? There will be no more Crusades. Not ever.'

The squire was stung by the page's superior air.

'You think you're important, don't you? But I'll tell you something. The only reason you're going to England is because your uncle is to marry Sir Arnaud's rich mistress.'

The page leapt upon his companion in fury. He bore him to the ground. The horse mail clattered to the ground. He sat astride the squire and pummelled him with his fists.

The squire laughed at his efforts. He clouted the younger boy, sending him flying. He grabbed him by the shirt and held him at arm's length. The page flailed at him ineffectually.

'That's right, isn't it? Sir Arnaud just wants a husband for her, who will wear his cuckold's horns lightly.' He pushed Wat backwards and stuck his forefingers out from his brow, wiggling them derisively. 'It's true, isn't it? Your uncle is the stalking horse. He's a decoy.'

He laughed at the page's fury. Young Wat charged at him, sending a rack of armour crashing to the ground.

'Stop!' bellowed the voice of Sir Arnaud. The sound reverberated in the stone-flagged room. He grabbed the boys by the collar, holding them apart like two dogs. He shook them as a terrier might shake a rat. They looked at each other, hoping that he had not overheard the discussion.

'What is this all about? So help me, if you have damaged anything, I will have the hide off your backs.'

'We were just having a discussion,' mumbled the squire.

'And what, pray, were you discussing?' Sir Arnaud spoke in that low courteous voice that the page had mimicked so well. It was the calm before a storm. The page hunched his shoulders, his mind a blank of fear.

'We were arguing, sire, as to whether Bruce was killed by treachery or in fair fight. It is said that Mappas fell upon him from ambush.'

'I see,' said the seneschal, releasing them. 'And what do you gentlemen think?'

'They say that he was tricked by an idiot jester,' replied the squire. 'I say that it was no fair fight. It was a shameful way to kill a knight, however wicked. There was no chivalry in it.'

'And you, sir,' said Sir Arnaud, taking Wat's chin between finger and thumb. He turned him this way and that, examining his swollen eye. 'What do you have to say about all this? Do you call it ignoble too?' In a way, he was pleased that there should be some taint on the killing of Bruce, even from the mouths of babes.

'I say that he is dead, sire, and we are alive. That is the important thing,' replied Wat.

'You are a practical young man, Wat.' He pushed him away with his mighty forefinger. 'We may make a politician of you yet. Or even a bishop,' he chuckled, ruffling the boy's hair. 'We must get some salve for that eye. Put on your bonnets, gentlemen, and tidy this place. Then, young man, I have some errands for you.'

He paused at the door, looking back. The boys were working in diligent silence.

'No more fighting now, mind.'

They nodded. Sir Arnaud whistled as he walked along the passageway. He liked a bit of spirit in his lads.

∽

'I can go no further with you, Spideog,' said Felim Bacach. 'I will go south again.'

'But do you not wish to see the king?' asked Robin, puzzled by Felim's sudden change of plan.

'I will find a better king in Munster, the man I told you about, FitzThomas. There is a man who could unite the hearts of Irish, Norman and Englishmen.'

'But what of the sea? Do you not wish to ride in a ship?'

Felim looked away.

'We could see the whole world,' persisted Robin.

Felim shook his head. The hank of hair fell across his eyes. 'I will not go in a ship,' he replied. 'Of all the things I dread, the water is the worst. How many good men lie at the bottom of the ocean? If I did not drown, people would accuse me of sorcery.' He gave a short, dry laugh. 'Either way they have you. No, I will not set foot on a ship. You have your holy picture to protect you. You have a good, clean heart. I have the soul of a thief, a murderer, a soul full of revenge and hatred.'

Robin smiled. 'You have the kindest soul of all. You are brave and honest. You saved my life. You are blessed. But you are afraid of water so we must part. You are entitled to be afraid of something in this world.'

Felim muttered, embarrassed by the praise. He grasped Robin's hand in both of his, visibly moved.

'Be careful among the English, my son.' It was the first time that he acknowledged how much the foundling child had meant to him. 'The English are not like us.' He spoke lightly to conceal his emotion. 'If I find myself in Kilkenny, I will commend you to your lady. I will tell him that Spideog sings her praise; that he has found his voice and sings her praise every day.'

Robin was pleased. 'Tell her that I will return when I have made my fortune. Tell her that I will return to serve her, like a true knight.'

'Well then,' said Felim, 'we must go our ways. I will tell her that you will come to her when she needs you. Go with God, Spideog.'

They parted.

❧

Bishop Ledrede sent for Henry the Smith. He commanded him to fashion a brand in the shape of a cross, about the length of two crossed thumbs and bring a brazier of coals. Henry assumed that the Bishop was marking Church property. He was known to guard jealously all property entrusted to his care and all rights proper to

Holy Church. He was known to check the accounts of all parishes in his diocese and to enquire into the incomes of all monasteries. This did not endear him to the friars.

Henry set up the brazier in the Chapter house. The fireplace had a good chimney. He scooped some live coals from the fire and used a small bellows to bring them to glowing life. He added some of the hard coal from the hills. He waited. The coal was stubborn, but worth waiting for.

The Bishop entered the room. He wore a long cope. A chaplain carried the end of the train to prevent it dragging in the dust. Henry knelt as the Bishop extended his hand. He kissed the jewelled ring. The Bishop sat down. The chaplain arranged the train of the cope to one side. He stood behind the chair.

'You may prepare the brand, my son,' directed the Bishop. He grasped the arms of his chair.

'It will take a little time, my lord bishop,' said Henry, urging the fire on with a few steady puffs from the bellows.

'Well then, we may talk.' He dismissed the chaplain with the back of his hand. 'We may speak in confidence. I know that the smithy is the counting-house for news in every town.'

'I am not one for gossip my lord bishop,' said Henry warily. He gave all of his attention to the coals.

'Indeed. But if I were to ask you directly, questions relating to the safety of Holy Church and the struggle against the Anti-Christ, it would be your solemn duty to answer truthfully.'

'I am a Christian man, my good lord,' said Henry. 'I am not given to lying, but there are matters beyond my understanding. I am a simple tradesman. I do my work and I say my prayers.'

'All very good,' replied the Bishop, 'but all Christian men have a duty to defend the truth.'

'I follow my conscience, my lord bishop,' said Henry. 'I try to live by my conscience and do no harm.'

'That is indeed commendable, my son,' agreed Ledrede, 'but

your conscience must be properly informed. As your bishop and spiritual lord, it is my duty to form your conscience. Just as your temporal lord may enlist you for war, I can enlist you in an even greater battle.'

'I am a free man,' Henry demurred. 'I am subject to no feudal levy.' He looked closely at his work, avoiding the Bishop's eye. He feared that he had spoken rashly. It did not do for a tradesman to correct a prince of the Church.

'In war you might lose your life, but if you decline to answer my call, you will lose your soul. You will give yourself over to be snatched by demons and roasted on a fire a million times hotter than that brazier. You will be in torment until the end of time and into the abyss of eternity.'

Henry was silent.

'Let us come to the point,' said Ledrede. 'What do you know of the lady Alice Kyteler?'

Henry chose his words cautiously. 'I know her to be a prosperous lady, a member of a good and respected family, skilled in many arts and leech-craft. I know her to be loyal to her friends.' He had an idea as to where the conversation was leading. He would defend Alice as a friend and benefactor, but he would not advertise any undue intimacy. He would not tread too far onto ground made shaky by gossip and innuendo. He knew that Alice had faults and plenty of enemies to point them out, mostly relatives of her husbands, heirs disappointed to see expected legacies diverted to her use and benefit.

'She maintains an inn of common resort, does she not?' The Bishop leaned forward. 'You may prepare the brand.'

The coals glowed, a mass of braise. A sweet odour pervaded the room and lingered on the tongue. Henry inserted the brand into the coals. It nestled among them, imparting a tinge of black to those it touched, but only for a second. Gradually the metal took on the colour of the coals themselves, turning from black to red, to yellow and then to white. Henry looked away. The image of the cross was imprinted on his eyes. It followed wherever he looked, turning from white to green. It lay across the Bishop's features, like a sign from God Himself. Henry blinked but the cross remained.

'Many skills?'

'She is skilled in the preparation of salves of various kinds. She understands the properties of herbs and flowers. She and her maid, Petronilla, have done many kindnesses to the sick and maimed.' Henry turned the brand until each arm glowed equally white. He turned again to the Bishop. Ledrede had hitched his cassock to the knee and was unwinding a soiled, wet bandage, to expose a vile and suppurating sore on his skinny leg.

'This is a mormal,' said Ledrede, 'an evil death. I command you to burn it from me, down to the very bone.'

'But, my lord bishop,' protested Henry, filled with revulsion, 'this is a task for a leech.'

'I command you, under pain of sin.'

'My good lord bishop,' Henry pleaded, 'this is not the way. I could go to the lady Alice and fetch some cleansing ointment to soothe your pain.'

'No,' snapped the Bishop. 'I will not be beholden to any sorceress. Now proceed.'

He leaned back and stretched out the diseased limb. 'I command it.'

Henry put on a leather glove. He pulled the brand from the fire. He hesitated.

'Go on,' commanded the Bishop. 'The Cross and holy fire will drive out the evil.' He clenched the arms of his chair. His knuckles showed white through the skin.

Henry plunged the brand into the mess of putrefaction. The metal hissed and smoked. Henry gagged. The room filled with the foulest odour ever to affront his nostrils. He turned his face aside. The Bishop snarled and ground his teeth.

'To the bone,' he urged, never flinching. 'To the bone.' His eyes started from his head. Drops of sweat formed on his brow, but still he did not draw back. 'Enough!' he gasped.

Henry withdrew the brand. A black cross-shaped blister smoked on the wound. 'You may go now, but I shall send for you again. I shall question you, under pain of mortal sin and you will tell me the truth. Send in my chaplain.' A spasm of pain convulsed him. He sagged back in his chair.

Henry gathered his bellows and tools. He picked up the metal cross.

'You may leave that. I will have use for it again,' said the Bishop, through clenched teeth.

Henry made no argument. He bowed low and withdrew, almost knocking the chaplain to the floor in his haste to breathe clean air again.

∾

'Beyond the Sea', that wonderful land, 'Outremer'. It was the kingdom wrested by the Crusaders from the heathen Turk. It was the land from which came the precious blue stones. He had crushed small fragments for Friar John, pounding them to fine dust and leaching out the astonishing blue. The Greek historian, Friar John told him, wrote about that land before the birth of the Saviour. In Outremer, men rode on camels whose genitals pointed backwards, unlike those of any other animal. Ants as big as dogs dug gold dust from the desert, to be harvested only when the heat of the noon-day sun drove the ants back underground. Then it became a race between men on camels and the ants, disturbed by the sound of men working overhead. The men rode recently calved she-camels. The camels' desire for their calves gave them that extra turn of speed to outrun the ants. Robin always loved the tension in that story. Life for the men on the camels was a daily race to earn a living. What if the ants caught up with them? What would happen to the calves, waiting and waiting for their mothers to return? What if? What if? He wanted to find out for himself.

In Outremer merchants sold silk that had been carried for thousands of miles from the kingdom of Presbyter John. Slow, plodding camels, he imagined, trudging in darkness through endless wastelands, their drivers gazing all night at the pilot stars, descrying the creatures of the Zodiac in the night sky. A man might go insane from loneliness or maybe he might meet God.

In Outremer, thought Robin, he might find the home of the mother he had never known. Her family would recognize him as one of their own. They would listen to his story and they would shed a tear for their wandering daughter. Beyond the sea lay all the wonders he had ever dreamed of.

He watched great white birds soaring in the wake of the ship. They folded their wings and dived like bolts from an arbalest. They made hardly a splash. He sat on deck, wrapped in a heavy woollen cloak. He closed his eyes. He could hear the shipmen shouting. He heard the creak of the mast and the thrum of wind in the sails. He felt the sea lifting him and rocking him gently to sleep. He was an infant again. He dreamed of Outremer, of castles standing in the sea, of swarthy men and mysterious women swathed in silken veils.

❧

Bishop Ledrede went across the river to visit the hospital of the Augustinian friars in Saint John's. He approved highly of the work of these good men. He rode a gentle mare, with his chaplain walking before him holding the bridle. His long cope covered the mare's hindquarters. He made an imposing figure. People in the street made their reverence to him as he passed. The guards at the Great Bridge went down on one knee. He was enjoying himself, despite the pain that never left him.

A lay brother examined the wound. He sighed in disapproval. He shook his head and murmured. Every man his own leech. It was always a cause of trouble. He applied some salve. The pain eased almost immediately.

'God bless you, good brother,' said the Bishop, raising his hand in the Sign of the Cross. 'God bless your skill.'

'Thank you, my lord bishop,' replied the white-robed friar. 'The credit belongs to God and, to some extent, to the lady Alice. She it was who gave me this receipt.'

Bishop Ledrede flinched. He was beholden to her after all. Was he in danger of falling into the power of a sortilegia? Sorcerers use devious means to achieve their ends. They can divine where people will go and what they will do. They can lay snares in the path of honest folk.

He flexed his leg. The skin no longer burned. The wound throbbed, but not as painfully as before. It was a puzzle. He rationalized. She had not made the salve. Her hands had never touched it. It was compounded by the humble friar, who still knelt before him. The friar was no sorcerer, he was certain. Nevertheless he had to renew his vigilance.

He walked with the prior, admiring the gardens and orchards. He leaned upon a stick, but his leg was definitely better. He blessed the poor wretches in the hospital, demoniacs, cripples, even lepers in their own secluded lodging. He prayed that God and His Holy Mother would have pity on them. Phrases of verse formed in his head.

He prayed in the Lady Chapel, distracted at times, by the glory of its windows. The walls were a lacework of light Caen stone, supported by a filigree of local limestone. The sunlight poured through clear and coloured glass, lifting his spirits, reassuring him that God had chosen him and was all the time guiding him on his way. This chapel was a lantern, a welcome light in a world beset by darkness.

Sir Arnaud was very small beer. He stood at the back of New Hall, among the stalls of the vendors of books and sweetmeats, straining to follow the proceedings. The hall, built by Rufus, the son of the Conqueror, was thronged with barons and the great nobles of England, for once putting aside their enmities to rejoice in the general good news.

There sat the king in ermine and gold. Beside him, but slightly lower, sat the De Spensers, father and son. There was no sign of the queen or her favourite Mortimer, sometime Keeper of Ireland.

A ship had arrived in the Thames. Bedecked with banners and flags, it surged upriver on a rising tide. It docked almost beside New Hall. Some wild Irish lords had arrived to present the head of Edward Bruce, pretender to the kingdom of Ireland, to the rightful monarch.

The barons looked at one another. They smirked at the unfashionable garb of the Irish lords. They raised eyebrows at their mangling of the French tongue. These were Normans gone to seed in a dreary and sodden land. But these men had done what many had tried and failed to do. The king was pleased with them. He beckoned them forward. Sir Arnaud stood on tiptoe to get a better view. His page darted forward, sidling through the forest of tall knights and stately nobles, until he came to the front of the crowd. He found a gap and watched, wide-eyed. This would be a story to tell to his compeers in the years to come.

The King gestured. De Bermingham stepped forward and went on one knee. He opened a leather case and tipped out the pickled head of Edward Bruce. It tumbled onto the flagged floor and rolled to one side. The crowd leaned forward, craning their necks like ganders.

The king rose, gesturing to all to be still. He paced towards the head and poked it with the toe of his elegant boot. He sent it bowling across the floor with a sharp kick. He laughed.

'You have done well, good sir,' he said to the still-kneeling de

Bermingham. 'I hereby create you Earl of ...' He turned to the younger De Spenser. 'Of where?'

'Of Louth, perhaps,' replied the suave counsellor.

'Earl of Louth,' proclaimed the king. 'And Baron of, of ...' He looked again to the smiling counsellor.

'Ardee,' replied De Spenser. 'Why not?'

'Ardee, our new earl and baron, saviour of our lordship of Ireland, we shall reward you greatly and those who helped you in this noble work.' He resumed his seat. He inclined his head to De Spenser, whispering. He nodded.

He called for Sir Edward Butler and commended him for his work. He consulted again. He laughed.

'Come forward Robin the jongleur, son of Art. Let us see something of your skill.'

Robin stepped out from the throng. He knelt awkwardly before the king.

'Look at us,' commanded the king.

Robin looked up. The king studied him closely. A flicker of a smile passed between him and De Spenser. Robin watched and waited.

'What you did was not the deed of a noble knight, but nevertheless it was a deed of courage and great daring, a great service to us. For this we shall grant you any reward you care to name.' He spoke extravagantly. De Spenser raised an eyebrow. He looked from the king to the strange young man. He recognized the smile on the king's soft mouth. He whispered to the king.

'My lord, De Spenser, suggests that you might stay with us as our fool and jongleur. You could entertain us with music and stories. What do you say?'

'I am no jongleur, Your Majesty. I have no skill in music. The only stories I know are in the language of the Irish. As a jester I would speak only the truth.'

'That we cannot have,' laughed the king. 'Well then, what can you do?'

'I can read, my lord, and write. I have skill in art. I can juggle and God forgive me, I can cut a man's throat, if need be.'

'Well then, Robin the artist, juggle for us now. Stand. Stand.' He gestured to Robin to rise. 'Proceed, proceed.' He waved his hand.

The page pushed his head between two burly knights. He stared transfixed. The strange young man was juggling before the king. He moved in a hypnotic dance. Five shining balls rose in an arc, higher and higher. The king was watching, entranced. The juggler stooped and picked up the severed head, incorporating it into the act. Eyes followed as the head of Bruce soared towards the rafters amid a constellation of shining balls. The juggler snatched the leathern case and concluded his performance, 'pthunk', by catching the head and 'pthunk, pthunk', the balls, one after another, holding the case at arm's length as if catching raindrops. The audience erupted in thunderous applause and laughter. Robin bowed.

'So Robin the great artist, name your reward.'

'I ask only your permission, my lord, to travel throughout this land and further, to study and to learn, wherever I go.'

'And so you shall. You will have letters patent under our seal, giving you the right to attend at any school in our realm and to study any skill with any master. As for beyond our realms, you have our good wishes, on the condition that you return to us at some time in the future and tell us what you have learned.'

Robin bowed. The king rose, signalling that the audience was at an end. The page scurried back to report to his scowling master.

'I could see nothing,' grumbled Sir Arnaud. 'A juggler, you say. The one who knocked Edward Bruce on the head? I'm sorry I missed that.' This page had all the luck. All he himself had to show for his journey was a reprimand and a call to military service. He wished that he might go home to Alice Kyteler's hospitable inn, a fire, a mug of ale and a warm bed thereafter. Maybe some of the newfangled beer. It was not too much to ask at his age. He had missed the tide of fortune.

FIFTEEN

Trino sumus certamine
Mundi carnis cum demone.
(We are engaged in triple battle, with
*   the world, the flesh and the Demon.)*
        —Richard de Ledrede

YOUNG WILLIAM OUTLAWE never missed an opportunity. Through his uncle, the Prior of Kilmainham, friend of the most powerful people in Dublin, he was able to advance a loan to the king himself. The house of Kyteler had arrived, under his stewardship, on the stage of European banking. His mother gave him a free hand. He outdid even her in business acumen. She was content to let him at it.

At a time of disastrous inflation, sometimes reaching eight hundred per cent, two thousand pounds was a trifling amount. The great wheel of the world would eventually turn and that two thousand pounds would regain its value and more. As a young man, time was on his side. He was exactly the same age as the fourteenth century after Christ. The century would belong to the house of Kyteler. He could have everything he wanted. With her staff and her rhymes, his mother had swept wealth to his door. She played her clients as an angler does a fish. She let them run into deeper water, giving them more and more line. Then she reeled them in, to flounder in the shallows and deliver themselves up to her. William admired her style.

But he himself had hooked the big one. The king had an insatiable thirst for cash. He quelled unrest among his barons. He fought Scots and recalcitrant Welshmen. He refused to pay tribute to France for his lands in Gascony. He conducted a running feud with his French wife, Isabella, daughter of the king who had crushed the Templars. The king was always in deep water.

But William could not have Petronilla. He could not marry the daughter of a drunken cobbler. He could not acknowledge the mother of his child. How many times had he stood outside her chamber at night, 'in extresme douleur', as they say, hungering for her white body. He pictured her naked in the moonlight on the other side of the door. Moonlight was the only explanation for her soft, ivory skin. He groaned inwardly with desire, but shame prevented him from forcing himself upon her. He remembered with mortification that Twelfth Night when his mother had arranged for him to lose his virginity. He blushed even now at the recollection. She teased him in a way that he knew to be inappropriate for a mother speaking to her son. She liked to shock.

'If I were a real witch,' she mocked, 'or even a Cathar, I could have done it myself for a fine of eighteen shillings.' She touched her knee to his. She could always throw him into confusion, but even she could not match him when it came to making money. He had money enough to set up his own household. He could get away from his overpowering mother and find a wife. Witches with their spells and magic were able to impede the conjugal action between man and woman. His mother could do it with a look.

It was Saint Augustine's Day. The Bishop was preaching in Saint Mary's church. William resolved to go there. This bishop always gave the faithful their money's worth. He had reinstated the practice of liturgical dancing. He was determined to reclaim music and dance from the lewd and degenerate populace. He put his own words to the popular tunes of the day, a practice that grated on the ears of purists, but he did not neglect the old forms either. It was worth going to hear the chanting of sacred song, but, more so, to enjoy the spectacle of Canon Bibulous and his fellow priests, dancing to a cantilena de chorea.

'You touched me and I burned for your peace,' began the Bishop in his penetrating, whistling voice. He spoke of Augustine the sinner and enemy of God. He spoke of Augustine's saintly mother and of the City of God, as distinct form the City of Man. William concluded that the Bishop was losing his teeth. He was a toothless old dog barking at the gate of the city.

'And there in the garden, he heard the voice of a child telling him to take up the nearest book and read. *"Tolle, lege"*, sang the child. It was Paul writing to the faithful in Rome: "Let us walk honestly, as in the day, not in rioting drunkenness, not in chambering and wantonness, making no provision for the flesh to gratify its desires." '

It was too much to ask. Augustine's mother was a saint. Augustine had a head start. William thought of the laughter of his daughter. He could never take her away from Petronilla or more importantly, from Alice. He realized that he could not be parted from her.

'You touched me and I burned for your peace.'

He could never be parted from Petronilla, although he burned when she was nearby. He resolved to wait. The great wheel of the world turns inexorably. The Bishop urged them to purge themselves of sin, to purge their city also and build anew a shining City of God. He declared war on heretics and those who defended them. 'To defend those accused of heresy,' he declared, 'is to share equally in their guilt.' He closed his book with a snap. The sound echoed in the silent church. The people shuffled their feet and coughed. The Bishop turned again to the altar.

∾

Alice actively disliked her fourth husband, John le Poer. His hands were cold when he touched her, which, mercifully, was seldom. His breath reeked of rotting teeth. He was seldom contented with anything. She despised him for the ease with which he accepted her adultery with his cousin, Sir Arnaud. It was advantageous to both of them. John received land and status and she could meet with the seneschal under the guise of a family gathering.

John's brother, Stephen, a decent and gentle man, was made a sheriff, an office he carried out with courtesy and diligence. Everybody gained.

There was, however, the matter of the fine. The Bishop was still demanding a fine and penance for the treatment of the reeve's clerk. Furthermore he pronounced Sir Arnaud guilty of an attack on the good Canon Godfrey and thereby guilty of compounding his original crime. He appealed to the sheriff as a representative of the civil power. The sheriff was in a quandary.

Sir Arnaud, freshly returned from the king's wars, was in no mood to entertain the ramblings of a deranged cleric. He was glad to be back in his seat of power. His cousin, the sheriff, explained the dilemma.

'It puts us all in an awkward position,' he said diffidently. 'If you need the money ...'

Sir Arnaud stretched. He had been long days at sea and long months in the saddle. He cracked his knuckles. That river mist was getting into his bones.

'There is no dilemma,' he explained patiently. 'I have influence in Dublin. I am a friend to Archbishop Bicknor and the Prior of Kilmainham. I will have this cackling rooster booted off that hill. In the meantime, my dear cousin, Stephen, you may return to Richard de Ledrede with my compliments and inform him that he has the seneschal's permission to go and fuck himself.'

The sheriff, Stephen le Poer, returned disconsolately to the Bishop. He explained the dilemma. He offered to mediate, to go up and down High Street, through Coal Market and Watergate as often as might be necessary, to avoid a clash between the civil and ecclesiastical powers. He reminded the Bishop of the chains that bind society togetherand also that Sir Arnaud had the ear of the De Spensers and thereby of the king. He pointed out the advantages of cooperation in turbulent times and how church and nobles had worked together to destroy the Scottish usurper. His arguments were cogent and reasonable. The Bishop nodded.

He took counsel; deliberated and prayed; read the law; reviewed the case in all fairness. He gave his decision.

By assaulting not one, but two members of the clergy; by refusing to answer a lawful summons to the Bishop's court; by refusing to seek absolution; by consorting with known heretics and by open and manifest adultery, Sir Arnaud le Poer had excommunicated himself 'eo ipso' from the society of all Christian people. He had shut himself off from grace, from the sacraments and even from Christian burial.

He directed his secretary to draw up the formal declaration. He signed it, Richard, Ossory and stamped it with his seal, as bishop of the people of Kilkenny and Ossory. He peered at the seal thoughtfully. The words were punctuated by a little cross, a Crusader cross. In this sign shall you conquer. The doors of the minuscule cathedral on the seal were closed. The line of the roof-tree was definitely sagging. That was another thing to attend to. To the inexpressible joy of Canon Bibulous, he ordered a preliminary enquiry into the case of Alice Kyteler, on foot of certain disturbing reports.

Sir Arnaud rode in fury to Dublin. His knights pounded the road, sending up a cloud of dust, with a great rattling of harness and coats of mail. Archbishop Bicknor was sympathetic. He explained his dilemma. Much as he disliked the man, Richard de Ledrede was appointed and consecrated by the Holy Father himself. The excommunication could be lifted only by the Holy Father, or by the Bishop who had pronounced it. He advised Sir Arnaud to use what influence he had with Prior Roger Outlawe of Kilmainham, a Franciscan like Ledrede. He spread his hands in a gesture of regret.

'Try to be reconciled,' he advised. 'This Ledrede takes offence very readily, but in the final analysis, he is a man of God. He will find a way to forgive.'

Sir Arnaud swore. He swore at the cunning and conniving churchmen. He swore at the inclement weather and the flooded roads. He swore at the lords Butler and Bermingham, who had wrong-footed him with the king. He swore out a warrant for the arrest of Bishop Richard de Ledrede. He whacked his seal upon the blob of wax, as one might crush a fly.

But he never swore at the young page, Wat. He liked the boy, the son of some member of his long-tailed family. Wat, with his hair sticking out and his propensity for fights and arguments, made Sir Arnaud laugh.

'Come here, Wat,' he commanded. 'Look at this and tell me what you see. Never mind the writing. Look at the seal.'

Wat scrutinized the smear of red wax. He turned the sheet of parchment this way and that. His tongue moved in a circle as he concentrated.

'There is writing, sire, but I cannot read it.'

'You must attend more diligently to your studies, my boy.' Sir Arnaud cuffed him playfully.

Wat nodded obediently. He was no scholar, but his quick wit

retained a great deal. He preferred the education of Castle Mede and the armoury. The sergeants and the unforgiving quintain were his teachers.

'The seal of the Commonwealth of Kilkenny,' explained Sir Arnaud. 'But what else do you see?'

'I see a castle,' said Wat, delighted with his discovery. 'There is a castle with towers and a man standing in the open door. There are two archers on qui vive upon the towers. There is a lion or an ounce, crouching before the castle.'

'A lion,' Sir Arnaud corrected him. 'A lion couchant, ready to spring, at the man's command. That lion represents the power devolved to me by the king. Now, boy, look more closely. What does the man carry in his hand?'

'A sword,' answered Wat. The man was an armoured knight, perpetually en garde at his castle door. He looked at his hero, Sir Arnaud, the real power in Kilkenny.

'That is how we began, when we first came to Ireland in the days of the great William Marshal and that is how we will survive.' Sir Arnaud clapped the boy on the back. 'Strong with sword in hand, the only way for a man to live.' Wat grinned. 'Now go, like a good lad and find me my sheriff. Tell him the hunt is up. He will understand.'

Wat scampered away. He loved the chase.

❧

Before he left for Kells to spend some time on retreat with the Augustinians, Bishop Ledrede gave orders that Alain Cordouanier should be buried in the nave of the cathedral. No one but the widow and the cathedral canons might attend and the funeral should take place at night. It was a secret, but a secret is no use if it cannot be told.

Some said it was a Christian thing. Alain had once been a master of his craft, deserving of respect. Others maintained that it was an affront to Saint Canice and his holy church, to inter in a place of honour a lowly cobbler, a drunkard, the father of a notorious harlot.

Whatever way the cat jumped, Petronilla did not attend her father's funeral. She heard about his death second-hand. She was ashamed to go and see her mother, but nevertheless she went. She was conscious of the looks and whispering in the street. She held her head up and clutched Basilia by the hand. The child trotted beside her on her little legs.

'You are walking too slowly,' chided Petronilla. She hitched the basket in her free hand.

'No, you are walking too quickly. *Trop vite.*' It was the song they sang together. *"Ton moulin, ton moulin."* Petronilla relented. She slowed her pace and looked the curious loiterers in the eye. They looked away, as if they had better things to think about.

The guard, Herebert, watched the pair as they crossed the Great Bridge. They paused to look into the river. Petronilla hoisted her daughter onto the parapet and clutched her with both arms wrapped tightly around the child's waist. She looked wistfully at the river. There was a time when she had contemplated ... no, that could never be. No matter what might happen, she could never be parted from Basilia.

Herebert nudged his companion.

'She can put a spell on me any time at all,' he muttered with a lascivious wink.

'Lecherous swine,' replied his companion. 'Anyway she can't be a witch. Don't you know that witches will not cross over water?'

'No, no, no, you're wrong. They can't drown, that's all. Why would they be afraid of water?'

His companion shrugged. 'They'd have a right to be afraid of fire though. They would be glad of a drop o' water if that mad fellow up there decides to set fire to them all.' He jerked his thumb in the direction of the cathedral. He laughed at the absurdity of it all.

'Sinful waste,' scoffed Herebert. 'Anyway I wouldn't mind having a go at her before she's roasted.' His eyes devoured the woman on the bridge.

'Not for you, my friend,' said his companion. 'Not for you.'

Petronilla moved away. The two men watched her until she dipped below the curve of the bridge. They slouched in silence, busy with their thoughts.

Helene shivered beside a miserable fire of twigs. She looked at the basket.

'I do not want your alms,' she muttered. Hunger gnawed at her. She looked again.

'It is nothing much,' murmured Petronilla. 'I am so sorry that I did not know.' The tears started from her eyes. She sniffed. Basilia looked up at her in alarm. When mothers weep then the world is awry.

'I sent for you, but you did not come,' retorted Helene. The bitterness choked her.

'And I sent for you and you did not come to me,' Petronilla said. She sat down on a stool and stared into the fire. Her tears glinted in the meagre light. She put her face in her hands.

'I tried,' said Helene. 'I tried, but she would not let me in.'

'Come away, child,' said Petronilla. Basilia was examining the shoemaker's tools. 'Come away.' She put her arm around Basilia and drew her close.

'Come away, child,' echoed Helene. 'Come away now. We can start again in another place.' She clenched Petronilla's hand in a fierce grip. 'Come away before it is too late. I will save you.' Her voice was desperate, urgent. 'I can save you.'

Petronilla shook her head. 'I cannot,' she said. 'She would never permit me to take Basilia away. I will not be driven out by gossip and slander.'

'But the Bishop?' Helene persisted.

'The Bishop has no complaint against me. Has he not honoured my father? Lady Alice has powerful friends.' Petronilla rose to depart. The smell of poverty and despair depressed her.

'You should stay,' insisted Helene. 'There is a storm coming.'

Petronilla declined. 'I must go back. Say farewell to your grand-mother, Basilia.'

Helene took the child's face between her two hands. She kissed her on the forehead. Her shoulders shook.

'*Au 'voir, grandmere*,' lisped Basilia, rather grandly. She had no idea who this withered grandmother could be. She already had a grandmother, better than anyone could wish for, not some shabby old woman in a tumbledown hovel.

Thunder rumbled in the distance.

'I must go,' said Petronilla again. She embraced her mother. 'All will be well,' she reassured her.

Helene nodded. She could not speak. She loosed her grip and let her daughter go.

The rain sprang upon them as they hurried over the bridge. A squall rushed downriver, soaking them instantly to the skin. They ran as fast as Basilia's legs could manage. Petronilla snatched her up, trying to shield her from the icy blast. She splashed through rivulets and puddles. Dung and straw swilled around the gatehouse. She paused, tempted to stand in and wait for the storm to pass, but she was already freezing. Lightning jagged, throwing the cathedral into dark silhouette. She ran on up the slope towards Hightown. A stream ran down Coal Market. At least the rain hid her tears from the few people in the street.

'She did that deliberately,' remarked Herebert. His companion was relieving himself into a puddle. He adjusted his breeches. 'That rain goes straight to my bladder,' he grumbled. 'Twenty years of standing here in the draught.' He retrieved his halberd and leaned on the handle. 'Twenty years in the service of the Bishop. If I served the seneschal, at least I might have had a bit of excitement. God's teeth, but I hate bishops. Standing here watching the whole world go by.' He spat in disgust.

'Did you not see her?' exclaimed Herebert. 'She did it on pur-pose to taunt us.'

'Did what?'

'She waited until she was wet through, then she stops here to let us have a good look. I could see everything. She might as well have been naked.'

'No, I didn't notice. My bladder was at me,' said his companion ruefully. 'And you think she was givin' you the eye?'

'Nothing surer,' asserted Herebert.

His companion laughed. 'You lecherous old goat. I tell you one thing. You'll never get your hands on the likes of her.'

Right enough she was soaked through, now that he thought about it. He resolved to pay more attention the next time she passed that way.

❧

Friar John noted that on that day a great storm afflicted the people. Some bridges along the river were swept away and a lightning bolt struck the cathedral tower. The pointed roof was destroyed entirely, letting the rain enter freely, to trickle down the winding stairs.

❧

Richard de Ledrede took strength from his days of retreat at Kells. The hard-working, devout Augustinians were putting the place back on its feet after the devastation of the Scottish war. It was almost a city in its own right. He thought that he might like to end his days in such a place, far from the turmoil and cares of office. The river sang with the waters of the recent storms. There were cattle in the fields again and the crop lands smelled fresh from winter ploughing.

He discussed his position with his confessor. He was reassured. It was as he had expected. The confessor put his hands inside his black scapular. He arranged it over his knees, twitching it into a tidy fold. His robe was white, but the scapular reminded him that they had been Blackfriars before the Dominicans usurped that colour. The Dominicans always got what they wanted. He did not care for them, but admired their zeal and their success. There was no one like a Dominican to pursue a point, or indeed a heretic, and shake it to death.

'Look upon your seal, my lord,' said the confessor. ' "Civium" if I remember rightly, "of the people". You are the ruler of the people of Kilkenny. You rule their hearts. You have care of their immortal souls. The seneschal is lord only of the state, of the abstract concept of citizenship – "civitatis". You see?'

Ledrede nodded. 'There is a difference. But people fear the power of the seneschal. He has armoured knights and men at arms to keep them in check. What can I do? I have some few sergeants and a modest gaol. I cannot go out in open battle against Sir Arnaud.'

'Have courage, good bishop. Have you not got the awesome power of excommunication and interdict? Is Sir Arnaud not already an outcast, debarred from Heaven itself?'

Ledrede considered the point.

'Do you think the people will turn from him? Do you think his men at arms will turn away from their allegiance?'

'Nothing surer,' said the confessor. 'When they feel the fires of Hell tickling their toes, when they think of their bodies cast out on the dunghill, their hearts will turn to you and to Holy Church.' He patted the black scapular over his knees. Not even a Dominican could have put it so succinctly. 'I urge you now to go forth and do the Lord's work with renewed courage. *Ego te absolvo, in Nomine Patris et Filii et Spiritus Sancti. Amen.*'

'Amen,' repeated Bishop Ledrede, suffused again with confidence and holy zeal.

SIXTEEN

Corda demulcens penitus
Vrens amoris fascibus.
(Softening our hearts to the core; making
us smart with the rods of love.)
—Richard de Ledrede

BISHOP LEDREDE LOOKED at the jackdaw. The jackdaw winked at him, with a sideways flick of the head, just as a corner boy might salute his betters. The jackdaw shifted from one foot to the other, an idle fellow, passing the time. It wore a sleek grey hood. It clashed its beak on the table and pecked at its talons, then suddenly, with a clatter of wings, it flew up to perch on a charred rafter. The rain fell in a steady drip, drip, through the tiles. The hall was a scene of destruction, but nonetheless better than the relentless rain and the biting wind outside.

Ledrede's holy zeal warmed him, raising his spirits. His companions, however, were soaked through. Out of his charity he was content to let them rest and wait for the storm to blow over. Thunder crashed directly overhead. Lightning flared at the shattered windows. The chaplains looked at one another and crossed themselves.

'What place is this?' enquired Ledrede.

'It is Outer Farm, my lord,' replied one of the priests. His expression was one of fear and apprehension. He feared more than the thunderstorm. His eyes roamed about the ruined hall. He swallowed hard, but his mouth was dry.

'And the village?'

'That was the village of Outer Farm, my lord, but sadly it is deserted.'

'But what of its lord? Has he not a duty to rebuild? Has he not a duty to his people?'

The chaplain coughed awkwardly. He was nervous of the ruined house, but fearful that this bishop would turn them out again into the fury of the storm. Straw fluttered from above. The jackdaw was busy with its nest. It poked its head out of a hole, where a truss had fallen away.

'It is the property of Alice Kyteler,' he murmured, 'and of her husband John le Poer, of course.'

'Aha!' exclaimed Ledrede, looking about with renewed interest. 'Aha!' It was a suitable place for witches to conduct their obscene and detestable ceremonies. He paced about, kicking at rubble and straw, certain that he would find some incriminating evidence, a graven image, a crucifix cruelly defaced, an infant corpse torn from the womb, but there was nothing save dust and desolation.

'My lord,' said the chaplain, breaking into his thoughts. 'There are people coming.'

Ledrede cocked his head to one side, just like the jackdaw. He could hear the jingle of harness and horses stamping in the mud of the bawn. His companions were afraid.

'They are armed men, my lord,' said one.

'Have no fear, my brothers,' replied Ledrede. 'We are in God's hands. Justice is on our side. Even if we be slaughtered here in this evil place, we will earn the glory of martyrdom.'

They were not reassured. Martyrdom might be all very well for bishops and other saintly men, but lowly functionaries preferred to keep their heads down, heads unworthy of a martyr's crown.

A flash of lightning illuminated a figure in the doorway.

'God save you, my lord bishop,' said the sheriff, Stephen le Poer. His teeth chattered. He removed his bonnet and shook water from the brim. He wore a simple surcoat and a riding cloak. 'I thought I might find you here.'

'God save you too, my son,' replied Lederde. 'Have you come to do us harm? You can see that we are unarmed.' He gestured at the white-faced chaplains. He smiled.

The sheriff shook his head.

'Heaven forfend that I should do you harm, my lord, but my duty compels me to take you to prison. I am sorry, my lord, but I have a warrant.' He reached inside his sleeve and withdrew a bedraggled parchment.

Ledrede held out his hand, gesturing impatiently. He shook out the roll and peered at it. The lightning obliged. He read the words and touched the seal with his thumb. He smiled again.

'So you have come with your posse comitatus, to arrest one old man and some terrified clerics.' He chuckled.

'No posse, my lord bishop,' replied the sheriff. 'Just a small escort to keep you safe. We can wait until the storm passes.'

'No, not at all. I would not keep you from your firesides longer than is necessary.'

The sheriff rubbed his chin. He scratched his beard. He hitched his belt.

'I am truly sorry my lord,' he began. 'You could return to Kells and claim sanctuary. I could say that we arrived too late.' It would be no great sin to deceive an excommunicated man.

The Bishop shook his head. 'No, my son. That would be a lie. I would not save myself by endangering your immortal soul. I will come with you willingly. Have you gyves for my ankles, pray?' He laughed aloud.

'No, my lord,' said the sheriff, embarrassed.

'Well then, let us go cheerfully. I know you to be a lover of music. Let us go along to prison and talk of music. I have some songs that I have set to the vulgar tunes. Perhaps we can sing as we go.' He laughed again.

The chaplains looked at one another. They shrugged. The thunder rumbled. They had precious little to sing about.

'My son,' began the Bishop as they rode, 'I notice that your men at arms carry hunting horns. Did you mean to raise a hue and cry against me?'

The sheriff made no answer. The thunder clouds rolled away. Fitful sunlight lit up the landscape, throwing fleeting shadows on the hills.

'You do realize that you have excommunicated yourself, *ipso facto*, by this arrest?' Ledrede persisted, 'and all those who follow you?'

'My lord,' replied the sheriff, 'I am bound by loyalty to Sir Arnaud. I cannot break my faith.'

'But you forget, my son, how Alexander, king of all the world, prostrated himself before the priest, Saddam, who carried before him the name of his god. Do you remember how Constantine made the Cross his standard and how his successors turned to the bishops and popes for the salvation of their souls?'

Sheriff Stephen coughed awkwardly. 'I am no Alexander, my lord. I am but a soldier. I do my duty.'

'My lord,' interrupted one of the riders. 'We will seize your enemies and drag them to your gaol.'

'No, my son,' said the Bishop gently. 'We will go willingly to prison. This is a day of great joy for the Church. We will suffer even torture in her defence. All I ask is that I may have with me the Body of Christ and one or two to pray with me.'

'That will be arranged,' agreed the sheriff.

'I do not hold you responsible for this, my son,' said the Bishop gently. 'You are a loyal knight. That is a good thing. However, all within my diocese of Ossory will suffer for the seneschal's crime. For forty days Ossory will be under interdict, until he comes before me as a penitent.'

They rode on in silence. As they drew near to the castle they could see already that a crowd was gathering, clergy and towns-people, hushed and anxious, frightened by the terrible thing that was happening. It was the first time in Ireland that such a monstrous crime had been committed against the person of a bishop.

Bishop Ledrede did not waste his opportunity. He stood up in his stirrups and addressed the silent crowd. He looked down at their upturned faces.

'Your seneschal has brought you to this pass,' he told them in the practised tones of the preacher. His sibilant whistle seemed to lend a greater force to his words. 'You are in mortal danger. For forty days the churches of Ossory are closed to you. There will be no sacra-ments, no forgiveness of sin, no Baptism. Those who die during this time will be cast into eternal fire. If in that time the enemies of Holy Church are not brought to book, this interdict will continue.'

He dismounted stiffly and allowed himself to be led through the gates. A murmur ran through the crowd and then a great cry of anger and lamentation burst forth. The men at arms formed a line, holding the people back from the gates. They drew their swords. The crowd fell back and parted to allow a procession of priests to pass through. Foremost among them, Canon Bibulous carried the Host. He held it aloft in a gleaming monstrance. The people crossed themselves and knelt in the wet street. The priests passed into the castle. The armed men followed. The gates slammed. The fright-ened people began to pray, and the sound carried to the Bishop in his dungeon below the massive walls.

Friar John went in darkness to the house of Alice Kyteler. He knew that he should not. He went in fear, as Nicodemus had gone to see Christ, climbing over the garden wall, afraid of what the Sanhedrin might say. It was a long time since Friar John had scaled an orchard wall. Sandals were not the best footwear for the task.

He skirted the fishpond and made his way between the fruit trees and the neat beds of herbs and roots. His cassock snagged on a raspberry bush. He tugged it free. He crept through the stable yard. He started at a black cat. The creature ran from him and seemed to flow up a wall. It perched in the dim light from a high window, watching him and flicking its tail.

He tapped urgently on the door to the basement. He tapped more loudly. He saw a thread of light below the door.

'Who's there?' whispered a voice.

His heart turned over. 'Friar John,' he whispered. 'Let me in.'

Bolts rattled and slid back. The door creaked open. Petronilla held up a candle. The light fell on her face. He was shocked to see how gaunt she had become. He stepped in out of the night.

'What are you doing here?' she whispered.

'I have come to warn you. You must go away from this town. All of you. Go away this night. This town is dangerous for you.'

'Where shall we go?' she asked, trembling.

'Your mistress is a wealthy woman. She must have friends everywhere. Go to Dublin. She has friends there.'

She gestured to him to follow into the kitchen. She sat down on a bench. Her shoulders drooped.

'My mistress will not leave,' she said. 'She is stubborn. She has sent William to Sir Arnaud for help. She has asked him to send armed men to protect the house. The Bishop has no authority here in Hightown.'

'He has the authority of God and of the Pope who consecrated him. There is no higher.'

She looked up at him in fear. 'What is to be done?'

He thought of sanctuary. Not even the Bishop could violate sanctuary. But then they would be doubly imprisoned, condemned forever to haunt the precincts of the cathedral. That was no life. They must leave. He took from his sleeve a silver pyx.

'I have brought you a consecrated Host. I should not do this, but there is no other hope. You may not touch it. I will place it on this high ledge, where none can see it. It will protect all within this house until this trouble is resolved. Then I shall return to recover it. You must say nothing about this to anyone.'

She looked in fear at the Host. 'I have not received Communion for a long time,' she murmured. 'I have felt ashamed and unclean.'

'I will hear your confession. Purge yourself of all sin and you need have no fear.'

She knelt and confessed. She told him of how she had thought Basilia was a child of the Devil and how she had turned away from her own infant. 'I thought that the Devil had lain with me in the form of a fox, but I was deceived. It was William. She gave me to William as a gift.'

He nodded. 'I know about William,' he said softly. 'There was no devil. You are innocent of all guilt. I fear that you have been much misused. There is no need of devils when there is so much evil in the hearts of men.' He absolved her of all sin and blessed her as she knelt, placing his hands upon her bowed head. 'Stay indoors,' he admonished. 'You will be safe now. Your heart is pure.'

He went out into the night, climbed over the wall and stood a long time with his back to it. His heart was in turmoil. He put both hands to his face, imagining that he could smell the perfume of her hair on his fingers. He trembled. Now he had risked sacrilege to the Sacred Host. His vow of obedience was broken, and he had harboured lustful thoughts for one whom he had taken into his spiritual care. He looked up at the stars. They whirled about in the darkness of chaos. They made no sense. The light glimmered at the top of the mutilated tower. It sent no message of comfort. To Friar John it was the eye of Bishop Ledrede, seeking out whom he might destroy.

∾

For a bit of peace Sir Arnaud retreated to one of his country estates. William sought him out.

'I will defend myself and my family in any court of justice,' said William. 'These charges have been laid by envious and malicious people. This bishop is a bitter and disappointed zealot. He will be satisfied with a fine. His greed for money is well known.'

Sir Arnaud rubbed his chin. 'It is not so simple,' he pointed out. 'He has terrified the people with his interdict. Not that I give a fig for excommunication, but it is bad politics to play into his hands. He will never submit to any civil court. The king's justiciar and my uncle, the Bishop of Leighlinn, urge me to set him free. God's curse upon him, for a jumped-up English peasant. He uses my castle as his own, summoning his priests and witnesses at will.'

'The people throng to him night and day,' said William. 'It is like a pilgrimage. They believe him to be a martyr.'

'This will never do,' said Sir Arnaud. 'I will return immediately and put a stop to all this. I will not have the people stirred up in this manner. I will clip his wings.'

'I will pay whatever it costs,' William offered. He had found in his relatively short career that money eased the way in most situations. 'I will endow a chapel, a window, whatever he wants. I will pay your knights and men at arms. Then we will make arrangements to be rid of him.'

Sir Arnaud nodded. So much good sense in one so young.

'What of your influence with the king, sire?' William explored an alternative approach.

Sir Arnaud shook his head. 'There is little to be expected from that quarter. He is engaged in war with his barons and with the queen. Mortimer has escaped to France to join with her. The lords De Spenser are embattled on every side. We must fend for ourselves. Return you to Kilkenny. I shall bring men to guard your house. I will have order in my town.'

SEVENTEEN

Better were be – at tome for ay
Than her to serve – the Devil to pay.
—Anonymous

HENRY THE SMITH, for the first time in his life, was frightened. He cursed the day that Walter Kyteler had advanced him money to set up his forge. He cursed his own skill and diligence, which had led him to prosper and fall into the circle of Alice Kyteler. He cursed his wife's hunger for social standing. He cursed his good looks and wit, which had always brought him to the attention of others. With his stature and strength, he had never feared another man.

Until now. He feared these two Blackfriars. They questioned. They took notes. They collated the information gleaned from witnesses, whom they questioned in secret. They used silence like a weapon. They conferred in Latin. Canon Bibulous sat to one side with the Bishop's secretary. It was their task to bring a report to Ledrede at the end of each day's proceedings. No others might attend these sessions.

'So, on this night you saw witches riding on broomsticks?' The Blackfriar leaned forward, his face a mask of composure, his fingertips joined. 'You were part of that rout in a remote ruin, far from the eyes of Christian people.'

'It was not a ruin then. That was before the Scottish war. It was a prosperous demesne. What was done there was done in sport.'

'In sport. I see.' The Blackfriar frowned. 'It was sport to consort with heretics? It was sport to allow renegade Templars to engage in lewd practices?'

'They were but clowns, reverend friar,' protested Henry. 'I set them on myself.'

'I see,' said the friar. 'You set them on yourself? And did you set on the dark man who transformed himself into a stag? Did you set on the woman Petronilla to cavort naked in the snow with this dark man?'

Henry shook his head. 'I know nothing of this,' he mumbled.

'Were you present when a fox was slaughtered and its entrails distributed about the room? Did you hear profane songs set to the music of our most sacred hymns?'

'These are common tunes,' mumbled Henry. 'Everyone uses them. Just different words.'

'Hmmm. Different words,' mused the friar. 'No doubt they were. So you did not witness the mockery of our Holy Father? You did not smell brimstone? You did not see the woman Alice dressed in peacocks' eyes or playing with the bones of executed criminals?'

'I … ' Henry began. 'I saw some clowns. I saw some bawdy sport. I saw no dead men's bones or peacocks' eyes.'

'Or the woman Alice exposing herself in nakedness to a demon in the form of a stag?'

Henry lowered his head. Canon Bibulous looked up, his interest quickening.

'My son,' put in the second Blackfriar, who all the while had sat in silence. 'You are a simple man, a foolish man in truth. You do not understand how the Devil works.'

Henry nodded, crestfallen.

'You have risen above what is normal for a common tradesman. You have been deluded. When you least suspect it, the Devil is there. He is there in convivial company, when you think it is nothing but sport. He is there in the temptations of women. They are imperfect creatures, women, but they have the power to entrap men's souls. We have spoken of your wife. She has wanted many things. She has demanded much of you. She has forced you into the company of wealthy and corrupt people. No, do not shake your head. Was she ever content to be the wife of a common smith? No, she was not. She has led you, by her avarice and ambition, to endanger your immortal soul.'

Henry slumped in his seat. It was true. She always wanted more. She had sent him to Walter Kyteler. It was not enough for him to work with the other smiths at the common forge. He must have one of his own, with apprentices and hired men turning out metal goods for the whole district. They had to live in a fine house and dress in fine clothes. They had to resort to the inn of the lady Alice and rub shoulders with the leading people of the town. Perhaps, after all, this good fortune had not come by honest means. He shook his head again. His brain was clouded with fear.

'You are distressed, my son,' said the second friar. 'You see now that you have been deceived. The Devil is the arch deceiver. You have allowed yourself to be influenced by cunning women. But ... ' he paused for a moment, 'but you are saved.'

Henry looked up. The friar smiled, a wan, sympathetic smile. 'You are saved by the power of the truth. You must go now and consider. You must try to remember. Say nothing to your wife about all this. Leave her to us. Return to us when you think of other evidence of evil-doing. Go now in God's name.'

Henry was dismissed. His legs shook so much that he stumbled on the stairs. He went down to his forge, ignoring the crowds on the street and the armed men patrolling on horseback. He ignored the procession of chanting priests and monks and the Bishop walking before them in his pontificalia, bearing the Body of Christ in a gilded monstrance.

The forge was deserted. His apprentices had run off to see the Bishop delivered from prison. They had even neglected to close the door. He worked the bellows, blowing the furnace to a pile of glowing coals. He heated a rod of iron until it was white. He hammered it into a hook, turning it this way and that on the anvil. The hammer rang. He beat the metal in panic and in shame. Henry the Smith was afraid for himself. He was afraid of two small, skinny men with whispering voices. His strength was of no avail to him now.

How his wife had laughed when Alice spoke of boiling men's brains in a pot, rather than in their skulls. How she had watched the dark man in the stag costume. How she hung on every word that Alice spoke, anxious to be agreeable. It was her insecurity that had brought him to a dark place. He had loved her, but the Devil had played with his love. She was pulling him down and down. He wanted to tear her hands from him, before he sank into the quicksands of heresy. Now he had delivered his love up to the two inquisitors, not by his words but by his silence. He quenched the red-hot iron. He took a length of harness leather and formed a noose. He attached it to the hook and stood up on the anvil. He put the newly-fashioned hook over a rafter and placed the noose around his neck. He stepped forward from the anvil.

He was cold when she found him. The fire had dulled to a pile of grey clinker.

∾

Bethany, the House of Affliction. It was aptly named, this home of Lazarus. It was a poor place, reflected Robin, hardly worth the twelve denarii he had to pay as a toll. Still, it was a place of pilgrimage and a place where pilgrims might find some sustenance. Twelve denarii also to the porter at the gate to the Mount of Olives. Everywhere he went in this Holy Land there were tolls and taxes. Although the land was ruled by the Sultan, it was the Christians who exacted most of the tolls. They fought among themselves for the best pitches, Greeks, Armenians, Georgians, Copts and Latins, often coming to blows over points of doctrine and vantage points from whence they might raid the purses of devout pilgrims.

There were Ethiopians to one side of the Holy Sepulchre. There were Nestorians, who preached to any that would listen, that Christ was entirely human. There were the black-robed Orthodox, who forbade the use of bells. They beat the times of daily prayer on planks of wood, sounding all over the land, setting the dogs barking. Robin was fascinated by their arguments. The Greeks hated the Latins even more than they hated the heathen Saracens. The closer they were in doctrine, the more they differed in garb. Some of the eastern Christians wore turbans and were indistinguishable from Muslims.

Through arrogance and internal conflict the Dominicans lost their custody of the tomb of the Virgin in Kidron, the Cenacle of Mount Sion and their toehold in the Church of the Nativity. The Franciscans moved in with the Sultan's permission, to see if they could make a better fist of things.

Robin recognized the grey robes. They were a welcome sight among the squabbling crowds. He listened closely to their conversation. They spoke in English, but with Irish accents. They were complaining that it had cost them four florins each to pass through Samaria. Four florins and that did not guarantee safety from rapacious villagers or wandering Bedouin. It was no wonder that Samaritans were so despised in the time of the Saviour.

Robin greeted them and introduced himself. 'Some call me Robin, the son of Art,' he said.

They looked at him in surprise. They had taken him for an Arab in his long white robe. They saw a lithe, dark-skinned man with a sparse beard.

He bowed. 'You are from Ireland, as I guess.'

'We are indeed,' they nodded. 'We have come here as pilgrims to see the holy places.'

Robin wondered if they might be like some others he had met, mad dreamers and fanatics, who saw themselves as the advance guard of some new crusade. There were those who rambled on about re-establishing the Frankish kingdom of Jerusalem and setting free those ancient knights, who still languished in the Sultan's prison in Cairo. The world, as he had found, was full of dreamers and madmen.

'I am Simon FitzSimon,' said one of the friars. 'Simon Symeonis they call me sometimes. I am from the friary of Dublin and this is my brother Hugh, known as the Illuminator. We have come here to learn and to find a way of bringing our erring brethren back into true obedience to the Holy Father.'

Friar Hugh shrugged ruefully. 'We will have our work cut out for us, I fear. Will you sit with us and share our bread?'

Robin was grateful. He had not eaten for a long time. He had almost used up the money granted to him by the king. Sometimes he found work, or earned money in the street as an entertainer. Sometimes he studied with a master or sat at the lectures of learned doctors. He survived, while all the time learning.

They talked of their travels and the hardships of not being permitted to ride horses in the Sultan's land. They talked of home and questioned Robin about his.

'I have no home anymore,' he told them. 'When I was a child I lived with the wild Irish in the mountains. I never knew my parents. I lived for a time with a shoemaker in Kilkenny. I learned his trade. I was a soldier in the Scottish war. Since then I have wandered the world, seeking knowledge.'

'Ah, Kilkenny,' said Simon. 'There is a wise man there, Friar John. Have you heard tell of him? An historian and scholar.'

Robin was delighted. 'Friar John! Yes, of course I know him. He taught me to read and write. He taught me many secret things.'

'Yes, yes,' said the second friar. 'He taught me how to illuminate. I learned everything from him and his assistant, old Brother Fergal. It is an art that must be passed on. It is as important as the knowledge contained in the words.'

Robin pondered for a while. He tore a piece of bread. He opened his satchel. It contained some books and the five steel orbs. He took out his picture of Petronilla.

'What do you think of this?' he asked, looking from one to the other. They studied the parchment closely.

'It is good,' said Friar Hugh, 'but of course she should have a halo.'

'A halo?'

'Yes of course. The Virgin must always be depicted with a halo.' He discoursed briefly on the different styles of illustration that he had witnessed on his travels. 'Whether in manuscript or in glass, the Virgin must have a halo. Beauty leads us to the love of God as surely as preaching.'

'That is a strange thing for a man of God to say,' remarked Robin.

'I know,' agreed Friar Hugh. 'My friend and I argue this all the time. He says that my work may lead to idolatry, but I say that, to ignorant people, too much preaching and disputation leads to confusion and heresy.'

'Argue is the word,' nodded Friar Simon. 'You are a son of art, young man. What do you think, Robin, son of Art?' He laughed at the name, 'Robin FitzArt, Robin Art his son?'

Robin grinned. 'That is my name. That is what I am. I like stories and I like to do things, but I do not like to argue the finer points. The stories of the Saviour are good enough for me.'

'So you have no time for the learned doctors, who explain to us the nature of God?' Friar Simon probed. 'How are we to avoid heresy, without the learned doctors and preachers?'

'Look about you,' answered Robin, shrugging. 'Who is right? Which is the true religion?'

'Ah!' they exclaimed in unison. 'There is but one true faith. All these wander in error.'

Robin did not persist. He looked at the scurrying priests of the various sects. Heretics all. Infidels and Jews, going about their business. One word was enough, like a spark in Friar John's saltpetre powder, to set them ablaze. He changed tack.

'What news do you bring from Ireland?' he asked.

'Well,' said Friar Simon, with an air of satisfaction, 'let me see. There is a new college in Dublin. Archbishop Bicknor has set up a *studium generale* in the cathedral of Saint Patrick. He has appointed learned divines and praeceptors in sacred studies.'

'A university in name only,' scoffed his companion.

'I have heard some of these teachers,' remarked Robin. 'I have sat in the schools and listened. I have been astonished by their learning, but confused by their message. It is always "you are wrong. I am right."'

Friar Simon chuckled. 'You have the makings of a learned doctor yourself, my son. Where would we all be if we kept it simple?'

Robin shook his head. 'But I thought it was,' he replied. 'I thought Christ's message was simple.'

'Simple yes,' said Friar Simon, 'but not easy.'

Robin pondered. 'Love your enemies. No, it is not easy.'

'No indeed,' agreed Friar Simon. 'If it were easy, Bishop Ledrede would embrace Sir Arnaud le Poer as a son. He would forgive the heretics in Kilkenny and bring them back to the truth through love rather than fire.'

'What heretics?' queried Robin. 'Who is this bishop? I remember an old man. I remember Sir Arnaud le Poer, a great man to argue and fight.'

'The seneschal,' said Friar Hugh. 'He is like Goll Mac Morna. Have you heard of him at all?'

Robin frowned. Goll Mac Morna? Something chimed in the recesses of memory, a fire, straw on the floor, the mountains locked in snow and frost, an old monk sitting on a stool. Goll Mac Morna. He fought Finn Mac Cool and his men. He was trapped on a rock joined to the land by a narrow causeway. His wife was with him. As Finn's men tried to cross the slippery causeway, he cut them down, one by one, or hurled them into the sea below. But he grew weaker and weaker as the days went by. Robin heard Brother Fergal again. 'Didn't the wife say to him to take the milk from her paps to keep up his strength? Didn't she tell him to eat the bodies of the men he had killed? But he would not. And why? Because he was under a *geasa* never to take the advice of a woman. That's why.' Brother Fergal always chuckled at this. 'There's many a man like Goll Mac Morna, especially in Ireland. So he was destroyed entirely by Finn.' Yes, Robin had heard of Goll Mac Morna.

'The seneschal has become entangled in heresy. The last we heard he was excommunicated by Bishop Ledrede. He turned away from his true wife, a saintly woman. She has pleaded with him to ask forgiveness and do penance, but he will not. He prefers to side with the witches.' Friar Simon shook his head sadly. 'As if there was not enough trouble in that unfortunate land.'

Robin felt cold fingers of dread clutching at his innards. 'What witches?' he asked quietly.

'A notorious sorceress, a sortilegia. The wealthiest woman in Leinster, Alice le Kyteler. She is accused of procuring foul weather, of causing the deaths of three husbands, of depriving children of their rightful inheritances. Abominations that I would tremble to name. She anoints her staff with magic ointments and rides upon it at night, ambling through thick and thin, or so they say.'

'Who says this?' Robin demanded. They were taken aback by his vehemence.

'It is common knowledge,' Friar Simon replied. 'Everyone knows about her. Her and her maidservant Petronilla de Midia. Even the maidservant's mother has accused her. But have no fear. The Bishop has the measure of them all, even the seneschal.'

Robin took the parchment and rolled it carefully, replacing it in his satchel. He stood up. 'I must leave you now,' he said abruptly. 'I thank you for the bread.'

'Where are you going?' asked Friar Simon. 'Where are you going in such haste, Robin, son of Art?' He said it lightly.

'Home,' replied Robin, turning away from them. 'I must go home.'

They watched him go through the crowd of hawkers, preachers and pilgrims outside the house of Lazarus. His dark hair caught the afternoon sun, almost as if he wore a halo.

❧

'It is a cause of grief to me,' said Sir Ivo, hanging his head. 'I betook myself from that house to live with an honest knight, her uncle Sir Guillaume le Kyteler of Ypres. It pained me greatly to lose both father and step-mother at such an early age, but it was intolerable to live under her roof.'

'We understand,' said Bishop Ledrede, with unusual gentleness. He looked at the two Blackfriars. They nodded. Canon Bibulous nodded. The chaplains nodded. A young man's soul had been saved from peril.

Sir Ivo sniffed. 'I thought it better to learn the profession of arms, to serve our lawful king in war against the Scots, than to live amid abominations and depravity.'

'Go on,' urged the Bishop.

'It is difficult,' went on Sir Ivo. His voice broke. 'My father was a good and Christian man, well regarded in this town.'

They nodded again, all together. There was no gainsaying that. William Outlawe the Elder was a generous man also, generous in giving alms to the poor and to the Church.

'I tried, in my duty as a son, well, a stepson, to be reconciled with her, but it was in vain. I saw such things.' He shook his head.

'You spoke before of several practices common in that household. Can you be more specific?' The Bishop waited.

Sir Ivo wrung his hands. 'I am ashamed to say what I witnessed. I did not speak out because at that time I was in fear. I was alone. There was no one to take up the challenge, to fight against evil. Not until now, my lord bishop. Not until now.'

Bishop Ledrede acknowledged the compliment with a slight bow.

'I saw witches at that vile Sabbath, riding on broomsticks. I saw the Devil disguised as a stag. He came in a cloud of brimstone. I saw my mother – it pains me to call her my mother – play with the bones of an executed murderer. She has enjoyed unnatural carnal relations with her maidservant. This is not hearsay. I saw this, to my horror, with my very eyes. I saw scenes of lewdness such as I can scarcely describe. In her house there are ointments and herbs to procure miscarriage in honest women, and the deaths of true Christians. I accuse her of poisoning not only my father, but two other husbands as well. Have you not spoken to her fourth? Is he not close to death?' His voice trembled with the fervour of a man greatly wronged. He tugged at the chain about his neck and pulled a crucifix from his breast. 'Had I not been armoured in the love of Christ, I should also have been destroyed.' He clenched the crucifix.

'You are a true and Christian knight and God will reward you,' said the Bishop. 'You may leave us now while we discuss what is to be done. We must use all our efforts to bring these sinners back to the true love of God.'

'But if they persist in obstinate heresy,' asked Canon Bibulous, 'what then?'

'Let us not rush to any conclusions, Canon Godfrey,' replied the Bishop, raising his hand. 'They will be examined and given every opportunity to renounce their evil practices. After some suitable penance and a fine, they will be readmitted with joy to the body of the Church.'

Sir Ivo paused as he was rising from his seat. That was not what he had had in mind.

'But what if they still persist?' Canon Bibulous asked again.

'Then,' replied the Bishop, 'they will be consigned to fire.'

Sir Ivo bowed and took his leave, well pleased with his day's work.

∽

Sir Arnaud called a council of war. He sat with his knights, sheriffs of the district and the king's justiciar, to discuss what should be done. He pointed out the danger of an all-powerful Church.

'We did not defend our lands and privileges from the Scots and the Irish only to hand them over to a renegade English peasant.' There was something about Ledrede that always got under his skin. The Bishop had not a drop of noble blood in him. He had risen by guile and cunning, a parasite sucking the blood and strength from better men. Even his accent grated on Sir Arnaud's ear.

'He abuses the law,' he went on. 'He listens to spies and informers. He condemns without proof and expects the civil power to do his dirty work. This I will not permit.' He clenched his fist. He paused. There were raised voices outside. The doors were thrown open. Two Blackfriars stood on the threshold. They strode to the bar and stood facing the seneschal. All eyes turned to them.

'The Lord Bishop of Ossory, Richard de Ledrede, demands the right to address this tribunal.'

The justiciar looked to Sir Arnaud. He was already on his feet. A vein stood out on his temple. In the foulest of language he ordered the friars to depart and tell their bishop to confine himself to his church and to his prayers, and to leave matters of law to those who knew better. The friars did as they were bid.

'I think,' suggested the justiciar, 'that this is a matter for the Archbishop of Dublin. I move that we ask him to summon Ledrede to put his case in Dublin.'

All agreed. Sir Arnaud was content. The vein at his temple subsided. He rubbed his eyes.

'Let us turn then to the matter of the lord Butler's massacre of the people in the church of Saint Molyng. This is an outrage which must be avenged. Twenty-eight innocent people, women and children. We must have justice.' In fact, it was the perfect excuse for Sir Arnaud. He hated Butler as much as he despised Ledrede. Butler with his overweening airs and his designs on Kilkenny itself. In the name of justice he proposed leading an army into Butler's lands and putting to the sword all those who might stand in his way.

The doors were thrown open again. Richard de Ledrede entered in full regalia, holding, as before, a monstrance. Beams of golden light radiated from the Sacred Host. He was followed by the two Blackfriars, a procession of Cathedral clergy and priests of the various parishes of Kilkenny town. The room fell silent.

'What do you want here, priest?' snapped Sir Arnaud.

The Bishop looked around. 'I call upon you all, as the representatives of the civil power and,' nodding to the justiciar, 'of the king himself, to assist the Holy Church in its battle against the forces of Satan.' He raised the monstrance and turned slowly in a circle, showing it to the entire assembly.

'Nonsense,' said Sir Arnaud. 'You have no business here. If you are to speak in this tribunal, it will be as a criminal at the bar of justice, for your persecution of innocent citizens, and for your greed and rapaciousness. Have you not deprived poor people of their village chapels and devoted their tithes to your own vainglorious ends?'

The Bishop advanced to the bar. 'This is the first time that the Body of Christ has been summoned to trial, since He stood before Pontius Pilate.' Christ was in him. He stood for the persecuted Saviour.

'None of your play-acting,' bellowed Sir Arnaud. He rose and grasped the Bishop by the shoulder, propelling him towards the doors. He pushed him violently over the threshold. Several knights stood up to intervene. The Bishop stumbled and fell. The monstrance dropped from his grasp. Sir Arnaud rounded on his knights. 'Sit down,' he snarled. 'And you lot, get out.' This to the horrified clergy. He aimed a kick at the fallen monstrance, sending it clattering into the outer hall. 'And take that trumpery with you.'

Some of the golden rays were twisted and bent out of place. The Bishop got to his feet, his mitre askew. He took the damaged monstrance in his hands. He tried to speak. His lips moved, but no sound came out.

Sir Arnaud slammed the doors on Ledrede and the astonished clerics. He turned to his silent and unhappy knights. They would not meet his eyes. He had slammed the doors on fealty and obedience and on his own salvation.

$$\sim$$

Bishop Ledrede climbed to the top of his roofless tower. He placed a lantern in the window. He looked down over the sleeping town. No lights showed anywhere, except for one in the distant castle. He wondered if the seneschal would answer his formal, legally binding request for the arrest of the heretics. Perhaps his knights had already gone through the darkened streets to beat upon the doors and drag those enemies of God to justice. He listened in the vast darkness for the sound of hooves and harness, but there was nothing save a great silence. He prayed for strength to do what was right. Perhaps the witches would send a demon to hurl him from the tower. Perhaps they would come themselves, whirling about his lofty eyrie, seeking to dash him to the ground far below. He fingered the pyx that he had brought for special protection. Christ's body steeled him for the conflict. Christ was with him on his lofty pillar. He waited and prayed.

He prayed and listened, but no demons came. Only the throb in his shin came to torment him, and the frost, a bone-chilling frost that gathered about him and settled on his heavy robe. He prayed for guidance and in the morning he rose to his feet, shaking the rime from his shoulders and rubbing it from his eyebrows. He knew what he must do.

The following night the Blackfriars went with armed men to arrest Dame Alice le Kyteler and as many of her sodales as they could find. They brought her with the chief offenders, to the Bishop's reeking gaol. Her son was lodged in the deepest dungeon of the common gaol, with two guards to watch him by turns, neither speaking to him nor sharing food, but noting everything he said.

The mad woman stood in the lane outside the Common Hall. She screamed all through the night.

'We had a bargain. Not my daughter. We had a bargain, Richard de Ledrede. We had a bargain.' Nobody answered.

Sir Arnaud lodged in Dublin. He spoke to Archbishop Bicknor. He laid the case before Roger Outlawe, Prior of Kilmainham. The prior explained that he had, in a sense, a conflict of interest, being connected by marriage to the lady in question. Sir Arnaud wrote to his liege lord, De Spenser, but the De Spensers had problems of their own. The English barons were smarting under their tyranny. Mortimer and the queen were poised to strike from France. De Spenser sent a curt reply to the effect that he had no time to clean up every cat's mess in his domain. If Sir Arnaud could not keep order, then perhaps he should reconsider his position as seneschal.

He pursued his case against Butler in the justiciar's court. He would prefer to settle the matter with weapons, but the times were growing degenerate. Pettifogging lawyers were deciding matters that should be settled on the field of battle. In truth he was not as sure as he once had been of the loyalty of his knights. He might lead, but would they follow an excommunicate? It was a dilemma; a gamble. At times Alice Kyteler floated into his mind. What would he give for a quiet life, a country estate, the pleasures of the hunt, a well stocked table, a decent cellar and Alice, warm and passionate in his bed at night. He was bewitched by Alice, but helping her was becoming more and more complicated.

EIGHTEEN

Videbitis qualis et quantus – mundi sit
Error in illecebris.
(You will see the nature and magnitude of
  the error that lurks in the allurements
  of the world.)
  —Richard de Ledrede

'LET US TALK, for a moment, about this cat,' began the Blackfriar. He shuffled some sheets of parchment, making a show of searching for a half-remembered detail. He put down the parchments, abandoning the search. 'Remind us, if you would be so kind, of the name of your cat.'

'Why?' queried Alice wearily, with the ghost of a smile. 'My cat is not on trial.'

'The name, please,' the friar persisted.

'Lucifer,' mumbled Alice. She was tired and cold. She wished for her sable coat. She was hungry. She looked at the faces ranged before her. With a square meal inside her and dressed in her finery, she would have scattered them all in confusion. But now she stood in a plain smock, too thin for the chilly weather. She shivered. The chains around her ankles were cold against her skin.

'Ah, yes,' said the friar. 'Lucifer. And why, pray, did you settle on such a strange name for a cat?'

It was ridiculous. Her explanation was even more absurd. It was the truth, but it was absurd. A flying cat! Flanders, the very seed-bed of heresy. The Blackfriar rubbed his chin. He blinked his lapidary eyes.

'Well, well!' he murmured.

Canon Bibulous cleared his throat. 'We have testimony that this cat shared your bed. Is it not a fact that you shared your bed with this demon, this flying cat?' There was something else in his eyes. She knew that he knew. He knew who had sent a snarling, spitting cat hurtling down upon him, bringing retribution from Heaven for his sin with the fallen woman. He had waited a long time. She could see the fierce anticipation in his bleary eyes.

She almost laughed. It was all so ridiculous.

'The cat is no demon. He is there to catch mice. I have stables. I have an inn. There is a river hard by. I must have a cat to keep the vermin in check.'

'The vermin,' repeated Canon Bibulous. 'The vermin must be kept in check.'

'If I may intervene,' put in Bishop Ledrede. 'Thank you, good Canon Godfrey. Now, before we proceed to the matter of flying, or this pretty boy dressed all in green, and the testimonies of witnesses to your manifold wicked acts, I urge you in God's name to make a full confession of your crimes. It is not too late, daughter. God's mercy is infinite. Confess now before this holy tribunal and you will escape torture and hellfire.'

Alice swayed. She staggered. The gaoler caught her by the arm, steadying her.

'I am no heretic,' she murmured. 'Nor am I a witch. These charges are brought against me by envious people.'

'Speak up,' said Bishop Ledrede. 'Speak up. Remember that a denial merely compounds your guilt. The more you deny your guilt, the greater will be your punishment. Confess now and save your-self. Perhaps you may even save those weaker spirits whom you have seduced into the service of Satan.'

'I am no heretic,' she murmured again. She hung her head.

'Very well,' sighed the Bishop. He turned to his secretary. 'Note, please, that the woman, Alice, has been given every opportunity to purge herself of her guilt. I hereby direct that she be examined for marks of the Devil and shown the instruments of torture.'

The secretary wrote.

'Take her away,' ordered the Bishop.

The gaoler took her again by the arm and led her out. The chains dragged along the floor. The inquisitors looked at one another and shook their heads sadly. The secretary's quill scratched on parchment.

❧

Friar John begged an audience with the Bishop. Ledrede received him warily.

'My lord,' began the friar, 'we are both followers of the gentle Francis. Our lives have been governed by obedience and service.'

The Bishop nodded. 'Your point, good brother?'

'I have come to plead with you on behalf of these, your pris-oners,' replied Friar John.

'There is nothing to be said,' replied Ledrede. 'There is a well-recognized procedure. The truth will come out.'

'My lord,' persisted Friar John, 'these charges are greatly exag-gerated. They are the product of envy and personal hatred. I know some of these people. They are not witches. As for heresy, most of them are unlettered and cannot argue fine points of doctrine.'

'It is the intention that matters. They do not have to be theolo-gians to be able to insult God.'

'My lord, much has been misrepresented. Things are done differently in Ireland.'

'I am aware of that,' said Ledrede. 'I have noticed.'

'No, my good lord. This was always an island of saints. Even before the Christian faith came to these shores, it was an island of wise men devoted to the law. Women were accorded great respect. Many women held power as queens and chieftains.'

'Nonsense,' snorted Ledrede. 'If that were the case, then it is as well that our people took control. These ancient laws and customs made this a land of barbarous heathens. If sorcery and witchcraft were acceptable previously, they are no longer permissible. We cannot allow a situation where unguents and spells supplant the healing power of prayer.'

Friar John touched the scar on his thumb. Ledrede sat quietly, pondering. The cicatrice on his leg was troubling him. He blamed the witch's ointment.

'My lord,' began the friar again. 'There may have been some sin involved, but it was the sin of ignorance only. Surely you can settle some penance on these misfortunate people. Perhaps a fine. I am sure that they would gladly pay.'

'I cannot accept money in matters of faith.'

Ledrede set his face against any such suggestion, possibly even temptation. The Devil has the power to use even the best of people to achieve his ends. 'I have been long enough in Ireland to know deceit when I see it. You are a good and holy man, my brother, but you are deceived.'

'There is no magic, my lord. The great teacher, Roger Bacon, has told us that there are many things we do not understand, but that does not mean that they are magic. We simply do not understand them – yet.'

The Bishop sighed. 'You are deceived again, my brother. He came close to heresy in these matters. He was imprisoned for his views. Do not risk the sin of pride in seeking to make God's ways amenable to our poor understanding. Remember pride was the sin of Satan himself. The lust for knowledge caused Adam's fall and brought sin into the world. I say this out of concern for you.'

'My lord,' said Friar John wearily, 'I see knowledge as a light sent by God, to lead us out of darkness.'

Ledrede tapped his fingers on the table.

'Do you presume to rebuke your bishop, good friar? Do you lecture me?'

'My lord, I do not. I merely make the case that you have been misinformed. Liars and those who envy are the true servants of Satan. There is evil abroad, but it is not witchcraft or heresy.'

'I have heard enough to make up my own mind, my brother. You may go now and pray for greater humility.' He gestured impatiently.

'My lord, I beg you. I have heard the confession of the woman, Petronilla. I have granted her absolution. She is no heretic.'

The Bishop froze. 'You overreach yourself, Friar John. You have no authority to absolve such sins. Those are sins reserved to a bishop or the Holy Father himself.'

'I cannot divulge the nature of her confession, my lord, but I found no such sins. She is innocent and absolved of her transgressions.'

'Then she has deceived you also. Of course I cannot ask you to break the seal of the confessional, but it is unlikely that a known heretic and sortilegia would confess crimes of such enormity to a mere friar. I tell you, you are deceived and, in defending her, you are complicit in the Devil's work. My dear brother, have a care for your own soul. You are a good but foolish man. You have been led astray by knowledge and enquiry. It is well known that Satan uses women to lead foolish men astray. I command you, under pain of mortal sin, to interfere no further in matters beyond your competence. Leave these things to those who know better. Now go and return to your duties.'

He held out his hand. Friar John knelt and kissed the ring. He rose dejectedly to his feet.

Friar John went through the busy streets and lanes of the town. He saw people going about their business. They haggled in the market-place. Carts lumbered past. Children played in the street.

Loungers, at street corners, gossiped and laughed. There was music coming from an alehouse. He returned to his scriptorium and to his annals.

'In that year,' he wrote, 'a great altar was consecrated in the abbey of the friars Minor at Kilkenny.' A great altar, an altar fit for sacrifice. The Devil whispered in his ear. 'It is all vanity.' He closed his eyes. The searchers had found the pyx and the Sacred Host in the house of Alice. He was afraid to admit that he had put it there. 'Have a care for yourself, Friar John,' whispered the Devil. 'Stick to your duties. Like the good cobbler, stick to your last.'

He wrote again. 'In that year also, a great murrain afflicted the cattle, causing distress and want in many parts of Ireland.' Distress and want. He could think of nothing else. He could have said that the trial of the witches had caused fear and alarm among good people throughout the land. He could have said that the seneschal, Arnaldus le Poer, was compelled by the king's treasurer and the king's justiciar to cooperate with the Church in every way in stamping out heresy and seeing to the just punishment of witches, wheresoever they might be found. But he wrote no more. He had failed in his attempt. He was of no importance. He lacked courage. All that he attempted was vanity. He lay down his quill, and putting his face into his hands, he wept.

∾

The gaoler rubbed his hands like a merchant displaying his wares. He spoke politely, as one might in the presence of one's betters.

'I know that all this is distasteful to you, reverend sirs, but it is my duty to show these things to you and to the accused.'

He nodded in the direction of the bound and gagged Alice. She would not look at the array of equipment. Her eyes rolled in horror. The Blackfriars grasped her head, forcing her to look.

'The rack, you may be familiar with,' the gaoler said. He pushed a handle. A wheel turned. The mechanism creaked. 'These are the thumbscrews.'

Ledrede moved closer. He placed one hand between the plates. His episcopal ring caught the light from a high window. He withdrew his hand.

'Usually it is not necessary to use anything else. Hunger, lack of sleep, privation. These usually produce the desired result.' There was a science to it all, cause and effect. Fear and apprehension of what was to come could produce a confession, before any corporal pain might be inflicted. With women it was easier. Showing the instruments was, in fact, an act of kindness.

'What is this?' asked Canon Bibulous, indicating a brass object. It was the shape of a pear, with a screw-threaded handle protruding from the base.

'Ah!' said the gaoler with a measure of professional pride. 'The pear of anguish.' He picked up the device and tapped it on the table. Dust fell from it. A mechanism rattled inside. Alice moaned. She struggled to look away.

'Look at it, witch. Look at it,' the Blackfriars hissed. Canon Bibulous caught her terrified gaze.

The justice of it all warmed his heart. He raised an eyebrow. She struggled frantically, but the Blackfriars held her tight.

The gaoler turned the handle. The tip of the pear opened like a flower. The mechanism squealed.

'As you can imagine, if this be inserted into any orifice of the body it will cause great pain and destruction.' He quite admired the exactitude of his language. 'While it may not cause immediate death, that will come in time, from infection and disease of those parts through which it entered.' That was good. If he could write, which he could not, he would write a book of instruction for the application of pain in the cause of truth. He tapped the sinister device on a bench. More dust fell from the brazen instrument. Alice slipped unconscious from the restraining grasp of the Blackfriars.

Canon Bibulous felt a stirring in his loins. It was an old familiar feeling that had eluded him for a long time, an old friend come back again. He shifted his weight from one foot to the other.

'We are greatly obliged to you, sir,' said Ledrede. 'I am sure that all this will not be necessary. I can see that the woman is very much in fear. I look forward to an early conclusion to this regrettable business. In the meantime, have her revived and brought back to her cell. We shall proceed to hear further depositions.'

❧

This has gone far enough, mused Sir Arnaud. He was being compelled to act against his own interests. Beset on all sides by enemies, he could rely on few friends. He went down to his armoury, ran his hands over the implements of war. He longed to be up and about, to go on campaign, to smite the enemy before him and ride home again in triumph.

The boy, Wat, was in the room, a kindred spirit.

'What age are you, young Wat?' he queried.

'Fifteen years, sire,' replied the boy. 'Well, almost fifteen.'

'What do you do here?'

'I come here, sire, when I am troubled. I like to burnish the armour and keep the weapons oiled and sharp.'

'Good lad. Good lad. An' it please God, you will have a chance to use them. You will make an excellent knight.'

'I am happy to serve you, sire, wherever you lead.'

Sir Arnaud sat down heavily. 'Ah, Wat,' he complained. 'What am I to do? I must obey the law and see this bishop triumph or lose my place and hand my lands over to my enemies.' He sighed.

Wat stroked the egret feathers of the crest of a helmet. It was a piece of vanity, for display and tournament, not a casque for the fury of battle.

'It seems to me, sire, that there could be a solution.'

'A solution?' Sir Arnaud smiled a bleak smile. 'What cunning stratagem have you got up your sleeve?'

'Well, sire,' said Wat, twitching the feathers. 'If she be a witch, then might she not just fly away? If she be not a witch might we not help her on her way? Without his witch the Bishop will have no case. The others are people of little importance. He will punish them and let them go. Then you may turn to matters of greater importance.'

This is a wise boy, reflected Sir Arnaud. He always saw a practical and pragmatic solution.

'Or you could do what King Henry did to Archbishop Beckett. Send some trusty men to silence him.'

Sir Arnaud chuckled. 'And turn him into a martyr? You know it might be an idea. This town would prosper as a place of pilgrimage. They would thank me for their prosperity, but I would not be here to benefit. I am no Plantagenet, my boy. I cannot go about chopping up bishops.' He struck his thigh in wry amusement.

'Well then,' urged Wat, looking closely at his work. 'I will serve you faithfully if you should decide on my first suggestion.'

'I shall think about it, Wat,' said Sir Arnaud, standing up. He clapped the boy on the shoulder. 'What could I not do, if all my men were as good as you? We will talk further on this matter.'

∽

Petronilla stood before the tribunal. Chains hung heavily on her wrists and ankles. The men spoke in Latin. She had difficulty in following what was going on.

'Tell us plainly, Canon Godfrey,' said the Bishop, 'how you believe the Sacred Host came into the possession of these women.' He spoke, for Petronilla's benefit, in English. The canon rose to his feet, breathing heavily.

'It was some years ago, my lord. It was my practice to stand at the door after Mass, to greet the faithful.' He joined his hands together, lacing his pudgy fingers. Candlelight glinted in his watery eyes.

'I greeted this woman and her mistress in a cordial manner, but this woman made no answer. She kept her mouth closed. Her mistress was engaged in unseemly laughter and mockery, so I concluded that this woman had stolen the Eucharist and concealed it in her mouth, as is the common practice among her kind.'

'No,' blurted Petronilla. She remembered. 'We were laughing about a cat that fell from the tower.' She looked defiantly at the canon. 'I remember it well.'

His eyes bored into hers, warning her to say no more about that matter. Petronilla dropped her gaze.

'Ah, the cat again,' said the Bishop. 'So this stolen Eucharist was kept in that house to be insulted. Is this not the case?'

Petronilla shook her head.

'Do you deny that there was a sacred Eucharist concealed in your house? Do you deny that it was in a pyx stolen from some church?'

The Bishop raised his voice. Petronilla shook her head again. 'Or from some priest, perhaps a corrupted priest?'

'I know nothing of this,' she mumbled, looking at the ground.

'We shall return to this another time.' He nodded to the Blackfriars.

One of them opened a bag and tipped out the symbols from the Jesse tree. She recalled how she had first seen them. She remembered warm spiced wine and the gifts that Alice had sent to their house. Alice had spoken about the wurzel of Jesse.

The other friar spoke. He held up the crescent moon and the wizened Sybil on the three-legged stool.

'Can you explain the meaning of these pagan symbols?'

'No, I cannot. They were always on the tree of Jesse at Christmastide.' She almost said 'wurzel'. A smile tugged at her mouth. She giggled. The wurzel of Jesse. She had no idea why it was so funny. She turned away from the tribunal, but the gaoler turned her back to face them. She shook her head, trying to stifle the laughter. She raised a hand to her mouth, but it was no use. She saw them in the candlelight, an array of shadowy men, looking at one another in puzzlement. She laughed aloud. Tears streamed from her eyes. She remembered the picture of Jesse in Alice's old book. Jesse reclined on a bed of flowers, with his enormous wurzel protruding from his robe. He looked rather surprised. She tried to wipe the tears away, but the laughter came again. Her chains clanked. It was all too ridiculous. She laughed. She wept. She sank to her knees.

'You see, my lord,' said the Blackfriar, 'how she mocks this tribunal. She refuses to admit to her crimes and laughs in the face of justice.'

Ledrede was furious. For the first time since the process had begun, his anger took over.

'Take her below and have her examined for marks of the Devil.' He stood up, twitching his long cope about him. He took his staff. A chaplain lifted the hem of the cope and followed his master.

Petronilla looked at him, a small, hobbling man in a ridiculous robe, with a lackey carrying the train. She could not help but laugh. The Bishop stamped his staff on the flagstones as he left the room.

'Examine her well,' said Canon Bibulous, as he passed in the wake of the furious bishop.

The gaoler tugged on the chains, pulling her to her feet.

'We'll see who has the last laugh,' he growled.

∾

William lay on the straw. The room stank of ancient misery and degradation. The heavy gyves chafed his ankle bones. He tried to occupy his mind. He reckoned his accounts, trying to list his creditors and debtors. The debtors would be in no hurry to have him released. They would be happy to see him go up in flames. They would pile the tally sticks around the stake and see their troubles waft away. But he still had money and creditors who would wish to prolong his life, if only for their own peace of mind. He had land and influence. It was only a matter of time and some considerable outlay.

He had no fear for his mother. She could handle any situation. He feared though, for the child, Basilia, and for Petronilla. They did not have the kind of steel necessary to withstand such a trial. Petronilla had no money, but he would look after that also.

The guard slouched in a corner, bored with his task. The days dragged by. His relief always came late. He would have preferred a turn of duty on the gate. All the world passed through that gate. The world and his wife.

William tugged at his ring. He licked his finger. The ring slid off.

'Take this ring to the seneschal. He will recognize my seal. Tell him that I will pay him generously to get us out of this situation.' He tossed the ring to the guard. The guard examined it in the dim light. He said nothing.

'When I am set free I will reward you also. What is your name?' William waited.

The guard tried the ring on his finger but it was too small. He slipped it onto his little finger, his *lúidín*, and twisted it speculatively. It was a nice fit.

'What is your name?'

'Herebert.'

'Well, Herebert, my friend, I shall pay you twenty marks when I am free.'

Herebert turned the ring again. 'For twenty marks, young master, I will set you free now. I will cut the gaoler's throat and take his keys. For twenty marks,' he chuckled, 'I will cut my mother's throat.'

'No, no,' protested William. 'I would then be a fugitive. I could not get my hands on my money. This must be done according to law. Some law. There must be some law.'

Herebert said no more. It was a good ring, a heavy ring. It would buy a good meal, plenty of ale and probably a woman. This young man was fucked anyway. There was no way out for him. He wished that his relief would come. He salivated at the prospect of an evening's entertainment. The young man was speaking, but Herebert paid no attention. He listened for footsteps and the jangling of keys. A plague on all witches and heretics who would keep a man from his meat.

~

The women came to Petronilla, four women of good character, four knowledgeable, experienced women. They stripped her and pinned her to the floor, kneeling on her spread-eagled arms and legs. She fought and screamed. They stuffed a rag in her mouth and with raised candles they examined every inch of her. Hot wax dripped on her white skin. They probed and poked and turned her this way and that. They shaved her head and body hair and then they found what they had suspected all along. Under her left arm they found a mole, a strawberry mark, a follicle, a nipple, from which she had nourished her demon, her succubus, Robin the boy in green. They crossed themselves in the presence of evil.

The eye at the peep-hole in the door withdrew. Canon Bibulous departed, anxious to be the first to bring the good news to the Bishop. The women hurried from the chamber.

The gaoler turned the key, then plodded back up the two flights of stairs, grumbling at the lateness of the hour. He looked up at the night sky. He saw stars. Something struck him on the back of the head; he saw bright lights and more stars before falling to the ground, unconscious.

When he awoke, he felt the cold gravel pressing on his face. The bunch of keys lay beside him. He sat up, putting his hand to his head. The pain blinded him for a moment as he probed the lump on the back of his head. He felt blood on his fingers. He stood up in alarm and hurried into the gaol. Everything seemed to be in order.

He took a lantern and peered into the cells. The few wretched prisoners blinked at the light. The doors were securely locked, but the last cell was empty. Turning the key, he entered, holding the lantern high to inspect every corner. He kicked at the straw, then looked up at the high, barred window. Everything was as it should be, but the witch Alice and the child Basilia were gone.

∾

If any further proof of guilt were needed, this was it. The gaoler recounted his experience to the tribunal. The cells were locked. The other prisoners were still confined. He had seen a blinding light and had fallen into a swoon. When he awoke the witches were gone, Alice and the child of Petronilla. However, the remaining witches were still available to justice. The Bishop sent for the minor offenders.

'Have them brought before us,' he directed. 'They have had time to reflect upon their crimes.'

The gaoler departed and returned with all but William and Petronilla. The prisoners shuffled into the presence of their judges. They were linked together by shackles. They were dirty and wan from fatigue and hunger. They stood in line.

Ledrede addressed them by name: 'Annota Lange, Eva de Brounstoun, John and Helena Galrussyn, Syssok Galrussyn, Robert of Bristol, who should have know better, Alice, wife of Henry the Smith, already damned by his own hand, William Payn of Boly.' He paused, looking along the line of wretched captives. 'You have been judged guilty of the foulest crimes, on foot of evidence and the testimony of honest and true Christians. You have offended against the teachings of Holy Church and caused pain to Our Lord Jesus Christ. All this you have admitted under examination. These are crimes which merit the detestation of all true men and the ultimate punishment of fire. If any deny this, step forward now.'

The prisoners did not move. None spoke.

'Good,' said Ledrede. 'Now kneel for forgiveness.' The prisoners dropped to their knees. Some had to be supported by their companions. Others shook with fear, but there was a glimmer of hope. They snivelled and waited.

'As Our Blessed Lord is infinite in His love and forgiveness, even to those who have offended against Him, so also must His Church be prepared to forgive and wash clean the souls of those who fall victim to error. Be grateful for His mercy. I must tell you that she, who seduced you into heresy and evil, is fled from here. By sorcery she has escaped from justice. She has abandoned you.'

The prisoners looked up at him open-mouthed. Ledrede nodded. 'I see that you are astonished, but be of good heart. It shows that there is no hope for you outside the fold. The false shepherd has fled, but you are saved.'

He reached down and picked up the branding iron from the floor. He threw it onto the table with a clatter. 'Be grateful that you have been given a second chance. All of you will be branded with the Sign of the Cross. You will be taken to each of the gates of this town. There you will be stripped and beaten with rods, as a warning to others and for the purification of your souls. Your properties are confiscated, half to the Church and half to his gracious majesty, King Edward. You are forever banished from the diocese of Ossory. Now rejoice that you have been shown mercy.'

He stood and blessed them. 'Rejoice that you have been saved.' He gestured to his sergeants to take them away. 'Hand them to the civil powers for punishment and report to me when all this is accomplished.'

The gaoler touched the lump on the back of his head. That lump had come from no supernatural power, but it was safer to say nothing about it. The prisoners shuffled out in distress, stunned by their good fortune in escaping hellfire and by the news that Alice had indeed been possessed of unearthly powers.

~

'Did you speak to the seneschal?' asked William again. 'Did you give him my ring?'

Herebert belched. He was under instructions not to speak to this prisoner. His head throbbed from wine and carousing. He wanted peace.

'What did he say?' William persisted.

Herebert felt a cold sweat on his forehead. He needed sleep. Soup. He needed soup. His stomach could take no solid nourishment. He lay down on the straw and turned his face to the wall.

'What did Sir Arnaud say? Did you tell him of my offer?'

Herebert rolled to his feet. He aimed a kick at William, sending him crashing against the wall. He punched him in the face, feeling William's teeth on his knuckles.

'In Christ's name be quiet,' he snarled. He squatted again with his back to the wall. He convulsed in a spasm of retching, but nothing came.

'You didn't see him,' said William, through swollen lips. He lapsed into silence.

'No I did not,' said Herebert, angry that he was forced to admit to his deceit. 'There is no point. Anyway, your mother the witch is gone. You are abandoned. So shut up and take your medicine. Now let me rest.'

He lay down again, gathering wisps of straw under him. His headache was getting worse. He rolled about, trying to find a hollow to accommodate his hip. He farted.

'Fifty,' said William.

'Fifty what?' asked Herebert.

'Fifty marks. I will give you fifty marks. I swear it. Speak to the seneschal.'

Herebert smiled in the half-light.

'One thousand,' he replied.

'If you break me, you will get nothing,' said William softly. 'You will stand at the Watergate until you are too old to hold a halberd. You will be thrown on the parish. You will die in a ditch and your miserable corpse will be gnawed by rats.'

Herebert was silent. There were rats inside his head. With fifty marks he could buy a bit of land. It was not too late to have a family, sons to work the land, a daughter to bring him a bowl of broth by his own fireside. A bowl of broth. He salivated. His belly rumbled. He sighed.

'Fifty-five,' he murmured. 'Fifty-five and I will carry your offer to the seneschal.'

'Fifty-five,' agreed William, 'and I will forgive the ring.'

NINETEEN

Egiptum adiens – prosternit idola.
(When he arrived in Egypt,
he destroyed their idols.)
—Richard de Ledrede

AMONG THE SEDGES of the water meadow, Robin found what he was looking for. It was a small dug-out cot of the type that had carried the river fishermen since time began. By good fortune the paddle was still there. He pushed it to the water's edge. He arranged some twigs and small branches in such a way as to suggest a drifting log, and launched it forth into the darkness, feeling the current take it. He lay low. In the great silence he heard the otters bickering. Like the cot men, the otters fished by night, diligent and secretive, making only the smallest disturbance of the water. He remembered well how he and Petronilla had watched those otters at play with their cubs. He had tried to swim with them, but they were too quick.

He listened for the cot men, but there was no activity on the river. He listened for the weir, clenching the paddle in his fist. He saw the light in the cathedral tower, a pinpoint in the darkness, a pharos guiding him home. No mangonel or malvoisin would be needed to take this town, just a few determined swimmers or boatmen, slipping downriver by night, to take the gatekeepers by surprise.

He could smell the familiar smells of the town. He saw the dim outline of the abbey tower. He swung, with a couple of deft strokes, into the dark cleft of the New Quay.

He was home. He stepped ashore and pushed the boat back into the river. He watched it turn and sway. Then the current took it. He smelled the dark soil of the orchard and decaying leaves. He moved silently, like a thief.

The stables were empty, the doors ajar. There were no lights in the house. The door to the kitchen stood open. He went inside. There was a smell of must and damp. Something pushed against his shin. He bent and stroked the cat's head. He scratched the animal's neck. The cat purred and pushed even closer, insistently, glad to see him again. He felt about in the darkness, touching the familiar furniture. His sandals crunched on broken glass. He sat down to wait for daylight, pulling his cloak around him. The cat sat across his feet, determined to keep him there. The cold of the flagstones penetrated his worn soles. He lowered his head onto his forearms and slept.

∾

Aptly named the Hounds of God, the Blackfriars were tireless in pursuit. By day they questioned Petronilla and each night they reported to Ledrede. The chief spokesman pushed back his cowl. His bright eyes glittered in the candlelight, like the eyes of a jackdaw.

'My lord,' he began, 'we have questioned her closely and applied such coercion as we deemed appropriate.'

'What have you uncovered?' queried Ledrede. 'What evidence have you found?'

'We find that she and her mistress were keepers of bees, like the notorious heretic, Leutard of Vertus.'

'Go on,' urged Ledrede.

'This Leutard was instructed by bees to reject legitimate marriage. Bees do not mate as other creatures do. This woman produced a child outside of marriage, contrary to God's ordinance. She is an affront to holy virginity. She expresses no remorse and refuses to name the father.'

The Bishop narrowed his eyes and nodded.

'As to her complexion,' continued the friar, 'it is well known that the Manichaeans also reject marriage. They avoid meat and fast to excess. This gives rise to an abnormally pale appearance. We are trained to read such signs.' His colleague nodded in affirmation.

'Have you questioned her on the teachings of the heretic Nestorius?'

'We have, my lord. We have applied the tormentum, to the extent that her limbs have sprung from their joints, but still she obstinately denies knowledge of such matters. She says one thing and immediately contradicts herself. As your lordship knows, everything comes in twos, one the obverse of the other, a dark witch and a fair one. At one point she acknowledges the divinity of Christ, but claims not to understand that the Trinity is one, namely by unity of substance, but three in sequence, in aspect, in manifestation. All this she appears to deny, protesting that she does not understand the distinction. This is a common practice, whereby error is reinforced by spreading confusion.' The Blackfriar was pleased with the clarity of his argument.

'What of baptism? Does she reject this also? Was the child, Basilia, baptized?'

'She claims that the child was indeed baptized by Friar John.'

'Ah yes! Friar John. Was she present at this baptism? Did she undergo the customary purification?'

'My lord, she did not. She absented herself.'

A silence descended on the room. The candles flickered. The Bishop breathed deep. He sighed.

'What is to be done?'

The Blackfriar spoke softly. 'Before the Conquest, when our people still lived in Normandy, Queen Constance struck out the eye of her own confessor with her staff. He had tried to corrupt her into heresy. She saw to it that he and all his associates were consigned to fire. That was three centuries ago, almost to the day, but no better way has been found to deal with such pestiferous people.'

'Well then it must be so, but first I shall send for Friar John. Now tell me. Has she said anything regarding Sir Arnaud le Poer?'

'No my lord, but we can examine her further if needs be.'

'All in good time,' said Ledrede. 'Justice must not be hurried. I have instructed Canon Godfrey to enquire into this matter. There is also the matter of the Sacred Host. Have you been able to ascertain anything about that?'

'No, my lord. She denies all knowledge.'

'So Christ is wounded again.' Ledrede spoke softly, his voice full of pain. 'It goes on from generation to generation.'

He waved them away. He took the candle and touched the wick of his lantern and climbed to the top of the tower, dragging his maimed leg from step to step. He knelt and prayed. Victory was almost within his grasp. The enemies of God were in full flight before him.

❧

Through a miasma of pain, Petronilla was conscious of the weight on top of her. She heard the creature snuffle and groan. She felt the pain between her legs. It was a boar. She had seen a boar mounting a sow, once, long ago. She remembered how the creature had grasped the sow with obscene hands; how it turned its head to one side with a hideous smirk; how it snuffled and thrust again and again and again, as if it would destroy its victim. She felt the boar give a long shuddering groan. The weight rolled away from her. It was no matter. She could not move. Her arms refused to answer. She recalled how some

woman had dragged her away. 'Come away, now. Come away.' The
sow was spattered with the seed of the boar. 'Come away at once.'

'When I return,' said the boar, 'you will tell me of the dark
man, who rides through the air on a crawfish.'

A door slammed shut.

'There's more than one way to skin a cat,' said Canon Bibulous.
'You may now apply the pear of anguish.' The gaoler chuckled. He
jangled his keys.

Not until I've had my turn, he thought. He chuckled again.

༄

Alice stood by the taffrail, feeling the rise and fall, as the river met
the sea. She looked back at Dublin and the elegant curve of its bay.
She watched as Ireland fell away to the west. She watched until the
tip of the conical mountain dropped below the horizon. The wind
stirred her dark hair. She put her arm around the shoulders of the
child, Basilia. The sail cracked overhead. She drew the child closer.
They stood in silence. The shipmaster observed them warily. He had
his suspicions.

The wind dropped in mid-passage. A long, slick swell ran from
the south-west. The ship rolled and wallowed. A great bank of fog
advanced from the eastern horizon. The ship faded into cold grey
obscurity.

༄

When he awoke his feet were warm from the cat, but the chill of
the house had penetrated his bones. Robin rose and stretched. He
swung his arms to take the stiffness out of them. He looked about
in the dim morning light. Everything was scattered about, but it was
as if nothing had been removed. Broken crockery was strewn on the
floor. Chairs were overturned but, strangely, the jars of unguents

and herbs were still on their shelves. They were no longer in the neat order that Alice had insisted on, but the lids were still closed, as if the searchers had feared their hidden powers.

He went quietly upstairs, his hand upon the pommel of his dagger. The chambers were cold and dank. The bedclothes were piled here and there in disarray. Alice's sable coat hung by the door. He remembered how proud she had been of her dusted sable. He stroked the coat. The fur fell away under his hand. It formed a dusty pile on the floor. He drew back with a shiver. Moths emerged from the fur. He stroked it again. More fur fell away, exposing the bare skin and the stitches that had bound the pelts together. He wiped his hands.

In Petronilla's chamber he found her red robe on the floor. He looked at it for a long time, remembering that Christmastide before Bruce's war, before everything began to go wrong. He picked up the robe and put it to his face, searching for her scent. It smelled of mould. He laid it gently on the bed. There was a cracked mirror. He looked at himself in the glass. The crack ran across his face like a scar. He saw a swarthy, bearded man, with little trace of the Spideog who had come to this town with gentle Friar John. The crack distorted his features into a wry grimace. He wore the hooded galvardine cloak of a pilgrim.

He heard voices in the street. A beast bellowed as it was driven to the shambles. He looked through the narrow window. The animal knew what was in store for it. It tossed its head and lunged at its tormentors. They restrained it with ropes and beat it mercilessly towards the shambles gate. Their feet slipped on the mud and dung. They shouted and cursed. The creature bucked and danced, trying to break free, but eventually the gate closed on the tumult and there was silence.

The cot men saw him standing by the New Quay, a tall pilgrim with a staff in his right hand. They threw a line to him. He made it fast around an upright. They lifted their baskets ashore.

'God's blessing on you, pilgrim,' said one.

Robin nodded in reply. 'And you too, brother,' he said.

'Have you travelled far?' queried the fisherman.

'Far enough,' replied Robin. 'Maybe I will settle here for a while.'

'Well then you have come in good time. You are in time to see the witch-burning.' The fisherman gestured towards Alice's house. He extended his index and little finger to ward off evil. He crossed himself.

'What witch?' asked Robin quietly.

The fisherman picked up a basket of fish.

'The one they call Petronilla of Meath, one of the worst of them.'

'Not as bad as Dame Alice,' put in his companion. 'It was often she caused us bad luck on the river, if we failed to pay her dues.' He laughed. 'It's an ill wind, as they say. Now we can use her dock for free.'

'Where is she now?' asked Robin. 'Is she also to face the flames?'

'Oh, not at all,' said the first man, hefting the basket impatiently. 'She flew away. Right out of the Bishop's gaol.' He looked around. 'She could be anywhere. She could be right here an' we wouldn't see her.'

He put down his basket, happy to enlighten the pilgrim, happy to let him see that Kilkenny was no backwater town; that matters of great moment could happen here also.

'You say there were others, what others?'

'There were twelve of them altogether. All condemned and punished. Two escaped, Alice and the little girl. The son, William, is still in gaol. He has money enough to save himself. They say he made a deal with the Bishop. They say he gave evidence against the woman. It will cost him a pretty penny, but yon William will not burn. Just goes to show.' He spat into the water. 'Just goes to show,' he said again. 'He bought the seneschal and now he'll buy the Bishop.'

'No,' his companion protested. 'This bishop is not for sale.'

'Every man has his price,' insisted the first fisherman. 'You'll see. The Bishop has his witch. He will be happy with the one and a steady income from the heretic.'

'What of the seneschal?' asked Robin. 'What does he say to all this?'

'Not much. He's away to the wars again. There is only one power in Kilkenny now. One power in Kilkenny.' He laughed. 'Do you get it? One power in Kilkenny and that's Bishop Ledrede.'

'There was another one condemned, the familiar, the boy in green.'

'Robin. That's right. He was the familiar demon. That makes thirteen, but they'll never lay hands on him. He could change into any shape he wanted, any animal. He deceived them all. He even deceived the good Friar John.'

'He was their incubus. He mated with them all. All, except the child.'

'Succubus,' protested his companion. 'They call it a succubus.'

'No, no, no, no, no! An incubus mates with witches and a succubus couples with men. Don't you know anything?'

'Well then he was both. He mated with the men and the women.'

'But not the child?' said Robin.

'Not the child. That's the rule with witches. The Devil never mates with a child under twelve. That's the rule.'

'So you tell me that the Devil, the father of all evil, respects the chastity of a child. Did you ever wonder about that?' Robin shook his head. 'Not much of a devil, is he?'

The fishermen looked at each other in silence. They shrugged and picked up their baskets.

'Well, he made up the thirteen anyway. I wouldn't want to run across him. The Bishop says he was a demon. The Bishop has the last word on everything.'

They left Robin beside the dock, a tall stranger in his pilgrim coat. They were anxious to get to market, to dispose of their catch and pick up the latest news. The cat came to scavenge among the scraps and fish guts by the weedy waters of the New Quay.

∽

The Bishop greeted him coldly, extending his hand in the most perfunctory way. Friar John knelt again and kissed the ring.

'Yes, yes, yes,' said Ledrede, gesturing to him to stand. 'I have called you here to clarify certain matters.'

The friar waited. Fear clutched his insides. The Bishop sensed his fear.

'Since I came to this town, I have been hearing disturbing reports of your behaviour and your opinions. I warn you. This is not a time to stray from the teachings of Holy Church. I caution you to answer honestly. We are alone. If there are things troubling you, confess them now. We are under the seal of the confessional.'

'My lord Bishop,' began the friar. 'I am troubled. I cannot reconcile what is happening here to the message of our Lord, Jesus Christ.'

The Bishop froze. 'Go on,' he said.

'I have prayed, my lord, and studied. Nowhere in the Gospels have I found anything to justify the cruelty meted out to these, our fellow human beings.'

'I see,' said Ledrede. 'So you set yourself up as wiser than the great doctors of the Church. You dismiss thirteen hundred years of tradition and learning.'

'I am a simple man, my lord bishop. I chronicle what I see. I am not qualified to dispute with the schoolmen. But I have read the message of Christ. It is simple also. There is no place in Christianity for cruelty.'

'Then you are fortunate that there are others to protect you. There are those who are prepared to challenge Satan and to do what is necessary for the salvation of souls. You may live your simple life, but remember who keeps you safe from the Devil and the snares he sets for Christian people.'

'Is not pride one of the worst of these snares? Did Christ dress in gorgeous robes with jewels on His gloved hands?' To hell with it, thought Friar John. This bishop's mind was like a toothed man-trap. He felt a fury rising inside him. 'I believe that Satan has triumphed here.'

The Bishop trembled with anger. 'Remember whom you are addressing.'

'I do remember. You are a man. You are one of God's poor children and you will stand before the judgment seat on the last day. Consider the possibility that you may be mistaken. I beg of you, do not torture this poor woman any further. She is no witch.'

'If I have not courage to carry out the law, then the followers of Satan will take heart. You are a foolish man, Friar John.' He sighed. 'This witch must burn. If I do not burn her, I leave the gate open to the enemy. I will overlook your impertinence for the moment. Go back to your abbey and go about your work.'

Friar John dropped to his knees. He coughed. His teeth chattered. He spoke in a whisper. Ledrede leaned forward, straining to hear.

'Then take me. Let me be the one to burn. I confess to you now that I gave her the Sacred Host. I gave it to her to protect her.'

'This is foolishness,' replied Ledrede. 'If this were true and she a true Christian, then she would have been safe. But we have testimony that she stole the Host. She has admitted it under examination. She has confessed to desecrating it in the foulest ways.'

'She speaks from fear and pain. I swear to you on the Cross, that I gave it to her.'

A flicker of doubt passed across the Bishop's countenance. 'Do you put your immortal soul in danger for this woman?'

'I am not afraid. I tell you the truth.'

'If it be so, then she has lied to us. Either way she deserves to burn. And you too, for wounding the body of Christ yet again, if what you say be true.'

Friar John lowered his head. His bowels churned. He was afraid that he might void himself in the presence of the Bishop.

Ledrede considered for a while. He spoke again with an unexpected gentleness.

'Your charity does you credit, my son, but it is entirely misplaced. This woman is a proven harlot and a witch. She has, no doubt, deceived many before you. She must burn.'

Friar John felt guilty relief whispering in his mind. He had told the truth and the Bishop had not accepted it. He would not have to burn. He clenched his hands. The scar on his thumb stood out. His fingernails were stained with ink. He remembered her gentle touch, her chiding. He touched the scar.

'But I did give it to her. I am the one who brought her to this sorry state. Let me take her place.'

The Bishop rose. He took up his staff.

'Enough of this foolishness. You will hear it from her own lips. Come with me.'

He limped to the door. Friar John rose and followed him. The staff rang on the flagstones with every step. It rang on the cobbles of the street and on the stairs to the dungeons of the gaol.

The armed guards stood aside. The gaoler opened the door. He held up his lantern and stood back to allow the holy men to enter.

She lay in the straw like a broken animal. The few rags that covered her were stained with blood and excrement. Her ankles were confined in enormous gyves. Her fingertips. Her fingertips were crushed and blackened. Her fingertips, which had soothed his pain. Oh God! Oh God!

Friar John knelt beside her. She looked at him through her one good eye. The other was bruised and swollen.

'Do not touch the witch. Remember that you are in the presence of evil.' The Bishop's voice crackled. 'Now tell her what you told me. Do not touch her.'

Friar John withdrew his hand from her brow. Her fair hair was gone. Her scalp was pocked with the marks of vermin. Her lips moved. He could see that all her teeth were broken.

'Let me die,' she whispered. 'Let me die.'

'When you acknowledge the truth, then you may die.' Ledrede struck his staff impatiently on the floor, calling the proceedings to order. 'Tell her what you told me,' he commanded.

'Petronilla,' began the friar. 'My poor Petronilla. I have told his lordship that it was I who brought the Host to you. I feared for you. I thought to keep you safe.'

He could not be sure that she heard him. There was no sign of recognition.

'If it be true, you will burn together.'

'Tell him the truth,' urged Friar John leaning close.

Her eye flickered. She held his gaze.

'This priest is a fool,' she croaked. 'I stole the Host and the pyx. Take him away from me.'

'No,' protested the friar. 'She is astray in herself.'

'She has bewitched you,' said Ledrede. The matter was settled. 'Take him away.'

Two guards seized the friar by the arms and dragged him to his feet. He struggled, but they held him fast. He looked back at her. Her single eye was following him in the flickering light. The Bishop ducked under the lintel. The cell door slammed. Ledrede stumped up the long flights of steps and emerged into the yard. The guards released their hold on Friar John. He looked at Ledrede. The Bishop was satisfied with his work. Friar John leaned forward and placing his hands on his knees, he retched, bright yellow on the stones of the prison yard. Despair overwhelmed him.

Ledrede looked at him with a measure of contempt. He had no tolerance for weakness.

'Now God's justice may be done. You may return to your books, good brother.'

He limped away without looking back. God's champion, ready for the fray.

TWENTY

Have mercie on me, frère,
Barfote that y go.
　　　　—Anonymous

ON THE THURSDAY within the octave of Saint Hilary, William appeared before the Bishop in a crowded Saint Mary's Church. The king's chancellor, the king's justiciar and the seneschal, Sir Arnaud, were there to speak for him. Sir Arnaud used what influence he had with the king himself, to secure learned advocates to speak in William's defence. But the king's star was fading, the influence and power of the De Spensers wilting under the remorseless pressure of the queen, the she-wolf of France and Mortimer, her paramour. Time was running out. Roger Outlawe, Prior of Kilmainham, sent the shrewdest teachers from the fledgling university to argue on William's behalf. They came, hotfoot from Dublin, barely arriving in time. Archbishop Bicknor dispatched his most eloquent scholars to confound and refute the arguments of the hated Richard de Ledrede.

More eloquently than all of these, money spoke out loud and clear, money and the throng of armed men, loricati in studded leather cuirasses, knights in coats of mail. They shoved the common people to the walls and occupied the centre space.

Ledrede spoke at length about the destestable crime of heresy. He spoke at great length. His tirade went on into the night. People shuffled and yawned. They knew all this stuff.

Ledrede beckoned to the prisoner. William was brought forward in chains. He knelt, his demeanour humble. He spoke as a penitent, publicly abjuring his heresy. He accepted the charges brought by the families of Alice's former husbands, and begged pardon of the hairless and gaunt John le Poer, the fourth of that unhappy group.

He knelt to the Bishop and denounced his mother and all her heinous practices. He admitted that she had used magic to secure her wealth, to raise tempests and floods, to blight the crops and cause miscarriage in Christian wives and in the beasts of the field. He told how she predicted the future with the bones of condemned murderers and buried the entrails of cockerels at crossroads at the midnight hour. He had seen her couple with demons, most especially the one known as Robin. In all this she had been assisted by the condemned witch Petronilla, obstinate in her heresy and entangled in wickedness.

The church was hushed. It was theatre. It was drama. Ledrede stood over the kneeling penitent. He spoke of his joy at the recovery of a lost sheep. He blessed William with holy water. William did not flinch. The evil was gone out of him. Ledrede told him the good news. He need wear the shackles for one month only and fast for one year. He would pay one thousand silver pounds to repair the cathedral roof and cover it in lead. He would pay for priests to say Mass in perpetuity in the Mary chapel. There and then, he would sign a new profession of faith, in French, Latin and English, so one could be in no doubt that the soul of William Outlawe had been snatched from eternal perdition. It was high drama. It was farce.

William was given into the custody of the civil power until his bond might be handed over. Ledrede decreed that all those vile instruments used by the witch, Alice, be burned in a public bonfire, along with her associate, Petronilla de Midia. All her unguents and wicked herbs, her poppets and her staff.

Honour was satisfied. The dignitaries were free to return to more important matters, the constant threat from the resurgent Irish, a tottering king with his power and authority fraying at the edges. Ledrede looked at the seneschal.

Sir Arnaud met his gaze. Excommunicated he might still be, but his men were loyal. There would be another day.

∽

The tanner was annoyed. That butcher again. The walls were scraped clean of the saltpetre. He might at least have had the manners to ask. Probably selling it on to all the other butchers, for a tidy profit, without so much as a by-your-leave. He grumbled. He dragged the gate over and locked it. There would be no work done in Kilkenny that day.

The coal merchant wondered why a pilgrim would need so much charcoal. The pilgrim had little to say. Probably became morose walking lonely roads, deep in contemplation. It was a lonely life for a pilgrim but, with luck, his reward would be great in Heaven. The coal merchant's reward would be more immediate. His reward for standing in the market-place in sun and rain, in dust and grime, was a prime site for witnessing everything of note that happened in Coal Market. He remembered the bear. That was by far the best spectacle. There was never anything as good as the bear. There was ale for everyone that day, the day the witch, Alice, wed her first husband, God be good to the poor man. There was ale and there was blood and guts. It was a mighty bear.

'You should have seen the bear,' he remarked. 'There was never anything like it in Kilkenny town.'

The pilgrim said nothing. The merchant shook the bag, tamping down the charcoal. He was in a generous mood. He added another fistful. 'An' a tilly for the cat, as they say.' He chuckled. 'Aye, the cat. That's a good one, seein' the day that's in it.'

He chuckled again. The pilgrim made no reply. A morose, blac-kavised bastard, thought the merchant. A bit like himself indeed, blackened to a shine, by his dusty trade. Still, it was no harm to be pleasant to a pilgrim. Maybe some of the sanctity would rub off. 'Chained to a stake, he was,' he rambled on. 'Just like that one over there where they are goin' to burn the witch.' He rubbed his hands. 'That'll be somethin', but I doubt if it will be as good as the bear.' He rubbed his hands again. 'Get it over with, I say. People have work to do. There's money to be made.'

The pilgrim looked at him impassively. He dropped a coin on the stall. It spun and spun. It came up tails.

∾

Herebert was glad to be out of that stinking cell. He was glad to be away from the heretic. He looked forward to the money promised to him, but sometmes he wondered if he had been duped. What value can be put on the word of a man who would denounce his own mother, even if she was a witch?

He stood ready by the tailboard of the tomberel. The smell of dung was clean and astringent, after the fetid air of the prison cell. It was the smell of land and honest toil. It was the smell of comfort and security. He breathed deeply and looked about. The street was crowded with people, craning their necks to see over the heads of those in front. Armed men lined both sides of the street. The Bishop and all his clergy formed up in front of the cart. The winter sun glinted on a tall crucifix carried by Canon Bibulous. For once the Church and the civil power were united in common cause. Herebert flexed his whip.

They tied her to the tailboard, barefoot and in rags. Her arms were like broken wings, her shoulders loose and awkward. Her head hung to one side. Her one eye looked at Herebert.

'Where are your pretty shoes now?' he taunted.

He raised the whip and brought the lash down across her shoulders. And again!

'Where are your pretty red shoes now, witch?'

The procession moved off. The canons sang. The Bishop limped, supporting himself with his staff. Canon Godfrey held the crucifix on high, as he led them down Vicar Street, Dean Street, up Watergate Street, across the bridge and through the gate into Hightown. The crowd flowed behind them. Urchins scurried through the throng, anxious to get a better view.

All the while, Herebert laid on with his whip. He was proud of his skill. He was proud to take such a prominent position in cleansing the town he had watched over for so many years. He gave good value. The lash stripped her of her few remaining rags. He exposed the white bones of her shoulder blades. He striped her arms and legs with bloody weals, she who had endangered his soul with carnal thoughts.

'Too good for Herebert, eh?' he goaded. 'No more dancing shoes for you.'

Her feet dragged in the dust, but still she looked sideways at him with her one good eye. Herebert put the thumb of his left hand between the first two fingers. He felt a twinge of fear. The witch was not dead yet. He brought the whip down with greater force. The crowd gasped. Again Herebert lashed her, expunging his own sins. Sweat stood out on his forehead. His eyes bulged. And again! The urchins nudged one another in glee. This was better than any bear. It got even better. The mad woman screeched at the Bishop, calling curses down upon his head.

'You will see my daughter's face for the rest of your life and into eternity. You will never have an easy day. Maggots will devour you while you live.' There was more, until she was removed. The Bishop stared impassively ahead.

The sergeants chained her to the stake, naked and bleeding, but still conscious. They piled straw and sticks around her feet.

'Not too much,' directed Ledrede. 'This must be done properly.'

The gaoler secured an enormous padlock. The sergeants piled bags and jars onto the straw. One man snapped a long staff and threw it onto the pile. A pilgrim carried a large cask to the pyre. Black dust spilled from a hole in the cask. No doubt the pilgrim had seen much of such matters in his travels. The pilgrim said something to the witch. She seemed to smile or perhaps it was just a grimace of pain.

Friar John, in deep distress, knelt before her. There had been talk about him too, something to do with the witch's daughter. Just idle gossip. The pilgrim seized him roughly by the shoulder and pushed him through the crowd. It was funny in a way. The friar's feet scarcely touched the ground. Canon Bibulous came into his own. He raised the crucifix in front of the broken sinner.

'*Maledicat Dominus*,' he called.

The gaoler touched a blazing brand to the straw. The fire crackled. The crowd fell silent. Smoke wisped around the witch. She twisted her head away. Herebert looped his bloody whip.

'It will be swift,' hissed the pilgrim. The friar was helpless in his grasp. The pilgrim pushed him into a side lane, confining him in a doorway. 'It will be swift.' There were tears in his eyes.

'Robin!' said the friar, astonished.

They heard the canon's voice again, echoing in the silent market-place.

'*Maledicat Dominus*.'

There was a thunderous roar and a blinding flash of light. Roof slates and debris hurtled past the narrow entrance to the lane. The friar staggered against the door. There was a terrible silence and then came the screaming. People rushed past them in panic. Some were bleeding or holding injured limbs. A man staggered and fell, his eyes hanging from their sockets.

Robin stepped out into the market-place. The stake was no more than a splintered stump. Petronilla was gone. Of Canon Bibulous there was no trace except for a smouldering shoe. A coiled whip lay on the ground beside a bunch of keys. The Bishop was wiping blood and excrement from his pontifical robes. The crowd in various states of shock and excitement, stood mute, keeping their distance. This was something to relate for many years to come, the witch's revenge, better by far than any bear.

༃

It was the day on which William was moved to the castle of Kilkenny, to be held until the first assize day after the feast of Saint Hilary.

Friar John wrote: *Hac eadem die combusta fuit Petronilla de Midia.* His tears fell on the parchment, blurring the ink. Her name was smudged, almost illegible. He thought of the boy, Robin, a pilgrim and fugitive, named by William as a familiar demon. Condemned to fire, if apprehended. *Combusta fuit Petronilla.* He repaired the smudged letters. The ink gathered into little feet, little dancing shoes. He wiped his quill and put it aside. *Combusta fuit Petronilla.* He could taste her ashes on his tongue. He closed the ink-horn.

༃

She would take the eyes out of your head. How often had he heard it said of the maid Petronilla. The coal merchant had time to reflect on it now. He used to see her in the market-place in the old days, herself and her dark-haired mistress. It was strange to think that they had posed such danger. He remembered her as a child with a heavy basket in the crook of her elbow. She came with her mother, the poor mad woman. He could have wept for her, but he had no eyes. It was strange. He could see her clearly still, but the Devil had dragged the eyes from his head, that day he came to claim his own.

265

The coal merchant lived now in the stygian blackness of the pit. He had seen it all, but had understood little. He longed to see the fair child again. He longed to weep for the broken creature at the stake. He longed to weep for the world, but he had no tears.

Friar John went every week to see the poor lunatic woman. She lived under the care of the good nuns, a wild, distracted wretch. Her eyes were those of a creature of the forest, brought to bay by hounds.

He was conscious of his failures over the years. He had not taken good care.

He always spoke gently to her, holding her hands, restraining her wild gesticulations. She wore the lightest of chains. She wore them for her own safety and the safety of those who ministered to her.

'Your daughter died in the grace of the Lord,' he assured her time and again. 'She is with God.'

Over time his words began to have some effect.

'She was guilty of no sin,' he reiterated. 'Your husband, the good Alain, lies in the house of God itself. You are safe here now with these holy women. Have no fear.'

Her eyes wandered, as if searching for someone.

'Robin,' she said. 'Did I harbour a demon in my house?'

'No you did not,' he said emphatically. 'You did a great kindness to an orphan child. You will be rewarded for it. Robin is gone now, but some day, when he has learned everything that is to be learned, he will come back. He has promised to return and vindicate your daughter's name.'

She nodded. The idea calmed her.

'And do worms devour Bishop Ledrede?'

Friar John shook his head.

'Think no more of Bishop Ledrede. He must live with his conscience.'

~

A worm had indeed begun to bore into the mind of Bishop Ledrede. A worm of doubt disturbed his meditations. It woke him in the long watches of the night, before the bell rang for Lauds. Like the ship-worm it gnawed at his certainty, sinking him down into the depths, threatening to drown him in an agony of doubt.

From the tower he looked down at the workmen on the cathedral roof. It comforted him to see them lift the chipped and broken slates. They dug out the worm-eaten timbers, replacing them with good oak. They sheeted the roof with a great expanse of lead, crimping the sheets together, flashing them around the central belfry. It cheered him to know that the expense was reducing William Outlawe to penury. He knew that William was indebted to his friends for a great sum of money. He knew that some enter-prising and zealous men had broken into the Kyteler counting-house in Coal Market, on the day of the great conflagration and had added the bundles of tally sticks to the pyre. He knew that the worm of usury was eating away at William's dwindling resources. It was all very satisfactory, but still the doubt nagged at him. Had he done wrong? Would he stand before the seat of judgment to be told that he had failed? Failed to remove all the rot from his diocese? Should he have burned the heretic, William, instead of accepting a fine? Had he sold Christ again for a handful of silver?

He reasoned with himself. Which was the greater good? It was more than a handful. The fabric of God's church was secure from damp and rot. There would no longer be nests of scurrying woodlice under the slates, lurking like heretics and witches, seeking to destroy the roof timbers. The idea pleased him. He had put the fear of God into them. On his lofty eyrie he prayed for a sign.

It came to him from the east. It was news that the queen and her general, the great Mortimer, had overthrown the king and his hangers-on. The De Spensers were no more. The elder was hanged and beheaded. The younger one suffered a hideous death, while the queen and Mortimer feasted jubilantly in his sight.

Hoisted fifty feet above the jeering crowd, he was hanged as a thief; disembowelled and quartered as a traitor. For securing discord between king and queen, he was castrated to show that his power was at an end. To the satisfaction of all, he emitted a long, blood-chilling howl of agony. The queen raised a toast to her lover and champion. The traitor was beheaded. Four deaths for all his crimes.

Within weeks the king was confronted with his many failings. He had lost Scotland, parts of Gascony and Ireland. He had injured the Church and many of noble blood. He had sold justice in return for profit, left his realm without good governance and taken advice from notorious enemies of the common good. He abdicated in favour of his son, Edward, a boy of only fourteen years, still under the control of his remorseless mother.

The best part of all was that the seneschal, Sir Arnaud, shorn of his power and influence, was left naked to his enemies. The Butlers came down upon his lands, burning and pillaging everything in their path. He enraged Maurice Fitz Thomas of Desmond by dismissing him as a mere rhymer, alluding to that lord's love of all things Irish. He barely withstood the onslaught of de Bermingham, the conqueror of Edward Bruce. He let Kilkenny slip from his hands. He stood at bay in Waterford.

But he could not resist the power of God. Ledrede denounced him yet again, as a heretic and excommunicate. The earth had tilted and the followers of the old king were slipping off the edge.

❧

The ingeniator studied the letter. He frowned and scratched his head. The parchment was worn at the edges. The wax was cracked. He could make out *Dominus Hybernie* and *Dux Aquitanie*. It was certainly the king's seal.

'Why do you wish to work here?' he asked.

'To learn,' replied Robin, 'and to earn my bread.'

'What were you doing before you came here to Salisbury?' asked the ingeniator. He saw a powerfully built young man, sallow and bearded. The accent was strange.

'I have been a scribe, a soldier, a scholar, a pilgrim, a juggler.'

The ingeniator snorted. 'A juggler!' He laughed. 'I have no work for jugglers.' He pondered. 'But if you can lift and carry, I will have work enough. I will start you on the crane.' He chuckled. 'You can learn from the ground up.'

Robin looked up at the bell tower. The clouds moved behind it, making it appear to topple.

'This will be the tallest spire in the kingdom,' declared the ingeniator with pride. 'You will help us to lift over six and a half thousand tons of stone into place. Are you prepared for this work, scholar?'

'If it be honest toil then I am prepared. If you will teach me also, then I will work for food and lodging.'

The ingeniator looked at him curiously. 'You are a strange one,' he said, 'but I will do as the letter directs.' He sniffed. 'Not that the king can do anything about it anyway.'

'Where is the king?' queried Robin. 'I made a promise to return to him and tell my story.'

'Well then, my son, you are too late. The king is dead. He did not live to see our spire.' He lowered his voice. 'His wife now reigns with her paramour and may God pity this kingdom.'

Robin did not reply. He thought of that glittering day in the New Hall, when he had performed before the king. He had reason to be grateful to the king, but now the letter had little force.

'He did some good,' said the ingeniator wistfully. 'He gave me plenty of work. Now, scholar, you can help me to complete it.'

Robin started on the treadmill, plodding like a beast of burden. The windlass creaked. The blocks were carried aloft. His companion grumbled at the folly of it all.

'They think they can build all the way to Heaven. When they build a bit, they move this crane up to the next level and build some more. It is folly. It will all fall down some day and we will be destroyed. You'll see.'

Robin was not dismayed. He studied the masons at work. He watched the ingeniator with the cross and plumb-line. He asked questions.

The ingeniator responded to Robin's enquiring mind. He showed him drawings. He liked the idea of having such an apt pupil. As the spire rose with every course of blocks, new features came into view below.

'Four hundred and fifty tonnes of lead on that roof,' he said proudly. 'The finest roof in all England.'

'How can that weight be supported?'

The ingeniator went on to explain buttresses and vaulting.

'Spread the weight. Deflect it,' said the ingeniator. 'My father was fond of a drink. In fact, he would never go aloft without a few drinks. No head for heights, you see. He put it this way. Two drunks coming home from the alehouse. They hold each other up by leaning together. Either one on his own will fall down.'

He formed an arch with his fingers.

Robin understood. 'Did you learn from your father?'

'That I did. I inherited his job.' He told how his father had climbed the high, spindly scaffolding one day in a fury over some slovenly work. He neglected to arm himself with drink. A plank fell from beneath him. The ingeniator had seen it fall, fluttering like an autumn leaf. He saw his father falling too. The head that carried all that knowledge, cracked open on the floor. Some knowledge survived in the son. The work went on.

'It is important that the knowledge is passed on,' said the ingeniator. 'I will teach you what I can.'

'It is all folly,' said the grumbling man in the wheel. 'Christ did not live in a great church. He built no palace. He lived by the work of his hands. His church was the open air. The day will come when there will be no palaces, no kings or nobles. People will hear the Word of God in their own tongue. No bishops. No gentlemen.'

He had a broad agenda. It kept his mind off the monotony of their task.

'How did the king die?' asked Robin.

'Where have you been?' asked his companion. He grunted at the interminable uphill journey.

'All over,' Robin answered.

'All over! So you have not heard?'

'No,' said Robin. The windlass groaned. A block landed with a thump on the platform. The man paused. He gasped.

'He died from buggery,' he declared. 'After a lifetime of buggery, that's what killed him.'

He was enjoying Robin's puzzlement.

'Some say that he was smothered, but I heard it as a fact, that she had him buggered with a white-hot poker.'

'O Jhesu!' said Robin. Robin never swore.

'I heard it as a fact,' said the man. 'She gave the orders herself.' They stepped out of the wheel to let the windlass unwind. The hooks fell downwards through the hatch. The windlass sang, freed of its burden.

∽

Far away, in his chapter house, Bishop Ledrede heard the news. He determined to write to the queen, expressing his loyalty to her and to her son, the boy Edward. He had a way with words. He would write before the archbishop got his foot in the door of royal favour. He would write a warm letter in courtly French, appropriate for a princess of that land.

'*A ma dame la royngne … et mon lige seignour le roy vostre fitz.*' He begged leave to come to England to look upon her face. He was not satisfied with the style. He put it aside. There was other business to be attended to first.

He began to draw up the charges against Sir Arnaud le Poer: heresy; violence against the persons of the Bishop and his clergy; refusal to repent and save himself from excommunication; consorting with known witches, to the injury of his virtuous wife; aiding the enemies of the queen herself. He had testimony from the virtuous wife and from the family of the unfortunate John de Bonneville, cruelly murdered by Sir Arnaud, a crime for which he had bought pardon both from the queen's enemies and by invoking the barbarous customs of the Irish. He had witnesses in plenty of the violence against his own person. He had a witness in the person of Sir Ivo, a noble knight in the service of the lord Butler, the rising power. There was some talk of riding through the air on a crawfish. That was too fantastical. Or was it? He deliberated. There were no witnesses. He left the crawfish out.

He put down his quill. He went over to his cathedral. He reckoned that a spire would look well, a Norman-French counterpoint to the Celtic tower. It was just a thought. He heard Mass in the Mary Chapel. Mass paid for by William, the repentant heretic. There could be some way of squeezing more money from that source. William was grateful to be alive.

He prayed silently after the priest departed. He sat in the saint's cold, stone chair. He listened to the sounds of the cathedral, a door rattling in a draught; the wind in the bell tower; various clicks and crackles; the new roof settling in, the architect assured him. He suspected that he was happy. A poem began to suggest itself to him, a poem of the Virgin and her son, the Bread of Life, a loaf in the oven of her womb.

He began to hum a popular tune. The words coming to him were a perfect fit. The building sang around him: *'Gaudens clamat ecclesia.'* The church cried out in joy.

∾

Sir Arnaud stole a march on Ledrede. He hurried to Dublin and
laid countercharges. He acquitted himself before the justiciar and
his court. He lodged in the Record Tower at Dublin Castle, an
honoured guest.

Ledrede delayed his coming to answer the case, pleading that
his life would be at risk if he were to pass through Sir Arnaud's lands.
Yet he came, by forest tracks and bleak mountain trails.

He sheltered one night in a great cave, where a monstrous cat was
said to lurk. He heard nothing but the timeless drip of water, in the
darkness of the void. Plink! Plink! all night long. There was no cat.

He raged against Sir Arnaud. Violent words flew back and forth
before the king's representative. All present knew that they stood on
shaky ground, not knowing which way to lean, or who might hold
them up.

Sir Arnaud sulked and raged by turns, alone in the Record Tower.
Weeks and months dragged by. He began to realize that he was a prisoner. Civility was thin on the ground. One morning he found that
the door was locked. He was hungry, but no food came for him.

Ledrede dispatched his letter to the queen. Victory beckoned
once more: *'Exultemus et letemur hodie.'*

The students in Archbishop Bicknor's college practised their
Latin maxims: in prosperity men have many friends. *'In rebus
secundis'*, and as always, the obverse of the coin. *'In rebus adversis
paucos amicos habent.'* Within a bow-shot of those students, Sir
Arnaud wasted away, deprived of the comfort of the sacraments.
His followers were scattered and powerless. Ledrede, the only one
who could have lifted the excommunication from his shoulders, had
followed his letter to England, in high hopes of an audience with
the queen.

Archbishop Bicknor washed his hands of the matter. The Prior
of Kilmainham, now acting justiciar, turned his face away. Worse

than the smell of death around Sir Arnaud was the lingering stench of the quartered De Spenser. Nothing should be done to antagonize the queen and Mortimer.

With none to mourn him or do him respect, Sir Arnaud le Poer departed this world. No one could bury him. The instructions were explicit: 'cast upon a dunghill like an hunde'. He lay for many months, a hideous warning to all who dared defy the Church and its implacable servant, Richard de Ledrede. At last, in the interests of public health, the putrid remains were cast into an unsanctified pit. Only Wat, a faithful young knight, attended the poor corpse to the grave.

∾

Mortimer, booted and spurred, on a warhorse splendidly caparisoned, was a man to be reckoned with, but in his nightshirt, hauled unceremoniously from the queen's bed, he cut a poor enough figure. He was given no chance to recover his dignity. The boy king wasted no time on a trial. 'Fair son, have pity on the gentle Mortimer,' pleaded the queen. The fair son was merciful. Mortimer, sometime ruler of England, defender of Ireland, Earl of March and holder of titles and castles the length and breadth of the realm, was hanged, without the customary torture, still in his nightshirt, on a cold November day. His white legs turned in the wind. The she-wolf herself, 'the gilfer', as they would have called her in Kilkenny, was sent to Castle Rising to live out her years in chagrin, chilled by the east winds off The Wash and by the thought of what she had lost.

Bishop Ledrede's timing was not great. He continued his journey to France and to the papal court at Avignon. Like his old adversary, the seneschal, he found that he too had become small beer. He drifted into the backwaters of ecclesiastical affairs. Few were interested in his triumphs. At times he longed for Kilkenny and his own cathedral. He longed to sit in the saint's cold chair and listen to the music of the stones.

He sought permission to return. He wrote abjectly to the boy king. His Holiness reminded him that his task was to spread peace and love, not rancour and discord. The Pope asked Ledrede to consider whether any of his actions or even his attitudes might have contributed to the turmoil and distress that seemed constantly to afflict the misfortunate island of Ireland. He found work for the Bishop, but delayed his permission to return. The new king sent no reply.

TWENTY-ONE

Et lux illa vera – quae caritate mera
Suo splendore – nos illuminat –
Celi divo rore – nos laetificat
Divino fulgore.
(That true light illumines us through love;
  we rejoice in the gentle dew of Heaven
  and in the splendour of God.)
                    —Richard de Ledrede

ON FRIDAY the eleventh day of June the priest in the Mary Chapel of the cathedral paused in the middle of Mass. He put down the chalice. He heard a moaning, as of souls in torment, a cry of despair, a droning of the great bells trembling at what was to come.

Dust floated in shafts of sunlight. Wisps of straw drifted down. Shards of pale blue, speckled eggshell, from nests not long deserted by newly fledged jackdaws, tinkled on the flagged floor. Particles of mortar rained down on the effigies of knights and noble ladies and on the slab covering the drunken cobbler, father of the witch Petronilla.

Oaken roof timbers cracked and gave way. The priest fled in

panic. Behind him, with an earth-shuddering rumble, the belfry, with its bells and a mountain of masonry, piled into the central nave. On top of this mountain of mortar and stone came tonne upon tonne of sheeted lead. The cathedral filled with choking dust, dimming the morning light from the tall lancet windows. It was, as Friar John was to note, a sight pitiful to behold.

It might well have been the work of witches. Wherever they might lurk, they still had power and the desire for revenge. The cathedral clergy made the best of things. They cleared the mountain of rubble and lead. They said Mass in the chapel, shivering as the wind howled about them and rain fell incessantly, puddling around their feet. They cursed the heretic William Outlawe for his cunning, but they could not touch him. The reformed heretic prospered again, but kept a wary distance from Kilkenny. Without the guiding hand of their bishop, the clergy were lost sheep.

Two years later, on the Feast of Tiburtius and Valerian, the burgesses and true men of Kilkenny began to pave their streets.

The pile of stone salvaged from the fallen tower began to dwindle. Without their bishop to put some steel into their backbones, the clergy were unable to protest. Men came with carts and drew away keystones and springers, beautifully shaped voussoirs from the vaults and arches and flagstones from the cathedral floor.

The cathedral was in danger of becoming a quarry. It was disgraceful and a scandal that cried to Heaven, but at least the people might walk dry-shod in the market-place in foul weather.

Friar John worked at his manuscripts. In his annals he chronicled the notable events of the times. Sometimes he pondered for a year or two, weighing the relative importance of one thing to another. His mood was as dark as the weather. It was all folly. He noted that John de Bermingham had been murdered by his own men. Along with the conqueror of the Scots perished Caoch O'Carroll, the wall-eyed bard and twenty players of the tympán, his pupils. O'Carroll was a famous musician, but twenty tympán players in one household!

Bang! Bang! Patapan pan! Twenty of them. It was, he reflected with bleak humour, asking for trouble.

He noted that his old friend Felim Bacach had reverted to type. After years of trying to live with the Anglo-Normans, he had gone back to his ancestral lands, blinding and maiming such kinsmen as might threaten his power.

He went to see the dedication of the new Market Cross. He walked slowly up the hill from the abbey. He rarely went to the market-place. It pained him to think of the terrible thing that had happened in that place, on the very spot where the fine new cross was standing. He was not at one with the excited crowd.

He could not appreciate the magnificent structure, with its towering central pillar and statues facing to the four winds. He was dismayed by the hysteria and fervour of men and women vying with one another to receive the brand of the Cross on their foreheads in order to be fit to go to the Holy Land. The smell of scorching flesh sickened him. He turned away from the throng, returning slowly to his books. It was all folly. It was pride to imagine that the weather would reflect the mood of a creature as insignificant as himself, but the grey Kilkenny drizzle entered into his soul.

The prior sent him to administer a small new community in Carrick. The change was designed to do him good. It was a small place indeed, built by James Butler, no doubt in expiation of his crimes. Friar John considered the bargain. Holy men and women were installed in monasteries and churches, to pray for kings and nobles too busy to pray for themselves. The prayers filled up a great reservoir of divine grace. The nobles and sinners, when their crimes became too heinous to be ignored, paid the holy men and women to turn the spigot on the reservoir, releasing a flow of healing grace, just in time to save them from the fires of Hell. It was, to some extent, a matter of timing.

Nevertheless, Friar John gave himself over to his new task. He found a new fulfilment in tending the poor, the sick and the many weary travellers who came to his door. He particularly enjoyed talking to the travellers. He heard news of the young king and his Flemish wife. The king had ambitions in France. He heard talk of a device that could reproduce copies of manuscripts by the hundred, by the thousand, if needs be. He thought that it would be interesting to see such a marvellous machine. If men were able to acquire knowledge at little cost, then surely the world was on the verge of a great enlightenment. It did not worry him that the patient work of his whole life might be surpassed in moments by some clever artificer. He began to believe that God had indeed a plan to raise men up from ignorance.

Almost all the time, it rained. He heard news of Bishop Ledrede, from travellers drying their soaking clothes by the calefactory fire. The Bishop was in Rome. He was in England. He was in Avignon. He was still arguing and demanding his rights. He was in prison for heresy. He was a jobbing bishop, assisting in the administration of various dioceses in England. He was in Salisbury when the great spire was dedicated. He was everywhere, except Kilkenny. The diocese of Ossory must fend for itself.

There came a great flood. Bridges were carried away throughout the land. The waters of the Nore rose and rose, until they lapped at the steps of the great altar in the abbey. They swept away the Great Bridge and drowned the garden plots and orchards of Irishtown and parts of Hightown. A palmer, on his way to Jerusalem, an intrepid man to be abroad at all, said that the waters had risen out of the New Quay like a fountain and flooded even the stable yard of what had once been the inn of the witch, Alice Kyteler. People had seen her cat perched on the ridge tile. It lent credence to the story that all the misfortune was the work of witches. Friar John withdrew his mind from the garrulous traveller. He was back again in the sunny orchard. He looked upon Petronilla's luminous face. She touched his hand. He looked at the scar. He would never be free of her. He asked permission to go home.

Peace came to him in the garden of the abbey. It was Brother Fergal's garden, where he had pursued the playful leaves with his rake and pondered his fantastical stories. He was home again. On a rare sunny day he sat listening to the rushing river. He had missed it. That was the sound in the background of much of his life, the bountiful Nore, sweeping imperiously from the mountains to the sea, brown with water from the great bog, turning trout and salmon to bronze against the gravel of its bed. He recalled pursuing a salmon that had lurked in a brown pool above the Bishop's meadow. He was glad now that he had not caught it. Maybe it was the Salmon of Knowledge. Knowledge had come to him the hard way, with maybe a little wisdom and a certain amount of patience. He concluded that he had grown old.

He stripped a handful of purple grass-seed from a tall stem, running the stalk between finger and thumb. Locked in every seed was the secret of the generations, God's plan for the future. He sat and lured the birds to him, flicking the seed in a semi-circle about his feet. First came the starlings, the corner boys of the garden. They strutted and squabbled, nudging their companions aside, always seeking the advantage. There was enough for all. Collared doves trundled aimlessly back and forth, grumbling to one another. A blackbird came with his wife, polite and demure. They looked about, always on the qui vive.

There was a saint once, up in the mountains, an Irish saint of course, renowned for his devotion to God. His cell was so narrow that when he stretched his arms wide to pray, his hands stuck out through the little windows. A blackbird came and built a nest in the palm of his hand. The saint was reluctant to disturb the gentle creature. He remained, kneeling there in prayer and cramp until the nest was finished, until the eggs were laid and hatched, until the brood fledged and high summer sent them out into the world. Now, that was patience. The saint was rewarded with the love of a growing family and with song from the bird's golden bill.

A robin hopped about, investigating freshly turned soil. He ignored the scattered seed. He was a confident fellow in his russet jupon. He looked about inquisitively, his black eyes glinting. He stuck out his chest, afraid of nothing. It was his garden. He tolerated the other interlopers. He came and went, disappearing only to emerge again.

'Ah, Robin,' murmured the friar. Those were the good days.

◈

The Bishop returned to Kilkenny in a kind of triumph. He was free at last from the authority of Dublin. He was free from the pestilential Archbishop Bicknor and all those who had accused him and tried to blacken his name before the king. He was vindicated on all counts. His body might well be frail, his eyesight dim, but his mind was clear. He remembered old slights. He remembered how much money was due to his diocese and what arrears had accrued during his long absence. He started rebuilding his maimed and shattered cathedral.

He brought the most skilled craftsmen from England, despising the masons and carpenters of Ireland. The hammering began again, the coementarii chipping and cutting under the watchful eye of Maistre Robin of Salisbury, ingeniator and artifex. It was said that he had built the highest spire in all of England. People wondered if a new landmark would rise over the town, dwarfing the old round tower. It would be a sight to behold. The hammering continued. It echoed through the narrow streets. It resounded in the broad concavity of the river valley. It rebounded from the castle walls and from Brogue-makers' Hill. It disturbed the feral cats in the deserted stable of the inn. The otters stood and looked this way and that. Knock, knock, knock, from dawn to darkness. The otters plunged. They had more important things to consider. They played with their young. They juggled shining pebbles. The cathedral healed. The skyline returned to normal. The hammering stopped. The bells rang again.

Ledrede was pleased. He knew that his name would live forever. He set more poems to music and directed his clergy to dance again in the sacred precincts. They danced before the high altar and the glorious east window. The Bishop, alas, could not join in the dance. He had to be carried about in a chair. The wound had spread, devouring the flesh of his calf, laying bare the shin bone. Maggots bred on the decaying limb, the despair of his leeches. It had gone too far to be healed by fire. He offered it up against Christ's own sufferings. He was content.

He called the artifex to him and pointed to the great window.

'It is very fine, Maistre Robin. You have shown us the life of Our Saviour better than any preacher could.'

Maistre Robin bowed. 'I am gratified, my lord bishop. I am glad that it meets with your approval.' He put his hands behind his back and looked up. The colours of the glazed panels fell upon his face and on his garments, blue and braise. He was illuminated like a figure in a holy book.

'But why,' queried the Bishop, 'is there no halo around the head of the Virgin?'

'Because, my lord, she was one of us. I reserved haloes for Christ and the angel. Her light comes from within. I beg you to come here at dawn when the rising sun strikes through the glass. My poor art is as nothing compared to the true glory of the sun.'

'Hmmm,' mused Ledrede. 'I would have preferred a halo. However, I have further instructions for you. I shall turn those lazy canons out of the Common Hall. I want you to demolish the hall and use the stone to build me a proper palace. I have endured hardship for too long.'

Maistre Robin bowed again. 'A palace it shall be, my lord. A prince of the Church should not live like lesser beings. Christ, I am sure, would have wanted you to live in a palace.'

Ledrede cupped his hand behind his left ear.

'What is that you say? Speak up, man.'

'I said that it would be an honour to build your palace. You are a prince of the Church.'

This pleased Ledrede. 'And another thing. I wish to be buried here within sight of the Virgin.' He pointed with a cane to a niche below the window. 'She will look down upon me through all eternity. I have been her servant all my life.'

'Indeed, my lord,' replied the artifex.

'And my effigy must show me in my Franciscan sandals. I am nothing more than a poor mendicant friar.'

'A humble friar, my lord. I shall direct my masons to prepare the effigy, although I pray that long life may attend you for many years to come.'

'As God wills it,' said Ledrede. 'I still have work to do.'

Friar John still had some work to do. He prepared more parchment. He wrote of the great war then raging in France. He wrote of the feuds that set one family against another. He mentioned Sir Fulco de Freyne, a valiant knight of Kilkenny who had fought at the siege of Calais. Sir Fulco once told him how five hundred children were expelled from the town to conserve supplies. The children died in the marsh between the two armies, a sight surpassing all other terrible sights in that war. Sir Fulco's companion, Sir Wat, a poor knight, was taken by the French. He had no one to pay his ransom. Friar John remembered young Wat. He was always young Wat, the seneschal's cheerful squire.

He wrote of the terrible pestilence afflicting the neighbouring island. It travelled in the air. Fortunately the wind blew mainly from the west in Ireland. The miasma would most likely drift away to the east, to Flanders, to Tartary and the land of Cathay. He felt guilty at the selfishness of the thought.

Robin came to him in the dark, before Lauds.

'You must come with me to see the sun rise.'

'My boy!' said Friar John, gripping him by the shoulders. 'My dear boy!' He could not contain his tears.

'Come with me now,' urged Robin. 'I must show you something.' He took the friar by the elbow. He noted how thin Friar John had become. He helped him through the dark streets. A dog barked in the silence. Birds began to sing, giving notice of the dawn.

They stood in the dark silence of the cathedral. A dim light indicated the position of the three tall lancet windows. The birds fell silent. The sun rose out of the river mist. It touched the upper panels, Christ ascending in glory, the disciples at the empty tomb, the disciples meeting Christ in the upper room.

The light slipped downwards. The Saviour's life played out in reverse: the Via Dolorosa; the Garden of Gethsemane; the Last Supper; the miracles; John the Baptist; old Simeon receiving the infant in the temple. In the panel closest to him, Friar John saw the Nativity, animals and doves and Joseph standing by. He recalled how as a child he could not pronounce the name. The letter J defeated him. He always said Seofis. He smiled at the memory. The sun struck through the image of the Virgin. She wore a red gown. The light dazzled him. He blinked. He opened his eyes. The face of Petronilla de Midia looked down upon him. He crossed himself and knelt in prayer.

'I thought you would want to see her,' said Robin softly. He went quietly away.

Friar John went every day to the cathedral. He knelt in prayer before the east window. A kind of peace came over him. He saw the pestilence devastate the town. Whole families died in one night. Nine of his brothers were carried off in one week. He wrote his hope that someone of the race of Adam might survive to use the parchment that he had prepared. He felt the swellings under his armpits. He burned with fever. He thought of Petronilla looking down from the refulgent glass. Lord, let your servant depart in peace, he thought. He laid down his pen. He closed the cap on the ink-horn.

Bishop Ledrede got his palace. He destroyed some few remaining enemies. He argued and disputed, until his voice deserted him. He deplored the decline of the English colony; how English custom was being corrupted by fosterage and gossipred with those of Irish blood. Children of English and Norman stock were forming bonds of affection with the barbarous Irish. They spoke their language. They sang their songs. They were becoming indistinguishable from the king's enemies. He saw the colony, battered by pestilence and the insolence of the resurgent Irish, beginning to fray at the edges. It was melting like spin-drift cast ashore by a winter gale. Nobody offered any hope. It was time to contemplate the end of earthly things.

He had his servants carry him to the cathedral to view the site prepared for his last resting place, if such a spirit could ever be at rest. It was fitting that he should lie there under the gaze of the kindly Virgin. He looked up in devotion. It was strange. Something nagged at him, a curse screeched at him by a mad woman. 'You will see my daughter's face in your dreams and for all eternity.' The maggots gnawed at his flesh. He knew that face. He had flayed and broken that woman. He had consigned her to flame. Fear gripped him. He struggled to speak. He struggled to free himself from the chair. His servants restrained him, uttering soothing words. Terror of what lay ahead gripped him. Error had sunk its fangs into his soul. It was too late. He was trapped in silence and immobility.

He lies there to this day, under the calm gaze of Petronilla de Midia, encased in his black limestone robes and wearing his simple Franciscan sandals.

GLOSSARY

Arbalest. A type of crossbow.

Artifex. A craftsman. (Lat.)

Baudekyn. Silk interwoven with gold or silver thread.

Bawn. An enclosure inside a fortification.

Bonhomie. Good fellowship. (Fr.)

Calefactory. A heated room in a monastery.

Caparison. Robes and trappings for covering horses.

Cantilena. A song or hymn suitable for dancing. (Lat.)

Chevaldoures. Iridescent flying insects. Lit: 'golden horse'. (Fr)

Coementarius. A stone mason working with stone and mortar. (Lat.)

Compline. The last prayers of the day.

Cordwainer. One who works with Cordovan (the finest) leather.

Cot man. A fisherman using a cot, a small boat common on the rivers of south-east Ireland.

Crockard. A coin of base metal, nominal value one-half of a penny. Outlawed in 1310.

Éiric. A fine, compensation, or 'blood money' recognized by Brehon Law.

Exegetes. Analysts and interpreters of texts.

Florilegium. An extravagantly illustrated book about flowers; an anthology of favourite writings.

Galvardine. A long coat.

Gaudy days. Days of special rejoicing.

Guerrier. A fighting man. (Fr.) Still in use in cycling parlance.

Gossipred. Relationship through sponsorship at baptism.

Gyves. Ankle irons.

Halberd. A mediaeval pike, equipped also with an axe-head.

Hobbelar. An Irish soldier mounted on a hobby, a small horse. No connection to a hobby, a type of hawk.

Homunculi. Inferior men. Lit: 'men of small stature'. (Lat.)

Ingeniator. Architect, engineer, designer. (Lat.)

Justiciar. King's deputy in Ireland. Lit: 'man of law'. (Lat.)

Kern. A light-armed Irish foot soldier.

Loricati. Men at arms, wearing leather breastplates. Lit: 'breast-plate'. (Lat.)

Lycanthrope. Werewolf. More common in the diocese of Ossory than in the rest of Ireland.

Mactíre. A wolf. (Ir.)

Mangonel. A siege engine designed to hurl projectiles.

Mattock. A digging tool rather like a pickaxe.

Mendicant. A beggar. Usually applied to begging friars.

Motte/Moate. A high mound topped by a fortification.

Murrain. A disease of cattle.

Orrery. A mechanical model of the solar system.

Ounce. An heraldic beast similar to a snow leopard.

Outremer. 'Beyond the Sea'. Eastern lands partly held by the Crusaders.

Patronymic. A name derived from a paternal ancestor.

Pharos. A lighthouse.

Pollard. A coin of base metal, nominal value one penny. Outlawed in 1310.

Purveyance. Levies of supplies and cash for the king's armies.

Quintain. A revolving target capable of striking back.

Refulgent. Gleaming, radiant. Lit: 'lightning'. (Lat.)

Reeve. Local agent of a great lord or king.

Saltpetre. Potassium nitrate, sodium nitrate, calcium nitrate.

Sarcenet/sarcanet. A finely woven fabric, often made of silk. 'Saracen cloth'.

Scaldy. An unfledged chick.

Scobaces. A witch sect that allegedly rode brooms. Lit: 'a broom'. (*Scopa* Lat. *Scuab* Ir.)

Seneschal. An officer in the service of a great nobleman. Sometimes given administrative and military command.

Spigot. A stopper or rudimentary tap.

Suit of Mill. The exclusive right to grind grain.

Tomberel. The final indignity for the condemned. Lit: 'dung-cart'. (Fr)

Trebuchet. A siege engine designed to hurl boulders at fortifications.

Usury. The practice of lending money at interest. Regarded as a serious sin by Christians.

Vaire. Squirrel fur. (Fr.)

Windlass. A lifting mechanism, like a horizontal capstan, using ropes wound around a revolving cog or drum.